the darkness in you

USA TODAY & *WALL STREET JOURNAL* BESTSELLING AUTHOR

BECCA STEELE

The Darkness In You

Editing by One Love Editing

Proofreading by Rumi

Cover photography by Michelle Lancaster

Becca Steele

www.authorbeccasteele.com

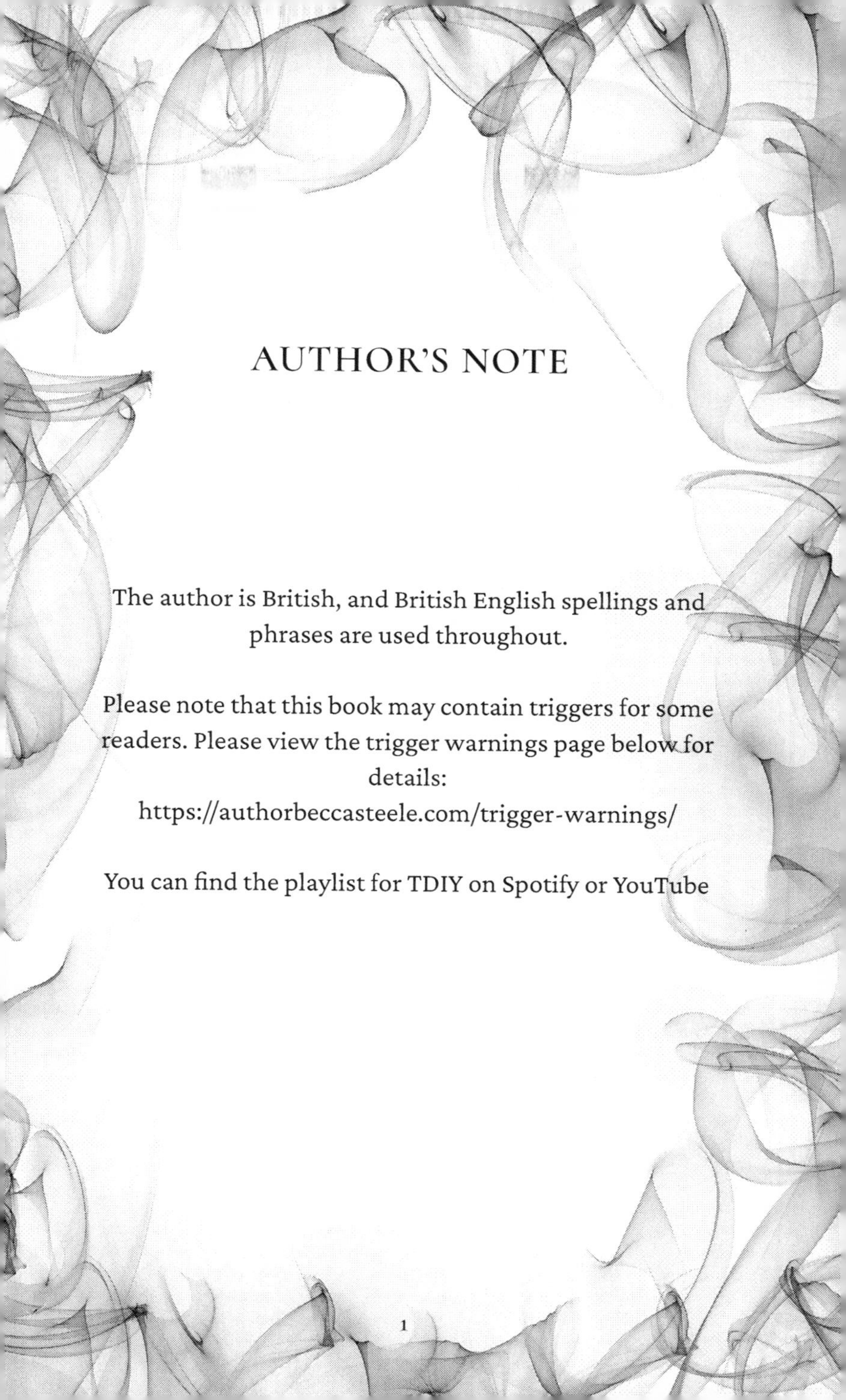

AUTHOR'S NOTE

The author is British, and British English spellings and phrases are used throughout.

Please note that this book may contain triggers for some readers. Please view the trigger warnings page below for details:
https://authorbeccasteele.com/trigger-warnings/

You can find the playlist for TDIY on Spotify or YouTube

For those who struggle in the dark.
May you find your light.

PART ONE

TWO YEARS AGO

"You never really understand a person until you consider things from his point of view... until you climb inside of his skin and walk around in it."

—Harper Lee, *To Kill a Mockingbird*

PROLOGUE

Tim. My brother. My confidant, my best friend, and my protector.

Zayde. My lover. My secret, my shelter, and my soulmate.

On Halloween, I lost them both, because of *him*.

He started the fire, and I burned with it. In one night, he destroyed my entire world, and ashes were all that remained.

1

fallon

My eyes blinked open, and it took me a minute to get my bearings. Oh, yes. I was in my friend Hailey's car. She'd come to pick me up from the train station for a surprise visit to Alstone. I was normally at boarding school during term time, but since it was half-term, I was making the most of no lessons and a chance to see my two favourite people. Even though it meant that I'd see *him*. "Where are we?" I asked, then took in the scenery outside. "Oh. Nearly home." I couldn't disguise the tremor in my voice, but I hoped that Hailey didn't notice it.

She smiled as she brought the car to a stop at the side of the road. "Happy to be back?"

That was a question with a complicated answer. "I'm looking forward to seeing Tim and Joe," I said, unclipping my seat belt. As I reached for the door handle, I forced a smile. "Thanks, Hails. I'll see you on Sunday?"

She nodded. "Yeah. Take care of yourself, Fallon."

Waving her off, I began to make my way up the long driveway that led to the Hyde mansion. My steps slowed as I neared the door and saw my dad's car was parked there.

What was he doing here at this time of day? I really hoped that one of my brothers was at home. Tim or Joseph, it didn't matter which. I loved both of my brothers, and they would protect me.

I made it all the way to the stairs without incident and ducked my head into Tim's room to see if he was around. The room was empty, but I heard noises coming from farther down the hallway, so I headed in the direction of Joseph's bedroom.

As soon as I pushed the door open, vivid memories assaulted me. Every time I came home, I remembered. Good and bad, all tangled up together, springing into my mind when least expected.

Nine years old, and I'd been standing here in Joseph's doorway when I'd tripped over...

"Tim!" I whisper-shouted from my bedroom door as soon as I heard my brother's footsteps on the landing. The footsteps sped up, and I moved back to let him into the room. A shock of red hair appeared, and then Tim's grinning face was focused on me. He flopped down on the fluffy purple rug next to my bed, propping himself up on his elbows, and I slid down to the carpeted floor to sit next to him.

"What's up?"

I bit my lip. "I heard you and Joe talking about me. I don't wanna go away, Timmy."

His face fell, and he moved to sit next to me. "I don't want you to go, either. I'll miss you. But it'll be safer for us all."

He was right. I was kind of clumsy, and if that wasn't bad enough, sometimes I found it hard to concentrate at school. When I dropped things or my teacher told Daddy that I wasn't paying attention again, he got angry. Daddy was different to other dads. He never punished me when I did bad things. He punished my brothers instead. Daddy said I was his princess, and it wasn't right to mark my skin. So he beat Tim or Joe instead and made me watch.

Watching my brothers cry in pain made my chest hurt, and it made me cry, too.

It was punishment for us all.

When I turned eleven, I would be sent away to boarding school. I didn't want to go. I would miss Tim the most—he was my best friend as well as my brother. He was only a year older than me, and we did everything together. Our older brother, Joseph, had nicknamed us "strawberries and cream" because of Tim's red hair and my pale blonde hair. Tim hated the nickname, but I didn't mind. It was better than our father calling me "Princess" because I knew that whenever he called me that, I'd done something wrong, and my brothers would be punished. Mummy never stopped him. She never did anything.

"It's a good school, Fal. Joe showed me on his computer." Tim put his arm around me. "Do you want to see?"

I nodded. "Okay." At least I didn't have to go away until I was eleven. I could still see my brothers every day until then.

As I followed Tim into Joseph's bedroom, where Joseph was sitting at his computer, I stubbed my toe on the door frame. With a cry, I tripped, falling forwards. I windmilled my arms, trying to stay upright, but I hit the side of Joseph's desk, and the globe lamp that was sitting on the edge of the desk fell to the floor with a crash.

I clapped my hand over my mouth as Tim scrambled to the floor. "I'm s-sorry. I'm so sorry." My lip trembled as I took in the broken pieces. The lamp had been a gift from Mummy and Daddy on Joseph's twelfth birthday, and I knew it had cost a lot of money.

"It's okay. It wasn't your fault." Joseph stood up, giving me a

hug, but I could see the worry in his eyes. "We'll get another one, and Dad won't know. If he finds out, I'll tell him I broke it."

"I can give you some of my birthday money towards it. I still have some left." Rising to his feet with the pieces of lamp clasped in his hands, Tim looked over at Joseph before turning to me. "It was an accident, Fal. You didn't mean to break it."

Joseph nodded. "Yeah. It's my fault for putting it so close to the edge of the—"

"Fallon!"

The three of us froze in place, and I clenched my fists to hide my trembling hands. Slowly, I turned, forcing myself to raise my head to meet Father's disapproving gaze.

"Princess..." He took the broken pieces of the lamp from Tim's hands. "Did you break this?"

I swallowed hard. "Y-yes." There was no point in trying to deny it—he'd obviously heard us talking. Either way, punishment was coming.

He sighed heavily, shaking his head. "You know what this means."

We all knew what it meant. In silence, we followed him through the house, dragging our feet until we reached the kitchen, where our father entered the utility room and then opened the garage door.

I took a seat on the stool in the corner of the garage, staring straight ahead of me while my brothers stood against the brick wall. It was cold and echoey in here. I hated this place.

Even though I tried to keep looking at the wall, I couldn't help looking at our father as he wrapped the leather belt around his hand, the long end dangling down. At least he wasn't using the end with the buckle this time. He used that when he was especially angry, and Tim had a scar on his lower back where the buckle had caught on his skin, tearing it open. The bleeding had lasted for so long.

Joe and Tim pulled up the backs of their T-shirts, hunching over.

Then it began.

First came the whistle in the air, then the thwack of the belt as it lashed Tim's lower back. Even though I knew it was coming, I couldn't stop myself from flinching. A deep red mark immediately bloomed where our father had hit him, and I bit down on my lip so hard that I tasted blood. If I cried or dared to turn away, Daddy would only hit them harder.

He always hit my brothers on their lower backs. I guess it was because the marks were easier to hide.

The lash sounded again, and again, and after three strikes, Daddy switched to Joseph. Tim stood silently, but his whole body was shaking.

When it was over, our father left us alone, slamming the door behind him, and the three of us finally let the tears fall.

I shook away the memory, blinking back the sudden moisture that had appeared, and focused on my brothers. Joseph was at his desk, frowning at his computer screen, and Tim was sprawled on his bed, playing on his phone. The sight made me smile. Even though I hated parts of coming home, I loved to see my brothers. And...someone else, someone who was very, very important to me.

I cleared my throat, and Tim was the first to glance up. His eyes widened, and then a huge grin overtook his face.

"Fal!" He jumped off the bed and threw his arms around me, spinning us around. "I didn't know you were coming home!"

"I wanted it to be a surprise," I mumbled into his shoulder, my smile widening as he continued to spin us around.

"Best surprise." Bringing us to a halt, he grinned down at me.

"Tim. The thing." Joseph cleared his throat, and Tim's face fell.

"Ah, yeah. The thing. Hey, Fal, I wish I'd known you were coming, but we have plans tonight and tomorrow night we can't get out of."

"Plans?"

"The Alstone Holdings fuckers," Joseph growled. "They've been stepping up their pranks recently—"

"So have we," Tim interrupted with a bright grin, and although I felt sick as usual at the mention of the rivalry between the Hydes and the Alstone Holdings families, I concentrated on the happiness beaming out of my brother's face. It was such a messed-up situation, and I knew the rivalry would never end. But how I wished it would.

"Yeah. So we need you to stay out of the way, Fallon. Promise me you won't try to get involved." Joseph's lips thinned as he stared at me.

"Okay. I'll stay away." It was already early evening, and if I were to be out of the house before either of them left, I needed to make a move now. I couldn't risk being left in the house alone with my dad. "I'll catch up with some friends. Are you going to be back late?"

Tim shrugged and then reached out to ruffle my hair, like he'd always done. "Not sure. Can we have sibling bonding time tomorrow, though? Halloween celebrations before I have to go out? We can watch *Hocus Pocus* and stuff our faces with popcorn?"

"Hey, hands off my hair," I said, smoothing my hair down while giving him a warning look. He just grinned back at me, and I couldn't help smiling. "That sounds good to me. I missed you both... It would be nice to do something all together."

"We missed you, too." Tim gave me another quick hug before collapsing back onto Joseph's bed. "Are you going back to school the day after tomorrow?"

"Yes, but not until the evening. My train leaves at six twenty."

"That's great. We can have the whole day together, then me and Joe'll drop you at the station, won't we?"

Joseph nodded, glancing over at me with a smile. "Yeah. I have some things to do for Dad in the morning, but I'll be around in the afternoon."

We made our arrangements, and then I slipped out of the house with the excuse that I was going to see my friends.

As soon as I was out of sight, I sent a text.

Me: Surprise! I'm back in Alstone for a couple of nights. Are you free?

While I waited for a reply, I carried on walking, pulling my jacket more tightly around me as the cool autumn breeze chilled my skin. As I cut through the alleyway that led to the ponds, my phone chimed, and when I read the message, I couldn't hold back my smile. Tapping out a quick reply, I increased my pace.

It wasn't long before the low roar of a motorbike broke the silence around me. Leaning back against a tree facing the road, I waited, butterflies in my belly.

The motorbike pulled to a stop, and I breathed in shakily. No matter how much time passed, he still affected me so powerfully. He was the boy I wasn't allowed to love, but I'd given him my heart anyway.

Zayde Lowry pulled his helmet off, hanging it on the handlebar before swinging his leg over the seat and moving to stand in front of the bike. He leaned back casually, folding his arms across his chest.

I took a moment to drink him in. His deep brown hair was tousled from the helmet, and his light eyes danced with rare amusement as I just stood there mutely, wondering how exactly I got lucky enough to call him mine.

"Uh...what?" I said eventually when my brain finally processed the fact that he'd actually spoken.

"Come here." Unfolding his arms, he crooked a finger at me.

When I reached him, he pulled me against his chest and tipped my chin up. Then he lowered his head to mine.

"Good girl," he murmured against my lips. "I missed you."

Winding my arms around his neck, I met his icy gaze, which held a hidden warmth that I knew he only shared with me. "I missed you, too, so much."

He lowered his head and kissed me, slow and deep, like we had all the time in the world rather than a few stolen moments. The smooth metal of his tongue barbell slid across my tongue, sending a shiver down my spine, and I pressed my body into his, tightening my grip on him as he deepened the kiss.

When he finally pulled back and released his grip on me, I smiled at him helplessly.

He studied me for a moment, and then his full lips curved into one of his rare smiles.

I melted into him. He was so beautiful. At first glance, you'd see a sexy-as-sin, tatted-up bad boy wrapped in leather, with icy eyes and a hard gaze. But when he smiled...

His icy exterior thawed, and it was like the sun coming out.

2

zayde

When I pulled up outside the house I shared with Caiden Cavendish and Cassius Drummond, I saw Caiden's younger brother Weston balanced on a ladder, screwing something into the wall above the front door. An electric drill was draped over one of the rungs, and a long piece of wire was hanging out of the wall.

"What are you doing?" I stared up at him.

He glanced down at me, screwdriver in hand. "Adding extra cameras. Remember? We talked about this. If those fucking Hydes think they can egg our house one more time, they can think again."

"Dickheads." A spike of guilt punched through me, like it did every time the Hydes were mentioned, but I was good at ignoring it now. What I had with Fallon had to remain a secret. Caiden, Cassius, and Weston were my best friends, my family, but they would never understand, and there was no way my dad would accept me if he knew. If I went public with Fallon, we could lose everything. And I'd never do that to her, anyway. She had even more to risk than I did.

I could still remember everything about the moment I'd found out about Fallon's family and how fucking sick I'd felt.

My first day at my new school. I was standing outside the golden stone buildings of Alstone High School with Caiden, who had somehow managed to get through my walls in a way that none of my friends had ever been able to. Maybe it was the fact that our dads had practically forced us together every day since we'd first met, sometimes with Caiden's brother, Weston, but mostly just the two of us. Or maybe it was the fact that I was completely out of my fucking depth, and he was the only person I was allowed to speak to who actually seemed to understand and seemed to instinctively know when to give me space. Whatever, we were friends now.

Now, I was glad of his presence as I looked around me. This school. Yeah, it was very fucking different to my last. I tugged at my uniform tie, suddenly nervous, although I did everything I could not to let it show on the outside.

"It's not that bad here." Caiden turned to me. "Stick with me, and you'll be alright. I know everyone. Not only that, but your dad's name means you'll be popular without even having to try."

"Thanks." I followed his lead, leaning against the wall at the top of the stone steps, arms folded across my chest as I watched him greeting people. He hadn't been joking about knowing everyone.

A pretty, red-haired girl stopped in front of us. "Who's your friend, Caiden?" She blatantly eyed me like she wanted to kiss me or something.

I made a face. I wasn't interested in kissing anyone. Not unless it was Fallon.

"This is Zayde. Zayde Lowry."

At Caiden's words, a sly smile crossed her lips, and she stepped closer. "Very nice to meet you. I'm Portia Thompson."

I was saved from replying by another girl with long, dark hair coming up behind her and grabbing her arm, shooting both myself and Caiden a smile as she pulled Portia inside.

"Cass!" Caiden lifted his hand, and I followed his line of sight to see a tall guy with dark blond hair approaching us. He grinned when he saw Caiden standing there, and they greeted each other with a fist bump, all grins and excited talking. I felt like a real outsider right then. What was I even doing here? I didn't belong. This wasn't my life.

"Z, this is Cassius Drummond." Caiden glanced over at me before turning back to his friend. He'd told me about Cassius and how the three of our dads owned this company, Alstone Holdings, and were the elite in this town. Whatever that was supposed to mean for me, I didn't know yet, but apparently, it made you kind of a celebrity around here. I wasn't looking forward to the attention. I preferred to stay under the radar if possible. My life so far had taught me that it was best to avoid the spotlight. If you went unnoticed, there was so much you could get away with.

Somehow, I made it through the morning. The classes were harder than I was used to, and I knew I'd have to pay attention if I had any hope of keeping up. By the time lunchtime rolled around, my head was hurting from all the new information I'd had to take in, and I needed a break.

"That's Joseph." Cassius was pointing out everyone to me, keeping up a running commentary while we ate. His voice hardened, and I gave him my full attention. "Stay away from him. Our families are enemies, and he hates us. Even though he's older than the rest of us, he's always trying to start shit with Cade." I followed the direction he was pointing in and saw a

group of guys standing at the side of the room, scanning the tables.

"Which one?"

"The one talking to the girl with blonde hair."

The boy turned around, and I gasped, my stomach churning as I saw the same face that had stared at me from the framed photo in Fallon's bedroom.

Joseph Hyde.

Fallon's older brother.

Cassius carried on talking, oblivious to the shock and nausea that was overtaking my body.

"His brother Tim's in our year. He's a wanker. And his friend Elijah, he's a fucking psycho. Then there's their cousin, James Granville..." He paused. "Guess he's not as bad as them. He stays out of it mostly; his family tries to play nice with both sides. Think they just want to suck up to everyone."

"The Hydes and their friends are fucking bastards," Caiden muttered, slamming his bottle of water down on the table. "Still holding a grudge and taking it out on us, just because our parents and grandparents had better business sense than them." The way he spoke, it sounded like he was reciting something he'd heard many times before.

With every word he said, the sick feeling in my stomach increased.

The Hydes were the enemy, which meant that Fallon and I were now on opposite sides.

The punch landed exactly where I wanted it, and I sent Elijah reeling back with a howl of outrage. Out of the corner of my eye, I could see Cade grappling with Tim, both of them getting in a few good hits, but I knew Caiden would come out on top. He always did. The bastards had tried to attack us after school, but they should've known by now that we were well prepared. Their reasoning for the ambush was probably because Alstone Holdings had beaten the Hydes to a contract, something to do with developing some land in the south-west.

Off to my right, Cassius and Weston were having a heated discussion with a couple of Tim's friends who'd been caught defacing our lockers. Why the fuck the Hydes had to drag their friends into it, I had no idea. We didn't drag any of our friends into our family shit. That wasn't anyone's business but our own.

The sound of a whistle blowing had us breaking apart and running for it. No one wanted to be caught out here fighting on school grounds. Even though our parents would ensure that it was dealt with, they'd come down hard on us. My dad's typical punishment was to lock down my privileges, stop my access to my account and the internet, and I'd usually be confined to the house outside of school-related activities. So I'd learned to be more sneaky, to hide what I was doing so he'd never know. He did the same, too. I'd heard the staff talking. I knew that he still slept around, although I was assuming he was more careful now than he had been with my mum. I knew that he spent a lot of his nights out at the Alstone Members Club, the boys' club in town that he frequented with Mr. Cavendish and Mr. Drummond. But he was nothing if not discreet, so I took my cues from him.

There was a part of me that knew he approved of me getting one over on the Hydes, because they were his hated rivals, but another part of him wanted to prove that he had a perfect son, a boy he'd taken out of a life that was going nowhere and was now being moulded into a future businessman that would one day take the reins at Alstone Holdings.

I knew the pressure I was under would be worth it in the long run. I had so many advantages here that I'd never even dreamed of. And it wasn't like he was hard on me all the time—only if I stepped out of line. Honestly, he left me alone most of the time. He wasn't at home much, always working, and he didn't seem to be all that interested in getting to know me as a person. We'd never done any father-son things, not that I'd ever had any expectations of that happening. I had my friends, and that was enough for me. Caiden, Cassius, and Weston. At school, they'd started calling us "the Four" since we were always together, and there were four of us. Bit of an obvious nickname, but it was good to be part of a group. We all had each other's backs, and it was different to when I'd lived with my mum in our council flat, on the twelfth floor of a tower block in a housing estate on the outskirts of London. Everyone looked out for each other there, but there'd never been anyone that I'd been so close to. Not even Mack and Creed, even though they were the people that had known me best growing up. Maybe it was because Alstone was smaller, so there were fewer of us. Maybe it was because I'd been yanked out of everything I knew and thrown in at the deep end, and I'd had to trust and rely on these three boys who had shown me the ropes and accepted me as one of their own without question.

Whatever it was, I was glad I had them.

And I still had Fallon on the other end of my phone. My closest friend. My secret.

"I can't fucking wait until I'm living here with you guys, away from that bitch Christine," West muttered. "Then I can monitor the cameras full-time. I've got an app set up and these alerts—"

"Tell me about it later, alright?" Once West got started on anything to do with computers or security, it was hard to get him to stop. Opening the front door, I placed my helmet on the console table and threw my keys down next to it. Then I headed upstairs to my bedroom, pulling off my leather jacket and gloves as I went.

As always, the darkness in my room calmed me. Cassius joked that it looked like a vampire cave, but it was my sanctuary—or as close as I could get it. My room, my house, away from the cold sterility of my dad's place. Throwing myself on my bed, I dragged my phone from my pocket and pulled up my text conversation with Fallon. She was under a code name, just in case anyone happened to glance at my phone, although I trusted my housemates not to go through my private shit. I had her listed as "Angel" because the first time I'd seen her, back when we were kids, I'd thought she looked like an angel. She'd been so fucking pretty. I hadn't ever noticed girls before, but I sure as fuck noticed her.

The bus dropped us off at the end of a long road with huge mansions spread out along the street. "Do people really live in these?" I stared around me, wide-eyed. "Why do they need so much space?" My mum ignored my question, puffing up the road, pulling a shopper loaded with her cleaning supplies.

I stayed rooted to the spot. This town, Alstone, was so different from the built-up area with the high-rise block of flats we lived in. As I watched, a kid around my age rode past me on a shiny blue bike, and the look on his face...it was so open and happy.

Weird. I couldn't imagine being that carefree. Not where I lived, at least.

"Zayde! Stop dawdling and get over here!" My mum's voice cut through my thoughts, and I sighed, shifting my backpack on my shoulders and trailing behind her.

We stopped at the gates of a large mock-Tudor mansion, and my mum pressed the buzzer. The gates swung open.

"Mum. I'll take the shopper."

She sighed with relief, and I grabbed the handle and followed her up the world's longest driveway to the front door.

When we were standing on the front step, she squinted at the piece of paper in her hand. "We have to go around the left side of the house and through the side door."

My attention was caught by the door knocker. It was so shiny I could see my distorted reflection in it.

I jumped when I was cuffed around the ear, spinning my head to see my mum narrowing her eyes at me. "Well, don't just stand there waiting! Come on." She huffed loudly, then stomped around the side of the house.

The door was unlocked, and we walked into some kind of cloakroom, then entered the biggest kitchen I'd ever seen, all gleaming white surfaces. Our whole flat was smaller than this.

When we'd come to a stop in the kitchen, the polished floor squeaking underneath my trainers, my mum began unpacking the shopper. "Let's get started."

Before we'd arrived, she'd informed me that I'd be helping her clean for half an hour, and then I'd have to do my homework while she did the rest. She wasn't normally on my back about homework, but I'd been in trouble at school, and if I didn't get my grades up and change my attitude, I was in danger of being expelled, according to my headmaster.

For the next half an hour, I helped her scrub and polish, and then finally, my time was up. I stretched my aching back before I grabbed my bag and headed over to the breakfast bar to get started. "Don't make a mess, and don't touch anything that doesn't belong to you," my mum warned me, then left me to it, heading out of the kitchen to clean wherever was next on the list. For a while, I stared at my textbook blankly, my mind wandering, before I bowed my head, getting started on my French homework.

"Hi."

I looked up with a start, not having realised that someone else had entered the room. My eyes widened as I took in the girl in front of me. Huge blue eyes, long eyelashes, a cloud of pale blonde hair around her face, and soft-looking lips. She looked like an angel or something.

"H-hi," I stuttered, my heart racing. Tilting her head as she stared at me curiously, she gave me a sweet smile. My heart raced even faster as she stepped closer to me.

"What's your name? How old are you? What are you doing? Do you want a drink? Are you here with the cleaner?" She asked the questions all in one go, the words tumbling over each other, and I found my lips stretching into a smile.

"I'm Zayde." I cleared my throat. "Uh, I'm ten. I'm, um, doing my homework, and a drink would be nice. And the cleaner is my mum."

"Zayde." She gave me a wide smile, showing me her perfectly white teeth. "Cool name. I'm nine, but my brother's the same age as you." Padding over to the cupboard, she lifted up onto her tiptoes and carefully took out two glasses.

I couldn't look away from her. I'd never seen anyone like her before in my life. She was beautiful.

"What's your name?" My voice sounded loud in the quiet kitchen.

Her eyes met mine, and she gave me another smile.

"I'm Fallon."

A slice of bright light hit the side of my face, interrupting my thoughts, and I turned to see Cassius in the doorway.

"I knew you'd be brooding in your cave." He grinned,

stepping into my bedroom.

"Fuck off."

"Cade got the new Call of Duty. Wanna play?"

Yes. Anything was better than lying here in the dark, thinking about things I couldn't change. If I didn't watch out, I'd let the feelings of inevitable despair and hopelessness that were always at the back of my mind drag me under, and then I'd be fucked.

My phone buzzed, and my screen lit up with the name "Angel." I dived for it before Cass could see, but he was occupied with examining the supplies on top of my desk. Thumbing open the screen, I read the message, the sudden strong beat in my chest reminding me I had a heart, even though it was damaged. I replied, climbing off my bed and glancing back over at Cassius. He raised a brow, holding up a petrol can.

"For tomorrow," I said. "I'm going out."

"You just got back."

"Yeah, and now I'm going out again." Shoving my phone into my pocket, I headed over to the door. "Don't wait up for me."

He smirked. "I'll be too busy tonight to worry about what shady shit you're getting up to. Hey, maybe you should try getting laid, too, once in a while. It might improve your mood."

"Thanks for the advice."

"Anytime." A wide grin appeared on his face. "If you want some help with the ladies, you know—" I shot him a look, and he stopped mid-sentence, shaking his head. "That serial killer stare is seriously creepy, mate. Do you practise it in the mirror, or does it come naturally?"

I left him without bothering to reply. I had somewhere I needed to be.

3

zayde

I had another fucking flashback when I reached the ponds and saw my girl standing there waiting for me, half in shadow, half lit by the street light close to the tree. This time, it was from the summer.

The sun was lowering in the sky, reflected in the series of ponds that lay in front of me. My back rested against the rough bark of the tree, and my arms were looped around my girlfriend's waist as she leaned back against me, settled between my legs. Music played softly from her phone, propped up against the side of my black motorbike helmet.

Fallon sighed against my chest, her fingers trailing across the blades of grass. "I wish we could stay here forever."

"Yeah." I leaned down to place a kiss to the top of her head, soft strands of hair brushing against my lips. The dying rays of sun caught her platinum-blonde waves, turning them a fiery gold. Fuck, my girl was so beautiful. My angel.

In the distance, I could see two people walking past, hand in hand. I swallowed hard, my jaw clenching at the reminder that there was no happy ending for me and Fallon. We'd never be able to be out in the open like other couples were. Not with the bitter rivalry between our families and the obligations that had been placed on us both.

If I were a better man, I'd cut all ties with her. Let her go so she could move on and be with someone that she could have a normal relationship with instead of these stolen moments we had to satisfy ourselves with.

But I was too selfish. I couldn't let her go.

My heart beat for her and only her.

"I know what you're thinking." Fallon twisted in my arms, pulling her legs underneath her and then shifting onto her knees so she could straddle my thighs. Winding her arms around my neck, she met my gaze. "That couple. I don't care about any of that. I want you." She punctuated her sentence with a soft kiss to my lips. Lifting her hand, she ran her palm across the tree bark just above my head. "Remember when we carved this?"

I nodded. We'd carved our initials into the tree, back when she was thirteen and I was fourteen. Back then, I was only a naive child, deluding myself that maybe we could make things work, but I was just kidding myself. There was nothing but heartbreak in our future.

I was no stranger to pain, but breaking Fallon's heart...I knew it would fucking break me, too.

"Let's forget about the future for now." Fallon stroked a finger across the back of my neck, making me shiver. "We have this summer. Now you've moved out of your dad's house, it'll be easier to meet up."

A few days earlier, I'd moved in with two of my best mates, Caiden and Cassius, and Caiden's younger brother, Weston, would be moving in with us the following summer once he'd turned eighteen and finished school. Our new house was close to the Alstone College campus, the elite business university college that Caiden, Cassius, and I would all be attending in September.

"Yeah...maybe." Hopefully. I knew Cade understood my need for space, how I had to get away from everything and everyone. Now I had my motorbike, I'd taken to riding it for hours at a time, sometimes revisiting my old haunts and friends, and sometimes, just being alone. But it was never better than when my girl was there with me, her arms wrapped securely around my body as she rested against my back, while the powerful machine thrummed beneath us, taking us wherever we wanted to go.

"Always so pessimistic." She rolled her eyes, but the sweetest fucking smile curved over her lips. "It will be easier."

Instead of replying, I leaned forwards, sliding my hand up into her hair and kissing her. She opened her mouth for me with a soft moan that went straight to my dick. I shifted, moving her on me so she wasn't brushing against my cock. We were out in the open, and although we were fairly secluded in this small clump of trees, there was always the chance of a dog walker or someone stumbling across us. We never had enough time together, and the time we did have was always at risk of interruption.

Always a mind reader, she drew back, resting her forehead against mine. "I want a whole night with you. Do you think...if I get Hailey to cover for me, we could have a whole night together?"

"Your dad won't let you, will he? He knows Hailey lives alone."

Her face fell. "You're right."

I couldn't fucking stand to see that look on her face. Fallon's friend Hailey wasn't an option, not now she was living alone with no one to answer to, but I had to make it better somehow. "I'll sort something out," I promised, even though I knew that the odds were against us. Fallon's dad...he liked to rule his household, and especially his only daughter, with an iron fist. When she was home from boarding school, he expected her to spend every night under his roof. If she dared to go against him... her brothers would be the ones to face the consequences. Her brothers toed the line—as far as he knew—and they were allowed all the freedom that she wasn't afforded. But if she dared to step out of line, they were the ones that were punished on her behalf.

I wasn't supposed to know anything about it. The Hydes kept everything close to their chests. But Fallon was mine, and I knew everything about her. In return, she knew all my secrets. I'd bled them all out for her, and she was the person who knew me best and accepted me for who I was. Even the darkest parts of me, the parts that I kept hidden from the rest of the world.

Fallon's phone beeped, cutting off the music that had been playing. Turning to the side, she picked up her phone and glanced at the screen.

"My dad. We'd better get back. I can't be late for the family dinner." She climbed off me, twisting her hair up and tying it back, then bending down again to pick up the helmet that I'd bought for her to use. Jumping to my feet, I lunged forwards and tugged her into me, slanting my mouth across hers. Just one more taste of her.

"Zayde." She whispered my name when we broke apart, her eyes wide and shining, reflecting the setting sun. "I wish I didn't have to go."

Yeah, I wished for the same, too. But wishes were useless in our world. I swiped my helmet from the ground and took her hand. "Come on. I'll take you home."

. . .

When I beckoned Fallon over and she kissed me, I remembered exactly why we kept up this forbidden relationship. We were both in too fucking deep to stop this now. She was *mine*, and even though I knew this would all come crashing down on us one day, I wasn't going to be the one to let her go.

"Good surprise?" She smiled.

"Always."

"My dad doesn't know I'm back home yet...and my brothers will probably be back late tonight. I told them I was going to see friends." Her lashes swept down, and she shifted on her feet. "Um...I was thinking that if I texted Tim to say I was staying with friends tonight, maybe you and me could...maybe spend the whole night together?"

The whole night together.

Fuck.

We'd never done that yet. Never had a whole uninterrupted night where it was just the two of us. Our whole relationship had been stolen moments, sneaking around, both of us constantly aware of the catastrophic consequences of us getting caught.

Where could we go? I racked my brain. Maybe...

Wasting no time, I pulled out my phone and dialled.

"Mack? I need a favour."

A low chuckle came through the phone. "If it's more of your pyro shit, you're gonna have to wait. You cleaned me out."

"Not that." I glanced over at Fallon, feeling that stab of guilt again. But this shit had been started by the Hydes and their fucking asshole friends, and they needed to be taught a lesson. Gritting my teeth, I clenched my fist around my phone. However I spun it in my head, the fact was I was going up against the family of the one person that I'd fucking die for.

"The warehouse. It has an office, yeah? I need somewhere to lay low tonight."

Mack laughed again. "I don't wanna know what shit you're in now. But yeah, you can crash there if you wanna. Want me to bring anything over?"

"Does it have a bed?" I asked, then swore under my breath, because he'd know—

"It's like that, is it, mate? There's no bed, but I can sort you out with one for the night if you want it. Got a futon I can drag in there for you."

He knew I didn't give a shit about sleeping in beds or being comfortable, and there was only one reason I'd ask.

"Appreciate it. This needs to stay between us, okay?"

His voice turned serious. "You know it. Give me a couple of hours. I'll leave the keys in the lockbox. The code's 14962."

"I owe you."

When I ended the call, I turned back to my girl, lifting her chin so her eyes met mine.

"The whole night?"

She nodded, a smile playing over her lips.

I tugged her over to my bike. "Get on. Helmet on, and hold on to me."

4

fallon

Even when I was a small child, I knew that what my parents expected of me was to finish school with respectable grades, then marry into a good family. Joseph thought the same, to an extent. Although he'd hated and disagreed with the way that our dad had treated us and he'd remained protective of me, he looked up to our father. Maybe it was something to do with being the oldest sibling and being groomed to go into the family business once he had his MBA. Who knew. But whatever the reason, he seemed to take it for granted that I'd finish school and then start looking for a husband.

There were two problems I had with that. One, I had no plans to marry anytime soon. I wanted to do other things first—move out of my parents' home, go to university if I could find some way to pay for it since my dad wouldn't pay, have a career, and enjoy freedom for the first time in my life. And two? The only boy that I would ever want to marry, the boy I loved with all my heart...he was the son of my family's rivals.

It was stupid, really. Way before I was born, before my

parents were even born, there was a dispute over land in Alstone. Three families banded together—the Cavendishes, the Drummonds, and the Lowrys—and formed Alstone Holdings. The company bought up huge parcels of land, and as for my family? They weren't happy with these developments, to put it lightly. They began acquiring their own land in retaliation, and soon, the rivalry was in full swing. From the information I'd been able to glean over the years, there was undercutting, shady deals, and backstabbing...and all the while, Alstone Holdings grew more influential, and my family grew more resentful of their growing power.

Nowadays, the board members were cordial on the surface, extending invitations to each other to social events and playing nice in front of other rich, powerful figures. But it was all a front.

Thanks to the long-standing rivalry, the children of any of the families that ran Alstone Holdings were off limits. To make matters worse, Caiden, Weston, Cassius, and Zayde—aka the Four—were actively involved in conflict with my brothers and their friends. Zayde held back as much as he could, especially with Tim because he knew what he meant to me, but my boyfriend had a bit of a thirst for vengeance, and he and Joseph hated each other. It was mostly childish pranks—nothing that would properly hurt anyone, and I knew that all our parents turned a blind eye to it. Our families were rivals, and I doubted that would ever change.

Zayde and Tim were the only two people that believed in me—that encouraged me, told me I could do whatever I could put my mind to, that I didn't have to follow the path my parents had set out for me. I loved them both so much, and it tore me apart that they were both on opposite sides of this rivalry.

One day, I knew I'd have to choose between my family and the boy I loved.

It was inevitable.

And had been, ever since the day Zayde told me that he was moving here, to Alstone, and the daydreams I'd had about one day running away with him all crumbled into dust.

I stared down at my phone, rubbing my eyes, but the words didn't change. The sick feeling that had been there ever since I'd opened Zayde's message was getting worse.

At first, when he'd told me he was moving, I'd been scared and sad—I didn't want to lose the boy who was pretty much my best friend. I'd asked him to find out where he was moving to, hoping with all my heart that he wasn't going to be far away. I was going away to boarding school in a couple of weeks, so I'd kind of prepared myself for not seeing him for a while, but I'd been consoling myself with the thought that I'd still be able to see him in the school holidays.

Now that hope had been shattered with two words that were on my phone screen.

Michael Lowry.

Zayde's dad was Michael Lowry, a member of one of the three founding families of Alstone Holdings and a bitter rival of my family. If anyone in my family found out...

I didn't want to lose my best friend, but it looked like I wouldn't have any choice in the matter. I would never be allowed to see him. It was one thing for the cleaner to bring her son to our house—my parents treated staff like they didn't exist, and my mum had barely paid any attention whenever he'd been there with his mum. I wasn't sure if she'd ever realised that he was there. But it was a completely different situation for me to not only invite a boy to my house, which I was sure wouldn't be allowed, but for that boy to be the son of Mr. Lowry? There was no chance we'd ever get to see each other.

Tears fell, thick and fast. I couldn't tell Zayde, not yet. I could picture his face so clearly, the way he would lie on his stomach, whispering his secrets to me. How he'd tell me how his mum had beaten him again, how he'd been in a fight with another boy on his housing estate, how he'd spent yet another night alone in front of a locked door, waiting to be allowed back into his flat after his mum had finished doing whatever she did. How he sometimes hurt himself. He'd speak like it wasn't a big deal, but he'd started to let me see the pain in his eyes, and in return, I'd shared how my dad would punish Tim and Joseph if I misbehaved and how I was scared to go away to boarding school but glad that it would mean my brothers were protected from punishments.

We'd grown so close, and that was why I knew that if I told him about my family right now, it would make everything a hundred times worse. Despite everything bad that he'd told me about his life, he was mostly content. He had his friends. There was an older boy called Creed who looked out for him and gave him jobs, and he never really seemed like he wanted anything more. I'd never heard him complain or say that he wished he was rich like I was. He just...got on with life. Accepted that things were the way they were and did his best with what he had. So I knew that this move would hurt him because it would take him away from everything he'd ever known, and he was going to be moving in with someone he'd never even known existed until today. I was scared and worried for myself, going to boarding school and leaving my brothers behind, but at least everyone else I'd meet would be in the same situation—all new to the school. Zayde didn't know anything about his dad or the rivalry...

Wiping my eyes, I sniffed, reading back through Zayde's message before typing a reply.

> ***Z:*** *Spoke to my mum again. My dad's name is Michael Lowry and guess what, he lives in ALSTONE. We can still see each other :D*
> ***Me:*** *That's great :):):)*

I ignored the lump in my throat and the guilt that was filling me. How could I tell him?

There was a knock at my door, and I quickly flipped my phone shut and placed it on my bedside table. The next minute, Tim's head poked round the door, a big smile on his face. It fell as soon as he saw me.

"Fal? What's the matter?" He crossed the room and sat next to me on the bed, putting his arm around me. We were so close, but I'd never told him about Zayde because I knew that neither of my brothers would approve of me being so friendly with a boy. They were so overprotective of me.

I couldn't tell him about Zayde, but I could tell him how I was feeling about boarding school. "I'm going to miss you so much when I go away."

He stared down at me, his big blue eyes shiny and his mouth turned down. When he spoke, his lip trembled. "I-I'm going to miss you, too. It won't be the same here without you."

Everything was changing. For all of us.

Slipping my arm around my brother's waist, I leaned my head against his shoulder and let myself cry.

Shaking off my melancholy thoughts, I wrapped my arms more tightly around Zayde's waist, pressing against his back as his bike flew along the coast road. The heavy motorbike helmet cradled my head, and the soft leather of the jacket I was wearing protected the parts of my body that weren't pressed up against Zayde from being buffeted by the wind.

We pulled into the entrance of an industrial estate that looked to be deserted. Zayde brought the bike to a stop outside a small warehouse, turning off the engine and putting down the kickstand. He indicated for me to wait while he climbed off, heading over to a lockbox situated on the wall. When he returned to the bike, after unlocking the warehouse garage door, he steered us inside. I climbed off, stretching and removing my helmet. After placing it on the seat, I glanced around the space. "Where are we?"

"A warehouse. It's not much...you deserve better, but no one will find us here."

He wouldn't look at me, and I rounded the bike, stepping up to him and sliding my arms around his waist. "I'm happy wherever I am if it means I get to be with you."

"Yeah, but you deserve so much more than this," he said, his voice low.

I knew he hated that he couldn't give me the things other people took for granted. I dreaded the time when his friends, all of whom were single, settled down. It would make things hit home for both of us. At least for now, we could hold on to the fact that we had something special, something that was just ours, something that I treasured with every part of me.

Reaching up, I placed a kiss to his stubbled jaw. "So do you. Come on, are you going to show me where we're going to spend the night, then?"

In reply, he took my hand and led me into the warehouse.

When we reached the small office and he'd flipped the

light on, my gaze went straight to the futon bed that had been placed there, the other furniture stacked or pushed against the wall to make space. I swallowed a little nervously because although we'd done things together, it had never been in a bed.

He looked at me, and I knew he could read the apprehension in my eyes. Leaning down, he brushed a kiss across my lips. "No pressure."

His words reassured me.

And I wanted him.

"I want this." Unzipping my jacket, I flung it in the direction of the desk, not caring where it landed.

His eyes, normally icy, filled with fire, and it made me burn. Shrugging off his own jacket, he stepped towards the bed and held out his hand.

"Come here, baby."

The first thing I saw when I opened my eyes was the tattooed arm slung over my waist. Then I registered the hard, warm body against my back, and a smile spread across my face.

This was the first time we'd spent the night together.

It had been the best night of my life so far, and I knew I'd never forget it.

My thoughts were interrupted by my phone ringing. Usually I kept it on silent, but since I'd been away from the house overnight, there was no way I'd risk anything. Even though I didn't think my parents knew I was here yet, if I was uncontactable while I was back in Alstone, it would be disastrous.

Automatically swiping to answer, I glanced at the

screen, covering the speaker and muttering to Zayde, "Please stay asleep." I cleared my throat. "Hailey. Hi."

"Hey, are you free today at all? I got some good news, and I feel like celebrating."

Twisting my head to look at Zayde, who still had his eyes closed, I lowered my voice. "Um...when?"

There was a small pause, and then she said, "Whenever. I'm free all day."

Next to me, I felt Zayde's body move. Long lashes blinked, and then suddenly, his eyes were open and focused on me. I shook my head at him, and he raised a dark brow. He looked so gorgeous, his hard edges softened with sleep. My breaths stuttered at the thought that maybe I was the first person to see him like this.

Placing my hand back over the phone speaker, I leaned down to him. "It's Hailey. She wants to meet me."

His gaze sharpened, instantly awake. "I'll take you. The Red Lion's close."

I gave him a small smile, trailing my hand up over the defined muscles of his bicep as I replied to Hailey. "Do you want to get lunch? Meet at the Red Lion pub?"

"Okay. Is twelve-ish okay with you?"

Twelve? I mouthed to Zayde, and he inclined his head in agreement. Returning my attention to my friend, I said, "Yeah. See you then."

When I ended the call, Zayde reached out, taking the phone from me. He placed it on the floor next to the futon, and then he lifted his hand to my face. His fingers smoothed back my hair, pushing the long strands behind my ear where they had fallen into my eyes. I shivered under his touch. Those hands that could be so cruel were so gentle with me.

He was only cruel out of necessity. He didn't take joy in causing pain when it wasn't justified...

Or perhaps he did, sometimes. Zayde was so complicated, and he'd been through so much. He'd experienced loyalty from his closest friends, but love?

Sometimes I felt like we were the only two people in the world. How could anyone else feel the way we did?

"Fallon," he murmured, pulling me down to him.

"Zayde..." My voice was so quiet because I didn't want to break the mood, but there was a niggling thought at the back of my mind that had been there ever since Joe and Tim had mentioned their weekend plans.

"Yeah?" His hand splayed across the small of my back, a hot brand against my skin.

It was hard to concentrate with the way he was touching me. "Um. Can you promise me something?"

His fingers stilled, and his gaze met mine again. "What?"

"Tonight. I...I know it's Halloween, and I know that something's going to happen between you and your friends and my brothers and their friends." I wasn't stupid; I could read between the lines, and even if Tim and Joseph hadn't said anything, I knew that Halloween would be a night that they'd all want to take advantage of. "Please...please, can you promise me one thing?"

His gaze shuttered, making it impossible to read him. It was difficult to read him most of the time, unless he let his guard down, which he so rarely did. On the rare occasions it happened, I felt so privileged because he showed himself to so few people, and somehow, I was one of them.

"What?" he eventually said.

"Promise me that whatever happens tonight, you won't hurt my brothers. *Please.*"

His gaze softened almost imperceptibly, but I was good at reading him now, and I caught it.

"I'll do my best to stay away from them, but I can't promise the same for the others. And they might not stay away from me."

I reached out and grasped his free hand. "I know, and I don't expect you to speak for anyone else. But thank you. It...it means a lot to me."

He didn't reply, but his fingers stroked across my lower back, and that was enough for me.

After Zayde had dropped me off at the entrance to the pub car park, I saw Hailey getting out of her car. She eyed me with curiosity as she locked the doors. "Was that you that just turned up on a motorbike?"

Oh, shit. Lowering my gaze, I bit down on my lip. What should I tell her? Eventually, I gave a small shrug. "If I say yes, will you promise not to tell anyone?"

Her eyes widened, and her mouth fell open as the realisation hit. "Wait, was that *Zayde Lowry's* motorbike? Fallon!"

I swallowed hard, staring at her, pleading with my gaze. "You can't tell anyone, Hails. Please."

She immediately rounded the car, coming up next to me and placing a hand on my arm. "I won't, but you'd better make sure your brothers don't find out. They'll kill you."

"I know," I whispered, and she sighed, slipping her arm around me as she steered us towards the pub.

"I promise I won't say anything, but I hope you know what you're doing." Thankfully, she seemed to sense that I couldn't explain myself...wouldn't even know where to start, and she changed the subject. "I have some news that might cheer you up. I finally have a buyer for my grandmother's house."

I shot her a grateful look, latching on to the new subject with relief. "Tell me everything."

5

fallon

"Perfect timing." Tim grinned at me from his spot on the reclining leather sofa in our theatre room. The scent of hot, buttery popcorn hung in the air, making my stomach rumble, even though it hadn't been long since my lunch with Hailey.

I flopped down next to him, grabbing a handful of popcorn from the bowl between us. Tim leaned forwards, pouring us glasses of Coke from the bottle that was sitting on the coffee table. When he was finished, he slid one of the glasses in front of me and pointed the TV remote at the huge flat-screen TV that took up most of one wall. The opening credits of *Hocus Pocus* began playing, and I settled back in my seat with a smile. I was so glad I'd decided to come back home this weekend. Even though it meant that I'd have to see my dad at some point—unless I somehow managed to get lucky—I'd managed to spend the whole of last night with the boy I loved, and now I got to spend time with my other favourite person. And I still had tomorrow to look forward to—a day with both of my brothers.

"Hey, Fal. I was thinking." Tim helped himself to the

popcorn, crunching for a minute before he continued. "How would you feel about me coming to pick you up from school at Christmas instead of you getting the train? We could go to Bath for the Christmas markets."

"I *love* Bath. That would be great."

"I know, that's why I suggested it. If I drive up early in the morning, we can have the whole day there, then drive home in the evening."

"I'd love that." With a smile, I curled my legs up under me on the sofa. "And maybe when I'm back at home, you, me, and Joe could do a day in London to see the lights?"

His own smile dropped as he considered his next words. "Yeah, I'll see if I can talk Joe into it. I think we need to stay out of the house as much as possible. Dad's getting worse lately. I dunno if it's work pressure or what, but he's on a really short fuse now."

"Has he been hurting you?" I whispered. When the silence stretched, I prompted, "Tim? Talk to me, please."

He sighed, running a hand through his tousled red hair. "There's no point in talking about it. I don't want you to be worrying about this when you're away at school. I can handle myself, I promise. And once you're legally an adult and can move out, we're all gonna move out, okay? You, me, and Joe. We'll find a place together or something. Even if Dad doesn't approve, I don't care. I know Joe has some... ideas about you finding a husband, like Dad expects, but I know that the two of us can convince him that it's better to wait." Pausing, he turned his head, his eyes meeting mine. "You should be free to live your life, Fal."

"I want that for you, too. I hate the thought of you being stuck here. You know I never wanted to leave you guys, but I thought that it meant we'd all get a break from Dad's punishments, at least. If he's punishing you even when I'm not here..." Tears filled my eyes. "I can't bear the thought of you getting hurt."

"I promise I can handle it." Moving the bowl of popcorn to the coffee table, he slipped his arm around me. "Please don't cry. It's okay.

I sniffed, blinking rapidly in an attempt to keep my tears at bay. "I just wish there was something I could do. I feel so...so...helpless."

He pressed a kiss to the top of my head. "We'll be away from this soon. Even if Joe ends up under Dad's thumb, I'll make sure that you and me get away, okay? We haven't got long to wait now. You'll be finished with school forever by next summer. You'll be over eighteen then, and we'll be free."

His words gave me some comfort, but I knew that the odds of our father allowing us to just walk away were slim. He was someone who was prepared to play dirty, and he liked to be in control. If we threatened that, I knew he'd come down hard on us.

But we would try. And I knew that it meant I'd have to come clean to Tim about Zayde. If, against all odds, we did manage to get out from under our father's thumb, then maybe, just maybe, there was a tiny chance that I didn't have to give him up. But only if I could make Tim understand how much he meant to me.

My mind was made up. I'd talk to Tim. I'd have to discuss it with Zayde first, and I needed to work out exactly what I was going to say. But I needed to take the time to sit down with Tim and do my best to explain how important Zayde was in my life, and I needed to do it before I finished school for good.

"Tim?"

"Yeah?"

"Not this weekend...but maybe at Christmas, can we talk? There...there's something I need to tell you. Something really important, and I—I don't know if you're going to like it. But I really want you to understand."

He drew back from me, his gaze searching. "You know you can tell me anything, right? I'll never judge you."

I nodded. "I know."

Whatever he saw in my gaze must have reassured him. His shoulders relaxed, and he shot me a small grin. "C'mon, then. No more depressing talk, okay? We've got a few hours until Elijah and Jason come over, and I wanna spend them with my favourite sister."

I returned his smile, some of the weight lifting from my shoulders. "Your only sister."

"Still my favourite. Just like we know I'm your favourite brother. We won't tell Joe." He shot me an exaggerated wink, his grin widening as he dug back into his popcorn.

Shaking my head, I turned my attention back to the TV. No matter how awful our parents could be, somehow I'd ended up with the best siblings I could hope for and a boyfriend who I knew loved me more than anything, even though the words were too hard for him to say aloud.

6

fallon

Joseph and Tim had disappeared, and I was alone in the house. I needed to think of somewhere to go before my parents got back. Hailey wasn't answering her phone, and both Zayde and my brothers had made me promise to stay away from whatever they were doing for Halloween night. As for other friends...I guess I didn't really have any of those around here anymore. The "friends" I'd had when I was little had mostly consisted of children from families that my parents deemed suitable. It had all been shallow, superficial children thrown together because their parents thought it would be advantageous in one way or another. It was attending parties that I couldn't stand, where I was forced to look and behave a certain way, in the hope that I'd make the right connections for the future.

A memory struck me then. I'd been ten, and it was back when Zayde was living with his mum, back when we were blissfully ignorant of the things to come.

. . .

Lying on the grass, I closed my eyes against the bright sun. Zayde was letting me rest my head in his lap while he listened to music through his headphones and I made a daisy chain. His mum was here cleaning, but we were out of sight of the main house, hidden behind the wooden summer house halfway down the garden. My dad and brothers were out, and my mum was napping, as she often seemed to do in the afternoons. For now, it was just me and him, on our own in this quiet, sunny space. We were hiding out of the way because we both knew my family wouldn't approve of me associating with the son of their cleaner. It was so stupid. Zayde was the best person I knew. Who cared if he wasn't rich?

My fingers faltered on the stem of a daisy, and I carefully lowered the chain to the ground. Bringing my hand up to shade my eyes from the sun, I looked up at Zayde. "I have to go to a stupid party with my family later, and I don't want to go. I wish you could be there."

He cocked his head as he stared down at me. Pulling his headphones from his ears, he said, "Did you say you wished I could go to a party with you?"

"Uh-huh."

"I don't like parties. Especially not the kind of parties your family goes to." Clearing his throat, he affected a ridiculous accent, his lips curving up as he spoke. "You can't drink all the champagne, sir! Have some caviar instead."

"What?" I scrambled to a sitting position, facing him, laughter bubbling up inside me. "What was that?" I managed to wheeze out, laughing harder as his eyes danced with amusement.

"My impression of rich people." One shoulder lifted in a shrug. "I would never fit in with those kinds of people. They're not like me."

Finally managing to contain my laughter, I smiled at him. "You fit in with me, though, and I like that you're not like them."

He made a huffing sound. "Yeah, but you're you. You're different to the others. I think..." There was a long pause, and I found myself leaning forwards. Just when I thought he wasn't going to finish his sentence, he did. "I think you might be my best friend?"

His voice lifted at the end, like he wasn't sure, so I nodded. "I think you're mine, too." My fingers touched the soft petals of a daisy, and I had an idea. Leaning over, I picked up my daisy chain and carefully looped the ends to form a circle. Then I shuffled forwards and placed it on his head. "I crown you as my best friend."

A tiny smile appeared on his face as he lowered his lashes. Curling the tips of his fingers around the circle of daisies, he lifted it up. "This should be for you. A halo for an angel." As he said the words, he carefully placed it on my head, his fingers sliding over my hair.

It had been true then, and it was true now. He was my best friend.

Making my way downstairs to the kitchen to get a drink while I decided where to go this evening, I lost myself in memories. He'd always been so soft with me, so careful, so different from the way he acted around everyone else.

Pushing the kitchen door open, I was greeted with a high screech and the sound of shattering glass. I clapped a hand over my mouth, my eyes widening as I was met with my mother's shocked, angry gaze.

"Fallon! What on earth are you doing here? Look what you made me do!" She pointed at the broken wine glass at her feet, dark red liquid pooling around the jagged pieces. Of course, her only concern was her glass of wine and the fact that I was somehow at fault.

I bit down on my lip hard, my fists clenching and my heart racing. Panic at the knowledge that my parents were already home warred with a familiar disappointment, the knowledge that my mother really didn't seem interested in me. Once I'd left for boarding school, she'd never contacted me, not like other parents did. Even when I came back home during the school holidays, she was never around.

"What's going on in here?" The loud, booming voice caused both me and my mother to freeze.

No. Not him. *Please*.

It was too late. My father strode into the kitchen, taking in the scene with one sweeping glance. His brows pulled together, his mouth setting in a flat line.

"It was her fault. I didn't even know she was here." My mother jabbed a finger in my direction, and for the first time, I noticed the slur in her words. That hadn't been her first glass of wine, then.

"What are you doing here, Fallon?" My father's voice was deceptively soft.

"I-I thought I'd come back home for the weekend. I wanted...I wanted it to be a surprise."

"Don't ever do that again." His words whipped across the room. "Your mother and I have plans for tonight, as do Joseph and Timothy, and we will not have you disrupting them. We don't pay for you to attend your school just so you can duck out on a whim. You aren't even eighteen yet. I do not expect this kind of behaviour from you."

"I'm sorry," I whispered. I *hated* how he affected me.

"I expect you back at Hatherley Hall tomorrow. I'll escort you to the train station myself." Taking a step closer, he held out his hand. "Come with me. You need to understand the consequence of your actions, Princess."

Something inside me cracked open, my body

trembling against my will. Was this what Tim had meant by our father being on a short fuse? Had he been dealing with the man completely overreacting to every little thing? I'd come back as a surprise, and yes, it was the first time I'd done so, but I'd never dreamed that either of my parents would react so harshly. At best, I thought they'd be indifferent.

Swallowing hard, I followed my father out of the room. My mother didn't even watch us go, too busy pouring a fresh glass of wine with hands that held a slight tremor.

We entered the garage, the dimly lit space cold and a little damp, and I shivered.

"Your brothers are both of age now, and I can't punish them for your mistakes any longer." His hand came down to grip my shoulder, and he turned me around. My body trembled again as my palms flattened against the cool bricks of the wall.

He lifted the back of my top with fast, rough movements, tucking the material under my bra strap. "Please, Dad. Please. Don't do this," I begged, my voice thick with the tears that were already beginning to fall. "It was a mistake. It's— All I did was come home as a surprise. Please. I didn't mean to do anything wrong."

"Be quiet. You need to learn that actions have consequences." His voice softened, but it was like a knife blade against my skin. "This hurts me more than it hurts you, Princess. Stay still."

The familiar, hated sound of his belt slipping out of its fastenings cut through the still air.

Then my world exploded in a burst of pain, lashing across my back.

I cried out, slumping forwards as the hot lashes flayed me again and again. Tears of shock and pain ran down my face unchecked. Was this what Tim and Joseph had suffered all these years?

My body lost itself to the stinging burn, my breath catching in my throat, coming in short gasps as he struck me over and over. He was using the buckle of his belt, his favoured implement with Joe and Tim when he really wanted to hammer his point home.

He held nothing back.

The lashes stopped as suddenly as they'd arrived. I sobbed, barely aware of my father leaving the room. How could he do this to me? To any of us?

When my tears finally ran dry, I straightened up, my movements stiff. With trembling hands, I pulled my top back down, wincing as the material brushed over the lacerations on my skin.

The mental and physical anguish had emptied my mind, and only one thought remained.

I needed Zayde, and I needed my brother.

No matter that they had both told me to stay away. No matter that even right now, they might be at each other's throats.

I was going to them.

7

zayde

Slowing down, I steered my motorbike onto the tree-lined lane to my right, looking out for the tall, rusted iron gates. Behind me, the wheels of Cassius' SUV rumbled along the overgrown track. My entire body was on high alert, ready for whatever the Hydes and their little group of overgrown children were planning.

All of us were prepared. These fuckers needed to be taught a lesson. If they thought they could lure us here and then get one over on us...they were about to learn that they were very fucking wrong.

We passed through the gated entrance of the huge, decrepit Victorian manor house. It was set away from the main town of Alstone, alone in the countryside, bordered by farmland on one side and trees on the other. From what Cade had told me, the house originally belonged to a lord who owned the surrounding farmland, but it had been condemned for as long as he could remember. It leaned to one side, the walls crumbling under the pressure. There were gaping holes where the windows had been, and if I were the kind of person who got scared by anything, the whole fucking haunted house vibe that this place gave out would be enough to have me running for the hills. Lucky for me, and unlucky for the Hydes' Halloween plans, an old building didn't even feature on my radar.

When I came to a stop outside the house and dismounted my bike, I pulled my helmet off and lifted my hood and tugged my skull bandana into place, leaving only my eyes uncovered. Cade came up next to me, also covered by his hood and bandana, speaking in a low tone. "There's smoke coming from the chimneys."

"Did you see the torches?" I replied, just as quiet, and he inclined his head in the barest nod.

"Yeah. They either think we're stupid, or they're trying to lure us in."

"Seems suspiciously quiet." Cassius' voice sounded from behind us, and we both turned to face him.

Caiden straightened up, his voice turning to steel. "We knew it would be a setup, but we're prepared. These fuckers will regret ever messing with us." He glanced over at me, his face shrouded in darkness, thanks to his hood, but I got the message.

I spoke softly, knowing they'd listen. "Keep to the shadows. We'll go inside, you two start the fire." The two guys we'd roped into doing our dirty work both nodded, and then I melted into the shadows with Caiden and Cassius. It wasn't a good idea to leave a trail, and as the sons of the most influential families in Alstone, we couldn't afford to get caught up in any shit. Our guys were hand-picked by me and Caiden, unassuming and unremarkable in every way—they'd fly under the radar, and no one would remember them.

As they headed over to the side of the house, crouching down on the ground, and I heard the whoosh of flames as they lit the fire, my lips curved into an approximation of a smile.

Cassius, Caiden, and I entered the house, completely silent. The glow of moonlight from the open doorway was enough to illuminate a long hallway with cracked black-and-white tiles. A tarnished chandelier hung at a crazy angle overhead, swaying slightly, reflected in the huge, cracked gilt mirror that was on the wall to our left. Thick layers of dust and cobwebs were everywhere I could see, disturbed in places by the footprints of those who had come before us.

As we'd planned, we split up in different directions. Pointing the light of my phone torch at my feet, mostly covered by my thumb so it only gave out the barest hint of light, I took the stairs, keeping to the inside edges, away from the missing spindles of the banister, testing each tread with the toe of my boot to avoid the creaks. Clouds of dust billowed through the blackness that was swallowing me the higher I went, but my bandana kept it away from my lungs.

I climbed the stairs to the first floor.

A pinprick of light winked in the darkness, and it was like a beacon.

My steps purposeful, I headed for it.

---

fallon

The burning stings of pain in my back grew easier to bear the closer I drew to my destination. My eyes were swollen and gritty with the tears I'd shed, but that wasn't important anymore. My only focus was getting to Zayde or my brother. I had no way of tracking Zayde, but Tim's phone location told me he was around here somewhere. And I knew where he was, Zayde was likely to be.

My bike wheels wobbled, my feet slipping on the pedals as I cycled over a bumpy track. The little light attached to the front of my bike barely penetrated the thick, heavy darkness around me. It felt ominous, but the darkness was less frightening than the monster I faced in the light.

My father's face flashed through my mind, the way there'd been an almost manic gleam in his eyes, how he'd immediately jumped at the chance to inflict punishment on me for something that shouldn't have even been worthy of punishment.

I *hated* him.

The realisation almost stopped me dead, and only the automatic push of my feet on the pedals kept me going as my mind reeled with the knowledge. I was an *awful* person. Who hated their own parents?

But now that the truth was out there, I knew that there was no way I could refute it.

I passed between two tall gates, probably wrought iron or something. Up ahead, I could see the shape of a huge, crumbling house, a black shadow backlit by the moon. My eyes caught a flash of light from one of the upstairs windows, and my heart rate increased, my breaths shortening as I drew closer.

After carefully placing the bike out of sight of the house, I turned on the little torch I'd brought with me and made my way into the dark interior.

As soon as I made it onto the upstairs landing, and I was debating whether to go left or right, I heard a soft creak which sounded like it came from the right. My heart was pounding so hard I could almost hear it, but I reminded myself that the likelihood was that it was one of my brothers or their friends. After all, my tracking had shown that Tim was here.

When I peered around the door frame, I immediately caught sight of a fire burning in the fireplace. Smoke was pouring out into the room, and I clapped my hand over my mouth, stifling a gasp. That wasn't good, was it? This room looked like it was one of the only ones with remaining windows, too.

Tugging my coat up over my nose and mouth, I ran for the nearest sash window, yanking it open. I gasped out a breath, the still night air filling my lungs, and as I did so, a sound came from down below.

A sound I was all too familiar with. The low, rumbling purr of a motorbike.

Zayde was here.

I needed to find Tim and speak to him before Zayde did. While Zayde had promised me that he'd stay away from my brothers, they hadn't made any such promises—since they didn't know anything about the two of us. And I knew that realistically, if my brothers did try anything with Zayde, he would be well within his rights to retaliate.

Turning away from the window, I made my way back to the corridor as quickly as I could and tried the next door.

By the time I'd reached the end of the corridor, I had to face it. There was no one in this part of the house. I should've gone left at the top of the stairs, not right.

Retracing my steps, I headed back to the staircase and then paused. Footsteps sounded overhead.

The third floor.

I had to go up.

When I reached the top, a cold breeze washed over me. This part of the house was in an even worse state than the floor below, whole sections of the roof crumbling, making the ceiling cave in, in places.

"I don't want to hurt you."

The voice was instantly familiar.

I crept forwards.

"Why? What's stopping you?"

Tim.

I swallowed hard. Neither of them was aware that I was here, lurking in the shadows. When I looked around the corner, holding my breath, I saw something that made my blood run cold.

The moonlight was streaming into the room in front of me. It seemed overly bright to begin with until I realised why.

Half of the wall was missing. Where the windows should have been was a huge, gaping hole.

Zayde and Tim were standing right in front of it.

8

zayde

I'd made a promise to Fallon, but it was going to be fucking impossible to keep it. Tim was on edge, his lip curled and his eyes narrowed as he clenched and unclenched his fists. Yeah, I probably could take him down without too much trouble, but if he did get hurt, then I'd have that on my conscience. My girl was pretty much the only person who gave me a conscience, so I knew it would be making itself known when it involved her brother.

The truth was, I was so fucking tired of this petty shit. Pranking each other was something that should have ended when we finished school. When you'd grown up in my world, you soon learned what was and wasn't worth holding a grudge over. But here in this privileged world of the elite with all the rich, vacuous bullshit, playing political games and smiling at someone's face while you stabbed them in the back, a generations-old business rivalry took on a whole importance of its own. Fuck my family name. Sometimes I hated being a Lowry. When I'd been a Smith, I'd been...well, I was just another kid on the estate. Not someone whose name was automatically associated with power and wealth.

"You really want to do this?" I raised a brow at Tim as he took a step towards me.

"Fight me, you bastard." There was a tremor in his voice. I had the feeling that Tim was just as tired of this as I was, but like me, he'd been sucked into this.

Tugging down my bandana so he could see my face and know that I meant every word, I met his gaze head-on. "I'm not gonna be the one to throw the first punch." Taking a step to the side, I moved away from the edge. I was close to the gap in the wall. Too close.

The loose, cracked floorboard under my feet squeaked, throwing me off balance.

Three things happened at once.

Tim's fist came at me.

Someone shouted Tim's name in a panicked, high-pitched voice, and both Tim and I twisted.

My. Foot. Slipped.

My fucking foot slipped on the broken floorboard.

Then I fell.

The floorboard snapped, wrenching my ankle around, and at the same time, Tim, already lunging at me, tripped, his jeans catching on a large, rusty nail that was sticking up from one of the boards.

I threw my body forwards, reaching for him, desperation giving me a speed I hadn't known I possessed.

But it was too. Fucking. Late.

One second, he was there, and his gaze connected with mine, pure terror in his eyes like I'd never seen before.

The next second, he was gone.

Tumbling through the gaping opening in the wall.

Falling.

Until he hit the ground far below, his body crumpled and his neck at an unnatural angle.

Fallon's scream chilled my blood, turning it to ice. She ran, and I was fucking frozen in place.

When I managed to climb to my feet, I raced after her, running headlong through the dark, praying I wouldn't fall, ominous creaks sounding behind me. By the time I made it outside, the fire our guys had lit was a raging inferno.

Thick smoke billowed into the night sky, choking the light of the stars. Cries and shouts echoed all around, the noise rebounding off the walls, and the flames reflected expressions of horror and fear on the faces around me. But all I could focus on was Fallon on the dirty ground in front of Tim's body, screaming over and over, her eyes wild and unseeing and her whole body shaking.

Sirens sounded in the distance as Fallon's friend Hailey ran to her, throwing her arms around her. Tim's best friend, Elijah, dropped to the ground next to them, taking Tim's limp, lifeless hand in his, his eyes filling with tears that spilled down his cheeks.

Fallon's screams turned to deep, racking sobs as she clung to Hailey. Seeing my girl in so much pain was like a knife to the chest. I couldn't fucking breathe.

Before I was aware of what I was doing, I found myself crouching down next to them, reaching out for Fallon.

"Fallon?"

She raised her head, and there was a split second where everything was okay. Then it wasn't. Her face twisted in hatred, and she flinched back from me like I'd struck her. "Get away from me!" she screamed. "Get away, get away, get away!" She spun away, throwing herself at Hailey, burying her face in her shoulder.

I fucking broke. Shattered, right there on the ground.

There was no coming back from what had happened tonight.

I sucked in a harsh breath, using every bit of control I possessed to lock everything down. My face settled into the blank mask I'd perfected. I was broken inside, but no one would see. No one would know that my entire fucking world had been torn apart.

"You need to leave," Hailey said softly.

I was dimly aware of Caiden running over and dragging me away from Fallon. Caiden's dad appeared, and then the police were there, and firefighters were dousing the flames that had broken out inside the house. Paramedics worked tirelessly, attending to Tim's broken body, even though it was too late. Elijah wouldn't let go of his hand, and Fallon was wild, shaking and screaming and hyperventilating.

"Fuck," I whispered, slumping back in Caiden's grip. "*Fuck.*"

"This ends tonight," he said, low and resolute. "No more. No fucking more."

I couldn't even focus on Cade's words as I watched the paramedics carry Fallon into one of the ambulances and a policeman forcibly removed Elijah from the scene. Then there was just the crumpled figure on the ground, the boy who'd been so full of life such a short time ago. My girl's brother and best friend.

"Give me a minute," I rasped out to Caiden. My unshakeable mask was fucking cracking, and I couldn't let anyone see it break.

He let me go, and I stumbled towards the trees. When I reached the cover of darkness, I turned back around.

The glow from the fire showed me a scene that would forever be burned into my mind. I watched, unable to look away as they covered Tim Hyde's body with a sheet and pronounced him dead.

My mask broke, and tears streamed down my face.

I fell to the floor, holding my face in my hands.

It was all my fault.

That was the first and last time I cried.

9

fallon

Flashes.

That was all I remembered.

Zayde's foot coming out and Tim falling over the edge.

Screaming until I couldn't hear my voice. Hands grabbing at me. The smell of antiseptic. The smell of death. The prick of a needle.

Blackness.

Home. Ripping my necklace from my throat, throwing it onto my bedroom floor along with my book and my phone.

My father. Being dragged downstairs.

Sobbing. A pain in my chest so powerful I could barely breathe.

"It's all your fault, you stupid little bitch. If you hadn't gone to look for him, he never would have fallen. If you hadn't come back here, none of this would have happened."

My father's hand coming towards me, a blur of movement.

A searing pain across my face. Then more, and more, and more, all over my body. Falling. My cheek against the rough carpet. A booted foot kicking out and a cracking sound and an agonising burn.

Then more blackness.

Itsallyourfault itsallyourfault itsallyourfault.

Wheels rumbling on a runway.

England's lights disappearing far below me.

It's all your fault.

But it wasn't my fault, was it?

It was Zayde's foot that ended it.

10

zayde

Three weeks had passed since my world had fallen apart, and I was fucking spiralling, sucked into a black hole with no way out. I'd shut myself off from the pain, made myself numb, but it wasn't enough. My knife burned a hole in my pocket, the latest cuts still fresh. But that wasn't enough, either. Nothing was working.

"Zayde. Zayde. Hey." Fingers snapped in my face, and I raised my head, staring blankly at Creed.

He turned away from me, walking a few paces to stand in the open doorway of Mack's garage.

"I saw your arm."

My gaze shot down to my arms, and I immediately noticed what I'd missed before—the telltale red stain that had seeped through the sleeve of my hoodie. *Fuck.*

"I don't...I wanted it to stop." It was easier to admit it when he wasn't looking at me.

His shoulders stiffening was the only sign he'd heard me. Closing my eyes, I slumped back against the brick wall.

"There are...safe ways you can hurt, if you're

interested." Creed spoke cautiously, and when I blinked my eyes open, he was in profile, and his gaze was sliding between me and the wall. "There are options."

I swallowed hard. "Wh-what options?"

The corner of his lips kicked up. "I enjoy inflicting pain. It can be done in a safe way. Not that I'm saying I would be the one to do it, but I could put you in contact with someone if that was something you were interested in."

Safe pain? But then I thought about the violence Creed enjoyed inflicting on those who crossed him...fuck...I didn't want to go down that route. Not with him. It was one thing for me to do this to myself, but that...that was something else entirely.

"What are the other ways?"

"I'm not an expert in this, Z, but I'll tell you what I think you could try. Tattoos—you know that works for you. Piercings. Working out—going hard until everything else fades away, and you get that high. Fucking girls. Weed, to take the edge off. I know you wouldn't try anything harder than that, not after—"

He cut himself off, but we both heard his unspoken words. *Your mum*. Growing up around drug addicts was enough to put me off anything stronger than a joint. It was one line I wouldn't ever cross, and we both knew it.

"I'll think about it."

"Good." Glancing at his watch, he hummed. "Mack'll be back soon. His tattoo station's already set up for me. Wanna get anything done while you're here?"

His voice was casual, but I knew what he was getting at. I shifted, my gaze dropping to the red stain on my sleeve. Fuck it. Maybe it was worth a try. I already had ink on my arms, so what was one more tattoo?

Pushing off the wall, I gave a single nod. "I might."

He returned my nod, heading towards the interior door of the garage. When he drew level with me, he met my gaze, his expression serious. "Z. Don't forget. We're all at least a little fucked up. And the people that say they aren't...they're just kidding themselves."

It took a long fucking time to get out of that pitch-black hole, and it was always there at my feet, ready to swallow me again. If it hadn't been for the rest of the Four and Creed, always there for me, loyal to the end, I didn't know if I would've made it through. There was no magic cure, though. Physical pain was still my default, and my darkness was a permanent stain on my soul. I'd never be fully free, and Fallon, my light, my angel, was gone.

PART TWO

EIGHT MONTHS AGO

"Revenge is an act of passion; vengeance of justice. Injuries are revenged; crimes are avenged."

—Samuel Johnson, *A Dictionary of the English Language*

1

zayde

Even when I started having more better days than bad, I never stopped thinking about Fallon. Wishing I could've done something, anything, to change things. Then Caiden's now-girlfriend, Winter Huntington, came into our lives, and we discovered just how far her mother, Christine Clifford, would go to take over Alstone Holdings...working with Roland Hyde. That was when I started having recurring dreams about Fallon. Not the nightmares I'd had at the beginning, but dreams that left me so fucking on edge every time I woke. Blonde hair, a teasing smile, her body pressing into mine. Then I'd wake, and she was gone. I had too many fucking reminders of what I'd lost lately, in our efforts to stop Christine and these bastards. Every time Roland or Joseph was mentioned, she was on my mind. I still missed her so fucking much, and time had done nothing to change that.

Standing in the shadows at the side of the van, I methodically checked to make sure my knives were securely attached to my belt. The clifftop ruins of Alstone Castle were visible up ahead, and my body was thrumming with anticipation. Ready to catch Fallon's dad in the act, to implicate her brother, to bring them down for daring to plot against our families with Christine fucking Clifford. That bitch had played everyone, and we were ending it tonight.

I went back over everything in my mind as we waited for the action to begin. The way everything had gone down was fucking crazy, and even though I'd seen more than my fair share of backstabbing, violence, and illegal shit in my life, I could never have predicted something like this happening. Winter had moved to Alstone to investigate her dad's death. We had reason enough to be suspicious of her in the beginning—especially because her mother had had an affair with and then married Arlo Cavendish, and despite Winter insisting they were estranged, we only had Winter's word for it. When it turned out that she had good reason for being here, for her own suspicions regarding Christine, we began to work with her. Somehow, we started to trust her, which was something else I'd never seen coming, and then my best mate had gone and fallen hard for her. When she was taken by members of the Strelichevo crime syndicate—the Belarusian gang that Christine was working with—we were all fucking frantic, and it was then that I realised how important she'd become to us all. She was one of us now. Someone I could call a true friend, and I didn't have many of those in my life.

When we got her back, we doubled up our investigative efforts. West managed to get into Joseph Hyde's email account, where we had a breakthrough, discovering the details of this meeting tonight at Alstone Castle—apparently to discuss the final details of Christine's plan—and we knew that Christine, Roland Hyde, and Joseph Hyde would all be there. Oh, yeah, and Arlo's fucking butler, Allan, of all people, was involved in the plan.

We'd managed to talk Creed into giving us some help, because there was no fucking way we were going in unprepared. They would have security at the meeting, and the Strelichevos were involved, so we needed to give ourselves as many advantages as possible. Creed needed to stay neutral because the Strelichevos had connections with the Volkovs, who were part of the Russian Bratva and also his business associates—so he couldn't afford to risk anything that might incur their wrath. But he agreed to help us indirectly, giving us every advantage he could get away with. So we had a van kitted out with the kind of surveillance shit that gave West a hard-on, we had Mack and also Obie—who had grown up on our estate and now worked full-time for Creed—and finally, we had all the equipment we'd hopefully need to bring these fuckers down.

Yanking my balaclava down over my head, I nodded to acknowledge Caiden's signal. It was time to go. Our objectives were straightforward—get in, get the targets, get out. My first target was up ahead. Melting into the shadows, I came up behind the guard, easily taking him out before he even saw me coming. When his body crumpled to the ground, I jogged back over to Cade. "Guard down," I murmured.

We'd previously agreed that Cade and West would go after Joseph Hyde, and Cass and I would go after Allan. It was easier for me to stay neutral when it wasn't a member of Fallon's family involved, and I needed to stay focused. I fixed my eyes on Allan, waiting for the signal.

The moment the fireworks went off, Cass and I moved towards him. I swore under my breath when he was in our line of sight. He was too fucking central—surrounded by others, including Christine and Roland, along with some of the Strelichevo fuckers. We needed to get him alone.

"What the fuck do we do?" Cassius hissed, peering around the crumbling stone wall we were using as cover.

I thought fast. "We need a distraction." Leaning down, I swiped a small rock from the ground and sent it hurtling through the air.

Heads turned in the direction it landed, but it wasn't enough. Cass had caught on, though, and we moved closer, crouched down in the shadows, sending more rocks skittering in the same direction. We were moving much slower than I wanted, but if we rushed in now, we risked being outnumbered.

Still, we drew closer to Allan. Smoke from the fireworks obscured my vision, which was good because it meant that the others would have trouble seeing.

"Now," I hissed to Cassius, circling my fingers. "We split up. I'll go that way. Meet back here as soon as they've seen me." He gave me a short nod, and we ran for it.

Coming to a stop at the far side of the courtyard, away from Allan, I curled my fingers around a rock and then smashed it against the stone wall next to me as hard as I could.

At the same time, there was a loud boom, and the courtyard lit up.

Fuck, yeah.

Mack, Winter, and Kinslee were on it, sending the Molotov cocktails right where we needed them, at exactly the right time. I darted back into the shadows, using my previous route to run from wall to wall. It took me under fifteen seconds to get back to where Allan was, and I leapt from behind, slamming the rag over his mouth while

Cassius immobilised him. Wasting no time, I grabbed the syringe from my pocket and injected it into his neck, tossing the empty syringe to the ground when I was done.

We grabbed his limp body between us, moving as quickly as we could across the stubby grass, towards the van. Something inside me sent alarm bells blaring, but before my brain had time to work out what the fuck was happening, a knife whistled past my ear, and then Cade was there, swiping one of my knives from its sheath.

"Faster," he said urgently.

Cassius' gaze swung to his. "Going as fast as we can."

Somehow, we made it to the van unscathed, and then we were on the move, the castle disappearing behind us, and Joseph and Allan bound and hooded and at our mercy.

2

zayde

We were utilising one of Mack's warehouses for our interrogation, beginning with Joseph Hyde. Caiden and I were in the warehouse with him while Cassius, Weston, and Winter watched via a feed in the office.

Cade wasted no time in ripping the hood from Joseph's head, and Joseph immediately kicked off.

"Untie me right now, you assholes! If this is some juvenile prank, I—"

Caiden punched him in the face, and I couldn't help feeling a sense of satisfaction because if he hadn't been Fallon's brother, I would've done that and worse. He deserved everything he had coming to him, and the only reason I'd been holding back was because of her.

Joseph jerked against his restraints, and I realised I'd zoned out for a minute.

"...Untie me right now! The joke's over."

I slid one of my knives into my hand. "It's not a joke." Stepping forwards, I palmed the blade, and I had the pleasure of seeing Joseph's face drain of colour.

"We want answers. You'd better start talking, otherwise, it's going to hurt," Caiden barked.

"What the fuck is this all about?" His voice was hoarse, trembling with fear as he realised what deep shit he was in.

Caiden got all in his face. "First question. Why did Christine pay you to split me and Winter up, and why was Granville involved?"

He glared back at Cade. "I'm not telling you anything."

"Z."

I was ready before Cade had even said the word. My knife sliced straight through the arm of Joseph's hoodie and into his skin, blood blooming along the shallow cut. Hyde roared in pain, his eyes wide and glassy. "You cut me, you fucking sadist! What's wrong with you?"

He deserved that and more, and I didn't have time for his theatrics when we were limited for time and badly needed answers. "I barely scratched you. Next time, though, I'll cut deeper if you don't answer my friend's questions."

"Psycho bastard," he muttered under his breath. I cut him a warning look, and he clamped his mouth shut.

"I'll say it again." Caiden straddled his chair, right in front of Joseph's bound legs. "Why did Christine pay you, and why was Granville involved?"

James Granville. He was Joseph's cousin, and he'd fucked with Cade and Winter's relationship, and yet he'd been here for us tonight, driving our getaway van for the first part of our trip. He'd made himself useful in other ways, too, as much as neither Cade nor I wanted to admit it.

Hyde stared at Caiden, his lips pursed, but eventually, he let out a defeated sigh. "Fine. She didn't want you together. She can't stand you. I hate you, I dislike Winter, thanks to her obsession with you and your friends, and I got paid to fuck with your relationship? Easiest money I ever made." He smirked, and I palmed my knife, ready to strike again. This bastard was walking a thin fucking line. Out of the corner of my eye, I saw Cade gritting his teeth.

"And you didn't give a shit that you were fucking up our relationship? Didn't even question why?"

He shrugged. "Not my problem."

"Are you fucking serious?" Caiden lunged forwards.

He was stopped by a voice. "Why, though?" Winter came around to crouch next to Hyde, right at his eye level. "Why?"

He stared at her. "You're back together." When she nodded, he turned back to Caiden, every word an effort, but he clearly realised he was outnumbered. "She didn't tell me why, but I'd imagine it has something to do with the not-so-secret fact that you've never seen eye to eye, and it's clear to everyone with eyes that you hate her."

I shook my head as Caiden's brows pulled together. "Can you blame me?"

"Whatever, don't give a shit about your family problems." The second the words were out of his mouth, my knife was back out and pointed at him, but Winter was already baring her teeth and growling.

His eyes flicked to Caiden. "Put a muzzle on your bitch."

Winter jumped to her feet and smacked him straight across the face, sending his head to the side. I grinned to myself because that was the least he deserved.

Tears filled his eyes, but he attempted a sneer. "Think it's fun to knock me around when I can't fight back?"

Winter sat on Caiden's lap, and he whispered something in her ear. She stared at Joseph, her gaze hard. "So she hates Cade. What about me?"

"I don't know. I do recall her saying that you having a

relationship with your stepbrother was distasteful, and it would affect her reputation. You're clever—I'm sure you can put it together."

Her expression grew thoughtful. "Hmm. Yeah, I can see that. She alluded to it before, actually. Maybe in her own misguided way, she thought she was doing me a favour. What about James, though? How did he end up being involved?"

The smug smile that curled at the edges of his lips had my grip tightening on my knife. "It was an easy way to drive a wedge between you, and I knew it would work. I knew Cavendish was a jealous, possessive hothead and would jump to the wrong conclusion—well, the right conclusion, for the outcome I wanted."

Caiden's eyes narrowed, his jaw clenching. "Why is it that every fucking word out of your mouth makes me want to put my fist through it?"

You and me both. When I thought back to that day, when he'd set Cade up, sending him a video of Granville and Winter supposedly kissing, rage fizzed through my veins, and I had to bite my tongue to stop myself from saying anything. It was more important that we got answers. And fuck him anyway, because Cade and Winter had got past that obstacle he'd thrown and come out stronger, and I for one was sure that nothing could tear them apart now.

Winter glanced back at Caiden and then leaned forwards, studying Joseph. "How did you persuade James?"

He shrugged. "A pile of guilt about family loyalty and our rivalry with the Cavendishes. A well-timed black eye when that didn't work."

This fucker was hiding something. It was blatantly obvious. Stepping forwards, I let him see the glint of my blade, and he immediately recoiled. "Okay, okay! I'll tell you the rest." He took a deep breath. "The black eye didn't work, either, so I had to get creative, and he realised he'd have to give in. The threat of me using my TA position to alter the records for the class you had with me so you'd fail was enough to persuade him. Oh, and fail your friend Drummond, too."

Winter gasped, her eyes widening. "You—you're a despicable person. Who abuses their position like that?"

"It's nothing personal. We're just on different sides."

She stared at him in disbelief. "That's the weakest excuse I ever heard."

Yeah, it was, but we couldn't go there now. I cleared my throat, hoping Cade would understand that we needed to move on because our time was limited. He got me straight away. "Next question. Why were you and your dad meeting with Christine tonight?"

Joseph's mouth thinned. "I can't answer that."

"Can't or won't?"

He shook his head. That was my cue. I stepped up to him, pressing the tip of my blade to the cut I'd made earlier, pressing harder when all he did was swear under his breath. He hissed in pain, a thin trail of blood running down his arm.

"Fine! I'll tell you. And you'd better make sure this doesn't get back to anyone. Not to Christine, and especially not my father, because my life won't be worth living." His body shook, his voice was raw, and suddenly, Fallon's face came into my mind. Roland fucking Hyde, who'd made the lives of all three of his children a living hell. And Joseph had taken the heat for Fallon, over and over again.

Fuck.

I straightened up, throwing my knife to the ground.

Then I yanked at the torn sleeve of his hoodie, applying pressure to the cut to stop the bleeding.

"What's going on?" Winter asked carefully, unable to conceal the surprise in her voice.

"His dad isn't a nice person," I muttered, unable and unwilling to say any more. It wasn't my secret to tell.

Caiden exhaled sharply, choosing to ignore my actions, which I appreciated. "Tell us what you know."

Fucking finally, Joseph gave us a piece of useful information. "She's been working with my father for a long time. They've been plotting to take over Alstone Holdings. I've never been privy to the ins and outs, but I know that there's the deal going down tomorrow with the De Witts, and she was going to make a move after that." Glaring at us, he added, "I probably would have found out more if you hadn't interrupted the meeting tonight and fucking kidnapped me."

It was the least he deserved. I exchanged glances with Cade, both of us on the same page, as Winter questioned him. "What move was she going to make?"

"I honestly don't know. My father keeps all his cards close to his chest."

"Is there anything else you can tell us?" Caiden bit out, near the end of his tether.

He shook his head. "Nothing, except those guys at the meeting tonight? I know she's paying them a lot of money, and I know they don't like her very much. I picked up that much from the short time I was there."

Caiden's arm tightened around Winter, both of them glaring at Hyde. I watched as Caiden took a deep, calming breath. "Why were you at the meeting, anyway?"

"I don't know exactly, but my father wants to bring me into the business. Not that I'd have anything to do with it if

I had any choice in the matter. I'm sure you can appreciate being groomed for the family business, being the son of the almighty Arlo Cavendish."

"Fuck you." Caiden lifted Winter off his lap, climbing to his feet. When he glanced at me, I was ready, anticipating his next question. "Tape?"

I handed him the roll, and he wasted no time in ripping off a strip and slapping it over Joseph's mouth. We carried him, chair and all, to the side of the room, where we seated him facing the corner.

Caiden and Winter took the lead in questioning Arlo's butler, Allan. As much as I fucking loathed him for working with Christine and the Strelichevos, I couldn't help feeling a small measure of sympathy for him. Not much, because he was working against us, after all, but the old bastard had obviously been manipulated and blinded by his family loyalty.

It all went to shit part way through the interrogation. Christine called to say she had Jessa De Witt hostage, and she wanted to trade her for Allan. If we didn't comply, Jessa's life would be forfeited. Jessa was a girl we'd grown up with, one of the elite, but she had a bit of a vendetta against Winter, and I had zero fucking time for that bitchy rich-girl shit. Even so, the only fuckers that deserved to die tonight were Christine, the Strelichevos, and anyone working with them against Alstone Holdings. Yeah, that included Roland Hyde, and maybe even Joseph, but I wouldn't play a part in the deaths of those two. Not when I hadn't been able to save Tim.

Caiden ended the call. His eyes were so fucking wide,

and there was an expression I'd never seen on his face before. It was uneasy, almost afraid. "I'll take Allan and Hyde. We've only got my car and the SUV here, so we'll split up, and when we get near to the docks, we'll pull over and I'll go in with them. I don't want any of you in danger." He was fucking joking if he thought that any of us would stay away. As his gaze went from me to Winter and then back again, his mouth twisted as realisation dawned. "Z, can you get hold of Mack on the way? We don't have any time to lose."

"On it." I was already tugging my phone from my pocket as Caiden turned back to Winter.

"Baby, can you get hold of Granville? See if we can get him to go to AMC if we can't get hold of Dad." He continued giving orders until West looked up from the computer.

"Everything's sent."

Caiden nodded. "Good. Let's go."

3

zayde

The rain was pouring. Lightning flashed, and thunder rumbled, but I was thankful for the storm. It meant visibility was decreased, which we could use to our advantage.

Caiden was already gone by the time we reached Winter. Even in the darkness and the pouring rain, I could see her stricken look, tears running down her face. Cassius pulled Winter into his arms as Weston and I came to stand by her side. The rain eased off a little in the minute we took to catch our breaths, but I couldn't allow us to wait too long. In the absence of Caiden, I was in charge.

"Let's go. We go in, avoid being seen, get Cade and Jessa out of there. Mack's on his way, but we don't have time to wait for him. Everyone ready?"

They slipped into formation behind me, and as we moved closer, I scanned every inch of our surroundings, calculating our best options. The entrance barrier was wide open, and I could see three cars making a U shape. Cade had driven Cassius' SUV inside, with Allan and Joseph in the back, and had stopped in front of them. Fucking

Christine was there, and Jessa was thrashing against a smirking Littlefinger. No doubt Roland Hyde was skulking around here somewhere, too.

Something twisted in my gut. We were running out of time. I signalled to Cassius and Weston to take one side, to get to Jessa, while I took the other. As Winter began following me, I pushed her back gently. Cade would kill me if anything happened to her. "Go. Hide behind the SUV. I don't want anyone seeing you."

Keeping to the shadows, I moved closer to the group of cars.

A hand clamped down on my arm, and I felt the cold metal press of a gun barrel in the small of my back. A deep voice growled in my ear, "Where do you think you're—"

Before he could even finish his sentence, I was twisting down and around, taking the henchman with me. At the same time, my fingers closed around the blade of one of my knives, pulling it free from its sheath. It was a matter of seconds before I'd incapacitated him, and one hard thrust to the back of his neck with my knife and he was down and out for good. Kicking his gun away, sending it skittering under one of the cars, I wiped my knife off on the henchman's jacket and straightened up.

Before I could process the scene, figures flashed across my vision, moving quickly through the shadows. *Arlo and James Granville.*

Gunshots cut through the night, and I was on the move. I was almost level with the SUV when the back door burst open, and Allan tumbled out. Then Arlo was there, and Allan was throwing himself in front of his body. More gunshots sounded, and I fucking ran, launching myself into the air with my blade in my hand. At the same time, Granville struck my target with a swing of his baton, sending his head to the side, and when my momentum propelled me forwards, slamming straight into his falling body, I drove my blade into his throat, twisting.

Another fucking gunshot sounded, and then I heard Winter screaming my best friend's name, over and over, her voice full of incomparable agony.

An icy chill stole the breath from my lungs.

No. Not again.

I should have been there to save Caiden, but I was too late.

The relief that went through me when I found out that Caiden was going to be okay brought me to my knees. Muttering an excuse, I pushed out of the hospital doors and stumbled around the side of the building. I collapsed in the shadows on the wet concrete, my back against the cold stone wall, and drew a shaking hand across my face. *Fuck.* We'd come so close to losing him. To losing more than just him. Winter, Arlo, Jessa, too. Even James Granville. All of us had been at risk in one way or another.

I fumbled in my pocket for the little tin, pulling out the joint, but my hands were fucking trembling too much to light it.

"Here."

I remained staring straight ahead as Cassius lowered himself down next to me, flicking the lighter. Inhaling deeply, I let my head fall back against the wall, my eyes closed.

When I exhaled, I passed the joint to Cassius. He took it with a sigh. "Thanks. What a fucking night."

"Yeah."

The cold seeped through my clothes, into my skin, but neither of us moved, swapping the joint until only a tiny stub remained. Cassius flicked it away and then cleared his throat. "You coming inside? Cade'll want all his family there when he wakes up."

All his family.

I was so fucking grateful for my boys, and for Winter, but I couldn't stop thinking about another night. Another night that had ended with the loss of a family member.

We climbed to our feet, and Cassius clapped me on the back. "Hey. You disappeared before Cade's dad mentioned the Hydes. They got away tonight, but Arlo's gonna pin some shit on Hyde Senior that'll get him locked up for a long time. He's not gonna get away with what he did."

For the first time since this clusterfuck of an evening had begun, the tiniest smile tugged at the corner of my lips.

"That bastard deserves everything he has coming to him."

We'd make sure of it.

PART THREE

PRESENT DAY

"The marks humans leave are too often scars."

—John Green, *The Fault in Our Stars*

1

fallon

"Here are your things, Miss Hyde." Selma placed the cardboard box into my arms. "Take your time."

With a small nod, I crossed the reception area of the facility—or the sanctuary, as it was referred to here—and sank down into one of the chairs in the far corner. The curved leather seat back cradled my body as I sat for a moment, tapping a finger against my thigh and counting to ten in my head, composing myself. Out of the corner of my eye, I could feel Selma watching me carefully, and that knowledge gave me the strength to open the flaps of the box and take stock of the contents inside.

There wasn't much of note. The clothes I'd worn on my arrival, so long ago. A battered paperback copy of *To Kill a Mockingbird*. My old phone, which was turned on and showing the time on the lock screen—someone must have charged it. And on top of it all, a necklace—a delicate platinum chain with a pair of angel wings, also platinum.

My breath caught in my throat before I banished the thoughts that were trying to break through. Making sure that I only touched the phone, I lifted it from the box, then raised my head and met Selma's concerned gaze.

"You can get rid of everything in this box."

A thinning of her lips was her only reaction. Crossing over to me, she took the box from my grip and headed back to the reception desk. I dropped my gaze, studying my phone. It had been a long time since I'd used this one. I had a new phone now, but this one...this one held memories. Photos. My social media accounts that I'd never installed on my new phone.

My finger hovered over the social media folder, and then I forced myself to look. Notifications began flashing up on the screen, too many for me to take in. I scrolled down, scanning over the names. People I barely knew wanting information about the incident.

I closed the apps and powered the phone down. There was nothing for me here now.

"Fallon?"

Raising my head, I took in the figure standing just inside the entrance door.

"Joseph." An unfamiliar feeling unfurled inside me, and it took me a moment to realise it was almost happiness. I was glad to see my older brother.

"Are...are you ready to go home?" He was chewing on his lip, unsure. He was normally the confident older brother, who I hadn't always seen eye to eye with, and it took me aback to see him so hesitant. Then again, we hadn't seen each other since his last visit, which had been months ago, and we'd never shared a close relationship.

Not like I'd had with Tim.

Tim.

Thanks to the months and months of therapy, I'd

mostly come to terms with my brother's death, but not the cause of it. I didn't know if I ever would. How could I?

As I followed Joseph outside into the night and the fresh mountain air filled my lungs and the sanctuary door closed behind me for the final time, I wondered.

How was it possible to still love someone that you hated beyond anything?

When would I ever stop hating myself for loving Zayde Lowry as much as I loathed him?

When?

Once, he was the love of my life. The cold, closed-off boy with the smiles he saved only for me.

My family's rival. My secret, my obsession, my protector.

I gave him my heart, and in return, he gave me his.

Then, he smashed me to pieces, leaving only fragments that I was still trying to put back together.

It only took one night to change everything.

The night he killed my brother.

2

zayde

Roland Hyde is behind bars.

The words had been playing in my mind on a loop ever since yesterday, when Caiden had informed me that he'd been charged with embezzlement, six counts of fraud, and various other smaller charges that would keep him locked up for a long time.

It was a piece of my past that was finally over. Justice had been served.

So why did I feel so fucking numb?

The loud thud of music reverberated through the house. Watching the party from the vantage point of my armchair in the corner of the room, it was like I was outside, looking in on a scene. I rubbed my hand across my face. This was supposed to be a celebration, but sometimes it took being in a crowded room to realise that you were lonely.

What I knew I should feel and what I did feel were two different beasts. Fucking hell, most people would kill to be in my position.

Focus. Focus on something good.

As I lifted my joint to my lips, my gaze zeroed in on the

group right in the centre of the action. Seeing Caiden, Cassius, and Weston—my three best mates—together with their girls, an unfamiliar emotion flickered to life inside me, penetrating the numbness. Infinitesimal, weak, but undeniably there. Something I hadn't thought I was ever capable of feeling again.

Hope.

I inhaled, holding on to that feeling. Maybe one day, I could move on from the past. Get rid of this darkness inside me. Break down the walls of ice I'd built around my heart.

And I hoped that wherever Fallon was, she'd been able to move on. I hoped that she was happy now.

With everyone's attention still on my friends, I opened my phone, pulling up the old message thread. Why did I torture myself? Fallon's account had been inactive ever since she'd left. I couldn't seem to help myself, though. It was a compulsion. Every fucking day. No matter how many times I told myself it was pointless. That I needed to let go.

Maybe now it was time. Roland Hyde was imprisoned, and everyone else was moving on with their lives. I was doing better now, wasn't I? I should move on, too.

My finger hovered over the Delete button.

I blinked at the screen.

What the fuck?

I grasped my phone so fucking tightly that it made an ominous crunching sound within my grip.

My world tilted on its axis.

There was a green dot next to her photo.

She was online.

Just as quickly as the dot had appeared, it disappeared. Almost like I'd imagined it, but I knew what I'd seen.

Memories crashed over me, a suffocating wave that dragged me under until I couldn't breathe. The noises of the party seemed to increase to unbearable levels, making my ears ring.

Fuck.

I had to get out of here.

Stubbing out the joint, I thrust my phone back into my pocket. Launching myself out of the armchair, I caught Caiden's eye. Without saying a word, he gave me a small nod, letting me know he understood that I needed to get away. He was my best mate for a reason—out of everyone, he understood me the best.

The ringing got louder as I pushed through the faceless bodies, aiming for the front door. The compulsion was there, the need for pain, so strong that I couldn't focus on anything else.

I thought I was doing better.

I thought I was fine.

Yet it had taken less than a minute for the cracks in my wall of ice to appear.

Less than a minute for my cold, dead heart to be revived, bringing with it an unbearable agony that tore through me, shattering the walls that I'd worked so fucking hard to build.

3

zayde

"Let me see him." I stared across the reception desk, my mouth set in a flat line. Natalie stared straight back at me, her glossy blue hair spilling over her shoulders and her arms folded underneath her tits, pushing them up. It did nothing for me. I'd slept with her once, when I was trying to forget about Fallon. It was no fucking use. No matter who I slept with, nothing changed. It had been almost two years that she'd been gone, but I knew I'd love her until the day I died.

I'd been lying to myself for too long, and that had all become clear the second I saw she was online. It had been a week since then, and although she hadn't shown up again, it was time for me to do some digging. Which was why I was here at Pope Industries in London, the home of Credence Pope's empire. If anyone could get me the information I wanted, it was Creed. Of course, I'd owe him a favour. But I'd been doing jobs for him long enough...since I was eight, in fact. I'd always be fucking grateful to him for everything he'd done for me over the years, how he looked out for me.

When I was around eleven, he'd started giving me different tasks, bringing me into his circle of trusted associates.

"Here. A fiver each. I've got another job if you're interested?" Creed handed two crumpled five-pound notes to me and my friend Lloyd "Mack" Mackenzie. I shoved mine in the pocket of my jeans before turning back to Creed. He was an older boy, around fifteen or sixteen, who often had odd jobs for the kids who lived on our housing estate, and we all looked up to him. I didn't know exactly what he did, but he told us he was building his empire, whatever that meant. Mack and I had just delivered some weed baggies to some of the flats in our tower block, and now Creed had another job for us? Yeah, that meant more money, which was always good. My mum worked two different jobs—one as a cleaner and one where men would come to our flat and she'd kick me out so she could do things with them that I wasn't supposed to know about. We still never had enough, though, and my mum spent too much of what we did have on alcohol.

"What's the job?" Tugging the sleeves of my hoodie down to cover my freezing fingers, I looked up at Creed.

"See that man over there? The one with the blue coat?" He tilted his head to the right, and I followed the direction. There was a tall man with black hair and a thick beard, wearing a blue puffer jacket and standing against the chain-link fence, talking on a phone.

"Yeah."

"Good. I want you to follow him and tell me where he goes. Make sure he doesn't see you, yeah?"

"C'mon, Z, he's moving. Let's go." Mack picked his fallen bike up and jumped on, already pedalling in the man's direction

before I'd even moved. I grabbed my bike and went after him, my brakes squeaking against the bent back wheel.

A loud roaring sound came from down the street, close to where the blue-coat man was walking. The noise immediately caught my attention, and I turned and watched, spellbound, as a shiny black motorbike came flying down the road, weaving around the parked cars with no effort.

The second I saw it, I knew. *One day, I was going to have a motorbike of my own.*

When the motorbike had disappeared from view, the rumbling purr still sounding in the distance, we followed the blue-coat man to a kebab shop, where he disappeared inside. Mack set up a makeshift ramp made from some rubbish in the alleyway next to the shop. We passed the time jumping our bikes on the ramp until the man came out again around half an hour later, now holding a Tesco bag. He walked fast, but we still had to pedal slowly so we didn't catch up with him, our bikes wobbling all over the pavement, thanks to our slow pace.

He finally stopped at a terraced house with a blue front door and used a key to let himself in. We waited around for a while, but when it looked like he wasn't coming out again, I saved the house number and road name on my phone before we cycled back to our estate. Creed seemed happy with the information even though nothing much had happened, and he gave us another fiver each.

After that day, Creed had started relying on me and Mack more often, seeking us out for tasks that involved surveillance and information retrieval, leaving the drug selling to other kids on the estate. Now...I'd stepped back from that life, out of deference to the Four and my fucking obligations that came with being a Lowry, but even the board of Alstone Holdings knew just how important it was to maintain connections with Creed. His reach was far, and he wasn't afraid to get his hands dirty.

"He'll see you now. He's in the basement." Natalie slipped into professional mode, and I was glad for it. Then her words caught up with me.

"Basement?"

A small, secretive smile played over her lips. "Mmm. Looks like you've made it all the way into Mr. Pope's inner circle. You know about the underground car park, right? Well...there's more to the underground than meets the eye. Parts that don't technically exist. They're not on the blueprints." She placed a black-tipped finger to her lips. "Shhh."

I rolled my eyes. She knew that I knew how important secrets were. How they were worth more than gold in our world.

"Understood," I clipped out. "How do I get there?"

"The lift. Use your card. You'll need the code. It's 24590." With a nod, I turned on my heel, striding towards the lift.

"Zayde?"

Her voice stopped me, but I didn't turn around. There was a pause, and then she spoke again, her tone softer than before.

"For what it's worth, I hope things work out for you."

My shoulders stiffened. I didn't need her misplaced sympathy.

"Zayde. I mean it."

I sighed, Winter coming to mind for some reason. If she was here, she'd probably have something to say about me being rude or some shit. "Thanks," I muttered grudgingly. I guessed it wasn't Natalie's fault that she wasn't the girl I really wanted, so I probably shouldn't take my shit out on her.

Still, I was glad to reach the lift and get away from the reception area. Pulling my black card from my pocket, I inserted it into the slot and then punched in the code that would allow me into the basement. As the lift descended, I wondered if Mack knew about the basement. There was no way of knowing, though, unless we both ended up down there at the same time. That was the thing about secrets—you couldn't discuss them. And Creed always played his cards close to his chest.

The lift spat me out into a cavernous space. High, arched ceilings soared above me, and mirrored walls stretched away into the distance. The floor underfoot was hard rubber, and over to my left, against the wall... I took a step into the room, and then another. Fucking hell. Overflowing racks of weapons stood proudly gleaming in the artificial lighting, both legal and illegal.

"Zayde."

I turned to see Creed striding towards me, a wide grin on his face. When he reached me, he shook my hand.

"I know you have questions for me."

"Yeah. How about you explain this?"

His grin widened, if that was possible, his golden eyes glinting with humour. "This is my training facility. We practise sparring, weapons training, whatever needs working on. There are changing rooms and showers through those doors over there," he said, pointing to the far side of the room.

"We?" I raised a brow.

"That's a question with an answer for another day. For now, I have something more interesting to show you." He spun on his heel, stalking across the huge space to a door at the far side. It was thick metal, almost like an underground bunker door. After he'd scanned his fingerprint and punched a code into the keypad, there was a click, and the door swung open.

"Welcome to the catacombs."

"Fuck me." I whistled, stepping onto flagstones worn smooth with years of use. "What is this place? Church ruins?"

He nodded. "Yep. Church crypts and the remains of a prison, from what I can tell. Maybe tunnels that were used by pit ponies back in the day."

"And now?"

"Now..." Drawing level with a tiny pad on the wall, he widened his eyes, allowing the scanner to work its magic. Opening another door, he swept his arm out. "Now, this is where I play."

Bloodstains arced across the floor, the pattern suggesting a spray, probably from a throat being slit. Creed followed my line of sight, shaking his head. "They should've cleaned up in here."

"Who was it?"

I hadn't expected an answer, but he gave me one anyway. "Remember how everything went down with Petr Ivanov? The Volkovs might have pulled in one or two of their London-based associates to make sure there were no more leaks in their syndicate. I was more than happy to offer the use of my facilities."

My jaw clenched as I remembered how Petr Ivanov had fucked with Cassius' girlfriend, Jessa. If he hadn't been dead before I could get to him, I would've killed him myself.

"We would've ended him whatever happened."

Intuitive as ever, Creed briefly clasped my shoulder, a fleeting touch. "I know."

We nodded at each other, and he dropped his hand.

"Zayde." Creed propped himself up against a long, low table with various instruments of torture laid out on the surface and glinting in the dim lighting of the overhead bulb. "I brought you down here to show you that I consider you someone I can trust. I hope you can extend the same trust to me."

"Yeah." I rubbed my hand over my face. It was so fucking hard to open up to anyone. It went against everything I'd trained myself to do. Blowing out a heavy breath, I spoke through gritted teeth. "The reason I'm here is because I need a favour. The Hyde girl. She..." Fuck. I couldn't get the words out.

"Hyde." His brows pulled together as he tapped on the metal surface of the table. "The one that had to be shipped off to the facility?"

I nodded jerkily, and he inhaled sharply. "That reminds me. Something I was going to call you about today. I've been given the details of Roland Hyde's sentence, if you want them. He's finally been charged, and it's about fucking time. Six counts of fraud, embezzlement, and some other minor shit that all added together should ensure he's locked up for a long time. They've frozen his business assets, too. There's a good chance he'll lose it all."

"I heard. Cade told me—his dad told him."

"Thought he might, but I wanted to be sure. I wouldn't be surprised if he tries to appeal his sentencing again to get the term reduced. I hate to say it, but that bastard has connections, and he's one slimy fucker. I'll keep an eye on the situation, though, and I'll let you know if and when I hear anything."

Fucker. "If he gets out, he'd better watch his back, or he'll be buried six feet under before he knows it."

Creed grinned, his psycho smile making an appearance.

"Creepy fucker," I muttered, which only made his smile widen. "Forget about Hyde Senior for a minute. The girl—"

"You want me to find out what's happened to her?" he interjected. "Consider it done."

"She was..." I stumbled over my fucking words. How could I explain the heavy weight of guilt that was a constant millstone around my neck? But fuck it. Creed wasn't someone to get personally involved in shit. Even if you were a friend of his. Yeah, he'd help out if and when he could, and he did what he could to tip the scales in your favour. But business was his number one priority, and he was good at playing people off against each other. So maybe he was someone neutral I could speak to about this. "This goes no further," I said.

"You know it won't."

"We were together for a while. The night...the night Tim, her brother, died...I was arguing with him...and I...and I..." Fucking fuck. I couldn't finish the sentence. Spinning away from Creed, I clenched my jaw so tight that my teeth were grinding painfully against each other. I couldn't lose control. Not now.

A hand came down on my shoulder. Creed's voice was completely neutral, which I appreciated more than anything because I was so fucking close to losing it. "Z. No need to say any more. Consider it done. I'll find out everything I can, and I'll have it to you within a few days. No favour in return, not for this."

My eyes fell shut as I bowed my head, slumping back against the table. The instruments rattled, clinking together. Blindly feeling next to me, I picked up a slim, metallic object. It had some weight to it.

Opening my eyes, I took in the handle I was grasping,

my gaze rising to the curve of the blade of the santoku knife. The hardened steel shone brightly as I curved my fingers more tightly around the handle, bringing the knife up to my arm.

It felt like I was outside of my body, watching as I tugged my sleeve up, turning my arm so my inner wrist was exposed. Then everything came back into immediate focus when I placed the point of the knife to my wrist and pressed down.

There was a sharp, familiar burst of pain, and I sighed with relief, dragging the knife across my tattooed and scarred skin, blood bubbling up in its wake. For a moment, all my problems disappeared, and the agony was all that remained. My mind was empty and quiet, my world narrowed down to this one perfectly still moment.

A moment of agony and ecstasy.

"Z." Creed's hand closed around mine. "I know there's no cure, and you're allowed to have good and bad days. But remember that you have other ways to deal with this."

Fuck.

He was right.

I'd come too far along this long, shadowy, painful road to go back.

I let the knife fall from my grip, and as it dropped with a clatter, the pain inside me came roaring back, dragging me under.

4

zayde

"Fuck you. I won." Cassius threw down his PS5 controller, turning to give Caiden a mock glare. To my left, Weston smirked as he tapped out something on his laptop. It was like old times today. Just the four of us. Me, Caiden, Cassius, and Weston. Their girls were all at Skirmish, one of Creed's places, where they were apparently practising archery or knife throwing or some shit.

I'd never cared that the rest of the Four were all pairing up. Yeah, there had been times when I'd thought about it, but I'd always known that I'd never have a relationship like they were all capable of. It was something inevitable—I was doomed to love Fallon, and therefore, I'd never have what they had.

I'd never cared *until*. Until it had become completely fucking obvious that the three of them were in serious relationships, and their girls were just as important to them as we were to each other.

Now I noticed the emptiness inside me.

Loneliness.

And then when I'd seen Fallon was back online, it made me think about things. Want things that I knew I was never going to have.

Tugging my knife out, I forced myself to concentrate on the repetitive movements as I flicked the blade in and out of the handle. It only took about ten seconds for me to realise it wasn't going to do anything to help. Shoving my knife back into my pocket, I scrubbed my hand across my face. Fuck. Wearing a mask had always come so easily to me, but now I was on the verge of losing my shit for the second time in two days. Climbing to my feet, I headed into the kitchen, pulling a bottle of water from the fridge to give me something to do.

"Z?"

I acknowledged Cade's presence with a nod but didn't turn around.

He sighed from behind me. "You know if there's anything on your mind, you can talk to me."

"Yeah."

"It stays between us, you know that."

I nodded again. When I didn't hear him move, I gritted my teeth, clenching onto the kitchen counter. There were things I couldn't tell him. Telling Creed had been risky enough, but at least I knew he'd stay neutral. Caiden was my best mate, but he was also very fucking anti-Hyde. As he should be, after the way Joseph had gone after Winter. Their cousin, James Granville, hung out with us sometimes, though. We owed him for helping Winter out, and Lena, if you wanted to go into detail. Even so, I wasn't sure if Cade would ever warm up to him, even though James had never been directly involved in our Hyde-Alstone Holdings rivalry, other than when Joseph had been blackmailing him.

And then there was the whole thing where Hyde Senior had been working with Cade's stepmother, Christine Clifford, plotting to take over Alstone Holdings. I hoped that it was just Creed's paranoia speaking when he said he thought Hyde might appeal his sentence. The charges he'd been sentenced with should be enough to keep him locked up for a long time. That fucker deserved to rot behind bars forever, as far as I was concerned.

"Wanna come with me to meet Mack? We're running low on weed." I couldn't say anything to Cade about what was going on with me, but I knew I could use the company.

"Yeah, okay. Let's take my car. I need to fill the tank." There was relief in his voice, and that meant he'd seen right through my act.

When we were on the road, with the rumbling purr of Cade's matte-black Audi R8 filling the silence, I cracked. "Creed spoke to me about Hyde Senior's charges. Said he thinks he might try to appeal his sentence."

In my peripheral vision, I saw Caiden's jaw clench, his fingers tightening around the steering wheel. "That fucker. If he dares to try anything... But how does he think he's gonna weasel his way out of his sentence? There's a mountain of evidence stacked against him. Surely they can get the charges to stick."

"Fuck knows, but remember he wasn't above working with your stepmother and the low-life scum she had doing her bidding. I wouldn't put anything past him. Creed said he'll keep an eye on the situation."

"Good. He'd fucking better." Caiden pulled into the waste ground where we were meeting Mack, bringing his R8 to a stop close to a group of hooded guys. I lowered my window, watching as one of the guys detached himself from the group, jogging over to us.

"Z." Mack's grinning face appeared. "And rich boy."

Caiden rolled his eyes but gave Mack a nod. "Alright, mate. What have you got for us?"

Mack handed me the baggies of weed, swapping them for a roll of notes from my pocket. When we'd completed the transaction, he leaned closer, sticking his head through the car window and lowering his voice. "I'm on a job for Creed. The name Hyde might've come up. Ring any bells?"

Caiden and I exchanged glances before I nodded slowly. As far as Cade was concerned, we were talking about Roland Hyde, not his daughter. "Yeah. We might know something about that. I might've asked Creed to look into it."

"Thought so." He straightened up. "If any shit goes down, you know where to find me." His eyes met Cade's. "If your girlfriend's hot friend is involved, don't even think about leaving me out."

Caiden smirked at him. "You're into Kinslee? Since when? You think you have a chance with her?"

Mack grinned again. "Who'd turn me down? I'm a fucking catch."

Caiden snorted. "If you say so."

"Z, I don't know why you hang around with rich boy so much. He's a dickhead."

"Takes one to know one," Cade shot back, his own grin appearing, and for a minute, I felt lighter. Almost normal, or what passed as normal for me. Until my gaze caught on the familiar tower block where I'd spent the first twelve years of my life.

What would my life have looked like if Michael Lowry hadn't discovered that he was my dad? I'd like to think I'd be successful in the way Mack was, but so many of our former friends were no longer around. Gangs, drug overdoses, stabbings, alcoholism...those things had been my reality growing up. Only the strongest survived, and sometimes being the strongest wasn't even enough. Death could come for any of us at any time.

I still remembered the day I'd found out about Michael Lowry, how completely fucking blindsided I'd been and how I'd had no idea just how much my life would change. The grey concrete structures loomed over me as I lost myself in memories, and I gritted my teeth, reminding myself that I was one of the lucky ones.

The electric meter beeped, a reminder that we were now running on emergency credit, and the key needed to be topped up ASAP. Last time it had run out, it had been late at night, and my mum hadn't been home. I flipped open my wallet to count out my change. I didn't have access to the online top-up facility, but the corner shop could top it up for me if I had cash.

Once I'd counted up my change, I had a total of £2.85. The minimum top-up was £1, so at least I had enough. Pocketing my wallet, I headed over to the meter. Before I even had a chance to get to the key, the door to our flat burst open, and my mum came running in.

"Mum? Aren't you supposed to be at work?"

Her eyes were kind of wild and crazy-looking, and she was breathing hard. Her gaze focused on me, and she pointed at the sofa. "Sit. Quick."

Staring at her, I took a seat, shifting to avoid the spring that was poking out of the corner. I was starting to get worried; she was acting weird. "Mum—"

"Shut up for a minute! Listen to me carefully, Zayde."

Taking a deep breath, she sat down next to me and put her hand on my arm, patting it lightly. I flinched, an involuntary reaction. My mum never touched me, other than to strike me when she thought I was misbehaving. "You're moving out."

I stared at her in shock, trying to make sense of her words. "What do you mean, I'm moving out?"

"Your dad."

What? "My dad? I don't have a dad. I thought you said he died."

"He might as well have been dead to me," she muttered. "He was a..." She coughed. "Client of mine."

"I-I don't understand..." My hands were fucking shaking.

"Turns out, he's rich. Very rich. Something he kept from me," she spat viciously. "Gave me a fake name and occupation, the lying bastard. Well, as it happens, he's the answer to all our problems, and he wants you to live with him now, you see?"

"But I...I don't understand. Why do I have to live with him? I don't want to go! I don't even know him. And w-why did he wait until now?" I dug my fingers into my thighs, pressing down as hard as I could while I tried to get air into my lungs.

"Ah." Her hand fell away from my arm. "He didn't know about you. I might have seen him in the papers when I was at Jean's house. So I contacted him once I saw he was minted. Can't look a gift horse in the mouth, can we?"

"But—"

"You don't get a choice. Didn't you hear me? He's rich."

"But—but I don't want to move away." I was panicking. Did she want me to leave? What about my friends? Fallon?

Her mouth set in a flat line, and she shook her head at me. "Don't be so stupid. You'll go to the best school; you'll want for nothing."

"But I like my school here."

"Too bad. He'll be here at ten o'clock on Saturday to pick you up."

I stared at her, my mouth falling open. Saturday? That was

the day after tomorrow. "I was going to help you with your cleaning job."

She laughed. "You don't need to worry about that. Your dad's set me up with enough money that I don't need to work anymore. I quit this morning."

There was a lump in my throat that I couldn't seem to swallow. "Won't—won't you miss me?"

"Zayde." There was silence for a long moment while she stared down at her hands, twisting her fingers together. I focused on the chipped red nail varnish on her index finger, trying to get myself under control.

Eventually, she raised her head and gave me a look that I didn't think she'd ever given me before. There was guilt and maybe even a little bit of sadness, but it didn't matter what her eyes said because her mouth was set in that stubborn line that meant she'd made her mind up. "It'll be better for you this way. You'll have opportunities that you'd never get here. Your dad...he's a successful businessman, and he'll do what's best for you." Patting my leg quickly, she tried for a smile. "Go and pack now. I expect you'll want to say goodbye to your friends, too."

In my bedroom, I stood still, that fucking lump in my throat refusing to go away. I didn't want to leave, but my mum didn't want me to stay. I was going to lose everything I knew, and I didn't give a shit who my dad was. I just wanted things to stay the same.

Everything inside me hurt, and I needed it to stop.

Throwing myself onto my bed, I balanced my left arm on my thighs, then placed my index finger to the skin above my wrist and dug my nail in. I scraped at my skin until it began to bleed, but it wasn't enough.

My gaze blurred as I dug my nail in harder, the blood welling around my finger in tiny bubbles. I sucked in a breath, focusing only on my skin and the superficial pain, and suddenly, everything inside stopped hurting.

Just like that, I could breathe again.

My hand fell away, and I used my T-shirt to soak up the small amount of blood. It would scab over, but I'd just wear long sleeves like I normally did when I did this to myself. When the bleeding had stopped, I grabbed my phone from the drawer next to my desk, the screen cracked where I'd dropped it, and sent a message to Fallon.

***Me:** Bad bad news. I'm moving away*
***Fallon:** Moving away? WHAT?*
***Me:** Mum dropped a bombshell on me just now. Said my dad's alive and wants me to live with him*
***Fallon:** WHAT!!! Wow. I wasn't expecting that. Are you okay?*

I pictured her sitting there on her pink bed, frowning at her phone and biting her lip. If only I could see her to say goodbye. This whole situation fucking sucked.

***Me:** I don't want to go. How will I see you?*
***Fallon:** Where are you moving to? Is it far? I don't want you to go either. I'll miss you too much*

Something warm curled low in my belly.

***Me:** I don't know yet. Mum said he was one of her clients so I guess he can't live too far away*
***Fallon:** Find out. You're my best friend Zayde. Even if we can't see each other anymore we can phone and text. I won't let you go*

Falling back on my bed, I forced myself to breathe in and out slowly until my heart rate calmed down. She was right. My mum might be making me do this, but I wasn't going to lose my best friend over this.

Me: *You're right. I've got to pack now but I'll text you again*
Fallon: *I'm always right ;) It's going to be ok I promise xx*

5

fallon

The house was empty, an echoing mausoleum with what remained of the furniture covered in dust sheets. I stared around me, horrified. I'd thought... I didn't know what I'd expected, but it wasn't this. My father was gone, locked up where he couldn't hurt me anymore, and maybe I'd been naive—maybe my therapy had made me too optimistic, if that was possible—but I'd convinced myself that being back here was what I needed to finally be able to move on with my life.

Joseph didn't even live here anymore. He'd left town, but he'd come back for me, or so he said. I wasn't quite convinced, but I appreciated his presence. I had to face the ghosts of my past, but I wasn't sure I was ready to do it alone.

"Where's Mum? What happened to all the furniture?"

Joseph shook his head, looking as gobsmacked as I felt. "I had no idea. She said...she told me she was having a clear-out after Dad's trial. This is..." He trailed off, shaking his head. "Come on."

We passed rooms that all told the same story until we

reached the kitchen. I stopped dead in the doorway, taking in the scene in front of me with dawning horror. Empty bottles littered the countertops, wine glasses with lipstick stains were crowded around the sink, and at the centre of it all, my mother.

She had a brightly patterned silk dressing gown wrapped around her, a cigarette dangling from her lips, and a half-full glass of red wine clasped in her hand. When she saw me and Joseph, she smiled.

"Joe! How lovely of you to pay a visit. And you..." She turned to me, her smile disappearing. "*You*. What are you doing here? You think you can stay away all this time and just waltz back in like nothing's changed?"

Her words were slurred, but the fact that she was clearly drunk in the middle of the day didn't soften the blow. A lump came into my throat, despite the fact that I'd prepared myself for this, as much as I could. I hadn't expected her to be happy to see me, but I thought that maybe... It didn't matter what I'd thought. I had to keep on moving on, and do what I'd set out here to do.

"Mum," Joe said, shaking his head. "That's not fair." A deep frown pulled at his brows, and I only realised then just how tired he looked. How much older he seemed. We'd stayed in touch during the time I'd been gone, but I hadn't been ready to face him in person until now. And that was because of my biggest, most shameful secret, one that my therapist had worked so hard on with me.

There was a small part of me that blamed myself for Tim's death. Deep down, I knew it hadn't been my fault, but I couldn't stop replaying the moment he slipped away, wishing I could have done something more to reach him in time.

My parents might have been the ones to send me away,

but I stayed away because of the guilt that their son was gone and I'd been there when it happened.

That, and my dad...

That night...

I'd been incoherent with grief. I'd found out later that the paramedics had sedated me, and after that, I...shut down. That's the only way I could describe it. It was like my mind went completely blank, taking me into a place where nothing and no one could touch me. I remembered my dad's rage, how he'd struck me, over and over, but it was like it was happening to someone else. The searing pain had eventually caused me to black out, but I hadn't been in my body at the time. Nothing could touch me.

When my parents had wasted no time in shipping me off to Switzerland, I hadn't even been upset about it. I'd wanted the same thing as they did, to get away, far away from anything and anyone that could hurt me.

Somehow, I'd managed to finish my A levels, but what I'd always considered to be the life that had been planned out for me had been left in ruins.

When my cousin James had called me to tell me what had happened, though, I felt like I could breathe again for the first time in almost two years. My dad was now in prison, where he could no longer touch me, could no longer make me march to the beat of his drum, and my mum... well, it looked like she was on the way to drinking herself into oblivion. For the first time, my life was stretching before me, open with possibilities, but instead of the elation I'd always thought I'd feel, I felt nothing but empty. That was why I'd come back here. I needed to face my past so that I could begin my future.

"I can say whatever I want, Joseph. This is my house, and I will not have you expecting me to just drop everything because she decided to swan back into our lives whenever it's convenient for her."

"She didn't—"

"Joe." Reaching out, I placed a hand on his arm. "It's okay. I don't need to stay here." Now that I'd seen the state my mother was in, I didn't want to stay. Had never wanted to stay to begin with. This house held too many memories.

I had nowhere to go, but I'd find somewhere. I'd managed to make it through the past two years, I could make it through anything. It felt right to be here, to get some closure.

Joseph glanced at his watch with a grimace. "Where are you going to go? I have a meeting in an hour, otherwise I'd stay." He lowered his voice as we both glanced over at our mother, who was now back to drinking, acting like we weren't even in the room. "I'll have to make arrangements, but I can come back here for a while if you need me to."

I shook my head. "Joe, it's okay. I can manage." Injecting as much confidence as I could into my voice, I told myself to believe my own words. And things would be okay. Life had fucked us all over, but I was slowly defeating the demons of my past, and I was prepared to face whatever the future decided to throw at me.

"If you're sure." He sighed. "Can I drop you somewhere?" I noticed that he didn't offer for me to stay with him, but I knew that he lived outside of Alstone now, and I guessed he assumed that I'd prefer to be in Alstone itself.

"Where does James live now? Can you take me there? I'd like to see him." It was as good a place to start as any, now that my friend Hailey had moved to Edinburgh to live with her boyfriend. There was no one else in Alstone I was close to.

Joseph's face cleared, and he nodded. "Good idea. We'll go there now."

When we'd left the house behind, both of us breathed a sigh of relief.

"I need to decide what to do with Mum. And you...we need to talk about what comes next. If there are any suitable families we could make a connection with."

My jaw dropped as my head shot around to face my brother. "No! I am not doing that, Joe. I don't even want to marry anyone, and definitely not someone I don't even love."

His mouth turned downwards. "I know that, but it's your duty. This family has been ravaged, and with Dad gone...it's up to me to pick up the pieces. Our business assets are frozen, and there's a high possibility that we could lose everything, you know. Everything that the Hydes have worked for, for generations. I wish there was another way, but we all have our part to play. I'm sorry."

Fuck. I didn't want to argue with him about this, not now. He was my brother, and I loved him, and I understood where he was coming from. But I had no interest in being treated like a pawn. Maybe there was something else I could do to help rebuild the family name. Something that would satisfy Joe without losing myself in the process. I had no loyalty to my father—to either of my parents, in fact—but I had loyalty to my brother. And to Tim.

"Joe, I really don't want to talk about this now. Please, just drop it, okay?"

He blew out a breath. "Okay. I'm sorry. I know that now isn't a good time to bring this up. Forget I said anything. We can revisit this conversation when you're more settled and when I've managed to get my head around the ins and outs of the business. I was a TA while I was doing my master's degree, but I took some time off from that, and it's a good thing. I'm going to have to move back here, you know, now that Dad's gone. Take on the business and find a girl for myself sooner than I'd planned."

"From a well-connected family, hmmm?"

He laughed without humour. "It's what's expected. I refuse to let our family's legacy be buried by those Alstone Holdings assholes."

Thankfully, the car came to a stop outside a large, Regency-style mansion house before I could come up with a response. Alstone Holdings was something that I wasn't ready to think about.

"This is where James lives. I'll call him now, let him know you're here." Joseph hit some buttons on the car's console, and the sound of ringing filled the car.

"Joseph. What can I do for you?" James' voice was wary, and I had the sudden realisation that things between the two of them had changed while I'd been gone.

"James, hi. I have someone here who'd like to see you."

We both heard his sharp intake of breath, and I smiled.

The wariness was gone in an instant. "Fallon? Fallon's here already?"

Something inside me settled, and a genuine smile appeared on Joseph's face at the obvious excitement in James' tone. Joe leaned forwards, closer to the car speakers. "We're outside your building."

"I'll be right down."

The call ended, and Joseph glanced over at me. "I'll call to check up on you later. Don't worry about anything for now. Just enjoy your time with James, okay? I've transferred some money into your account, too. It should be enough to tide you over until we can make more permanent arrangements."

I nodded. "Okay. Thanks."

Climbing out of the car and taking a deep breath of the fresh air that carried a light tang of salt from the sea, the smile remained on my face. I never thought I'd feel this way, but to my surprise, I found that a part of me was happy to be back in Alstone.

6

fallon

"Are you sure you're going to be okay?" James eyed me hesitantly. "If I could get out of this, I would, but it's been arranged for a while. I'll only be gone for the weekend, though."

I smiled up at him from my position on his comfortable two-seater sofa. "It's fine. I appreciate you letting me stay here. I'll sort something else out as quickly as I can."

"You're welcome to stay as long as you need," my cousin assured me, but we both knew that this wasn't a feasible long-term arrangement. For a start, James only had one bedroom in his flat. He'd insisted on giving me the bed while he used the sofa, and I wasn't going to take advantage of his hospitality for longer than was absolutely necessary.

"Thanks, James. I know it's not ideal. But the house..."

He grimaced. "I know. My parents have mentioned a little about what's going on with your mum, although I haven't been able to find out much. You know what our families are like. If we don't talk about it, it doesn't exist."

"Yeah. Remember Lady Greenway's coke habit? I could

never understand why people would turn a blind eye at those parties, but then I realised that she wasn't the only one. It's just never mentioned, therefore, it doesn't exist."

"Exactly." His shoulders slumped. "There's a lot of fucked-up people in this town. And the richer you are, the worse it seems to be."

"Do you know what? It turned out that being sent away was good for me," I mused. "It allowed me to see things from an outside perspective. I knew the world we lived in wasn't normal, but I hadn't realised just how abnormal it was until I saw it from the outside."

He hummed in agreement. "Maybe I should do the same. But I doubt I'll ever get out of this life now." His lips curved upwards. "Honestly, though, I like this life. Mostly. Not the shit that's happened with...in the past. But knowing I don't have to worry about money, that I can walk into a good job when I've finished my degree—those are privileges that a lot of people would kill to have."

"You're right. It's...I know that it's a life a lot of people want. I guess it's just the expectations. They feel like a burden to me."

"I get it." Crossing the room to the sofa, he squeezed my arm before fishing in his pockets. "Before I forget. Here's my spare keys, and this one's my car key. My dad's driving us up north, so you're welcome to use my car this weekend."

"Thank you." Standing up, I hugged him. "I'll be fine. You don't need to worry about me. I've been living on my own for almost a year now. I had a room in the sanctuary to begin with, but then they let me have a little apartment close by. I'm used to fending for myself. I even taught myself to cook."

"Tim would've been proud," he said softly as he released me.

The familiar ache went through me, an ache that would never go away, but now I was able to smile when I thought of my brother. "I'd like to think so."

"Can you hold the door, please?"

I paused in the apartment building doorway at the breathless call from behind me, turning to see a pretty girl with long dark brown hair weighed down by several supermarket bags. I vaguely recognised her...Jessica? No... "Jessa? Jessa De Witt?"

The girl's eyes narrowed as she scanned my face, biting down on her lip, and then her eyes widened in wary recognition. "Fallon Hyde?"

I nodded. "Before you say anything, can I just say something? I'm not here to defend my dad for what he did. As far as I'm concerned, he can rot in prison."

Her whole demeanour instantly relaxed, and she came up to stand beside me. "You heard about what happened, then?"

I indicated for her to go ahead while I held the door open for her with one hand, with my own small supermarket bag in the other. "I've been out of the loop while I've been away, so I don't know the ins and outs. But I heard that he was plotting to overthrow Alstone Holdings, and from the face you made when you recognised me, I take it there's a lot more that I don't know. My brother...he...uh, he didn't want to tell me. He thought I was too fragile or something." My mouth twisted.

She glanced over at me. "There is a lot more...but you need to know something. Your brother...he was working with your dad. He was...he did some bad things. I'm sorry, I shouldn't—"

I cut her off with a wave of my hand, attempting to act casual, even though my heart was sinking. I had to be realistic, though, as much as it pained me. "I know what Joseph's like." It would be naive of me to think he'd go against our father. Of course he'd be involved in whatever had happened. And now I thought about it, maybe my supposed fragility wasn't the only reason he hadn't given me any details. Maybe he knew that whatever he told me wouldn't paint him in a good light. Taking a deep breath, I squared my shoulders. "I know it's unfair of me to ask, but if you know what happened, could you tell me? Please?" I turned to face her, laying all my cards on the table. "I know we don't really know each other, and you don't owe me anything, but I came back to Alstone to get closure, and I would really like to have all the information about what happened while I was gone. The only reason I felt able to come back was because my dad's not here anymore. He... we...I *hate* him," I whispered fiercely. "I owe him nothing. I just want to be able to move on with my life."

Jessa studied me for a long time, and then she finally nodded. "Okay. Are you here visiting James?" At my nod, she continued, "Why don't you drop off your bag and come up to my apartment? I'll open a bottle of wine because, believe me, we'll both need it to get through this conversation. It was...well, it was a very traumatic time for me. I've only recently felt like myself again. Or a new version of myself. A better version, I hope."

I stared at her, my mouth falling open. I'd had no idea she was involved. "Are you sure you want to relive it?"

She nodded once, decisively. "Yes. Talking about it is good for me. And I believe you when you say that you want your dad to rot in prison. I've been around false people enough to be able to tell when someone's lying. I should know—I used to be one of those people."

"Yeah, you always came across as a bit of a bitch." I laughed lightly, teasingly, and her lips curved into a wry smile.

"Oh, I was. I like to think I've changed, though." She shifted the bags she was gripping from one hand to another. "I need to go and get this shopping put away. I feel like my arms are about to fall off. I'll meet you up at my apartment in a few minutes?"

I nodded, and she gave me her apartment number, disappearing off up the stairs while I remained in the large foyer, lost in thought.

I knew that my dad was in prison, and I knew that it was all to do with Alstone Holdings. Which meant that I was going to have to prepare myself for potentially hearing about Zayde much sooner than I'd thought.

I was definitely going to need that wine.

There was a long silence after Jessa had finished recounting everything that had happened—or everything she knew and was prepared to share with me, at least. It was so much to get my head around, and while I knew that my dad wasn't a good guy, I had no idea he was capable of so much bad. And Joseph...I was so, so disappointed in the part he'd played. I cleared my throat, trying to dislodge the lump that had appeared. "If I didn't hate my dad already, I'd hate him for what he did to you all. And I'm so sorry about Joe. He's my brother, and I love him, but I'm not excusing anything he's done. *Anything*. It's beyond wrong. I'm so sorry that you went through all that pain. Getting kidnapped...fuck, Jessa. I can't even—"

She took a large gulp of her wine, her voice wobbling a little when she replied. "I know. You don't need to be sorry, though. None of this had anything to do with you."

"Even so..."

"Some good came out of it, anyway. I got a new group of friends. Good friends. Good *people*. Not the false friends I had before. I have a much closer relationship with my brother now, too. And best of all..." Her gaze softened, her wobbly smile turning bright and happy. "I fell in love with the most amazing man, who loves me back. I still can't believe it's real sometimes. He's...he's everything."

I couldn't help returning her smile, even as I desperately suppressed thoughts of the person I'd fallen in love with. The man who had shattered me into tiny pieces that I was still putting back together. "Was this after everything?"

She nodded. "Yes. There was more that happened after your dad was involved. Other things. The guy that took me...he came back for revenge. And Cassius...he became my rock."

Dread settled low in my belly. I already knew the answer to the question before I asked it, but I had to get confirmation. "Cassius? Cassius who?"

"Cassius Drummond. My boyfriend."

Cassius Drummond.

One of the Four.

"Oh," I croaked out.

Her astute gaze arrowed to mine. "Hey, don't worry. Look, it was obvious from the minute I met you again today that you were different to your dad and Joseph. I'm confident in saying that the Four won't hold your family against you. James is friends with them, after all. Kind of."

That hadn't even occurred to me. Maybe she was right, but that wasn't a concern that was even on my radar. The only thing that I could think about was the fact that the Four meant Zayde.

My heart beat faster, and my mouth went dry.

"Fallon? Are you okay?"

I nodded once. I wasn't okay, far from it, but I couldn't even begin to hint at why. Not when Jessa was in a relationship with one of the people closest to Zayde.

"If you want...why don't you come with me tonight? There's a party at their house. Another one," she muttered under her breath, but she was smiling. "It's open invite, and I know there'll be loads of people there. You won't have to worry about having all the attention on you."

Seeing Zayde again...

I wasn't ready to face the man that had torn my world apart.

But my mouth was already forming the word.

"Okay."

7

zayde

The house was packed. Music pumped through every single room, and people filled every corner of available space, spilling outside into the garden. I could take it or leave it. Crowds weren't my thing, but I was in the mood to get fucked up tonight, so a party was just what I needed.

Sprawled out on one of the wooden chairs on our deck, I absent-mindedly flicked my knife blade in and out of the handle with one hand, the other lifting the joint to my lips. I inhaled deeply, smoke curling in the air as the weed worked its magic. Fuck, yeah.

"Hey, Z."

I eyed the girl who'd spoken from beneath my lashes. What was her name again? Amber?

"Yeah?"

Whatever she said in reply turned to white noise as my gaze slid past her to the person standing in the open doorway.

My mouth might've fallen open. I wasn't even aware.

What. The. Fuck.

Our eyes connected. Her expression was haunted but hostile, brimming with so much fucking agony, and she made no effort to hide it from me. On my part, I called on all my experience and locked everything down, even though it took everything I had. Even though I wanted to fucking shout, to scream, to rage. My past was colliding with my present, and I had *no fucking idea* what to do.

My breath caught in my throat as I raked my gaze over her, drinking her in. She looked so fucking good standing there, the same but different. Long, platinum hair cascading halfway down her back, her skin so smooth and pale, and her eyes so blue, piercing right through me. She was even more beautiful than I remembered. Even with hate radiating from every part of her, directed at me.

My angel.

Except she wasn't *my* angel anymore, was she? And I was her demon. The monster who'd destroyed her life in one night.

"Zayde? Zayde!"

"Fuck off," I muttered to the girl who was trying to get my attention. I ignored her sharp intake of breath and the mumbled "Rude" as she stormed off, my gaze never leaving Fallon's. Before I knew what I was doing, I was climbing to my feet and taking a step towards her.

She took a step back. A single tear slipped down her cheek, and it was like a knife through me.

"Fallon?" Jessa appeared at her side, her eyes wide with concern as she noticed that Fallon was crying. What the fuck? Since when did Jessa speak to Fallon? *And why was Fallon here*?

Jessa's gaze shot to mine, her eyes narrowing, and I spun away from them both, stalking across the deck and down the steps into the garden. When I hit the deep shadows of the tree line, I breathed out, trying to make sense of what I'd just seen. I dug around in my pocket for my phone, my hand shaking as I dialled Creed via the secure line we used for communication.

"Z." Amusement sounded in his low, smooth voice. "Are you psychic? I was just about to call you. Had my phone in my hand and everything."

I wasted no time. "What did you find out?"

His amusement disappeared, his tone turning businesslike. "According to my sources, Joseph Hyde collected Fallon Hyde from the facility in Switzerland earlier this week. She'd been sent there after the incident with her brother."

I clenched my jaw at the sudden gentleness I could hear in his voice, completely unaccustomed to it coming from Creed. He never handled me with kid gloves.

"Yeah. I know she was sent away." She'd disappeared from the face of the earth, and the last memory I had of her was of that night, when she'd completely broken right in front of me, right next to the body of the boy that had died way too young.

"Okay. She was an inpatient for the first six or so months of her stay; then she was treated as an outpatient. Lived in a place close to the facility, with minimal supervision other than mandated therapy sessions. While she was there, she finished studying for her A levels via remote learning and managed to achieve top grades." Pausing, he cleared his throat, and I could hear the sound of a mouse clicking. "What else...she passed her driving test. Driving on the right-hand side, so she'll need to exchange her licence eventually—"

"That's not what I'm concerned about," I interrupted, my voice hoarse. Even though I wanted to know every single fucking detail about what had happened to her in the time she'd been away, what I wanted to know the most was what she was doing back in Alstone. "Why did she come back?"

There was silence for a moment, and then I heard him sigh. "Honestly, I can only take an educated guess, but the fact that the arrangements for her to return were made right after Roland Hyde's sentencing, and we know what a piece of scum he is, then I would assume that has everything to do with the timing of her return to Alstone."

I thought back over the things Fallon had confided in me in the past, whispered confessions when I was holding her in my arms, of how her father would punish Joseph and Tim every time he thought *she'd* done something wrong and make her watch.

My fist clenched around my phone. That fucking bastard deserved to fucking die. Even prison was too good for him. I'd never forgive him for any of it. Not only for Fallon but for plotting against us, putting our lives at risk, being a completely reprehensible human being. Christine and the Belarusian syndicate members were gone, and he was the only one left who needed to pay. If he got out, I'd make sure he'd fucking regret it.

Forcing my mind back to the conversation, I spoke brusquely. "Okay. Anything else?"

"Nothing of use. You can find my intel on the secure server to peruse at your leisure. Nitro will know how to access it."

I smirked at his use of the words "peruse at your leisure." He'd come a long way from the boy on the estate that had first hired me all those years ago. Although it was just as likely that it was a front. Creed was a chameleon—he had an ability to fit in with anyone, to get information out of everyone from the smarmiest businessmen to the hardest criminals.

I ended the call without saying goodbye, shoving my phone back into my pocket as my mind shuffled through the details he'd given me.

"Zayde."

The voice from behind me made me freeze in place.

I hadn't heard my name spoken by her in so long.

And I'd never heard it spoken this way before.

Hate dripped from the word, raw and savage.

I turned around, meeting those blue eyes that had always been so soft and warm but were now so fucking cold.

"Fallon."

8

fallon

My entire body was trembling, and I felt sick to my stomach. How could I still have feelings for the person that I hated? How could I love and utterly despise someone at the same time?

"Fallon." He spoke with a deceptively gentle tone. His icy eyes were shuttered, and I envied his ability to lock everything down, to give nothing away.

Opening my mouth, I inhaled shakily, trying to get air into my lungs. "Why did you do it?" Once the dam had been broken, the words came pouring out in a torrent, words that I'd been holding back for so long. "Why, Zayde? Why did you kill my brother? You took away the most important person in my life, and I'll never forgive you." My voice dropped to a whisper. "*Never*. My brother's gone, and I'll never get him back."

"Fuck." He ran a hand over his face, his knuckles white under the tattoos that covered them. Against my will, I began noticing things about him. His hair was still a tousled deep brown mess, falling over his forehead, and his eyes were still that same icy, pale blue-grey, fringed by those thick lashes that had always given me butterflies whenever he looked at me. His lips were full and tempting against the shadow of stubble that darkened his jaw, and I knew from memory how soft they felt when he was kissing me. There were differences, though. He had way more tattoos and more piercings than he had the last time I'd seen him. His body had more muscle definition, the body of a man rather than an eighteen-year-old boy. The sleeves of the black T-shirt he was wearing pulled tight around his biceps, and his black jeans hugged his quads in an almost indecent way. The tip of the handle of what I knew would be a wickedly sharp flip knife peeked from his pocket. Even when we were younger, he'd had knives. Maybe it was a product of his upbringing, knives being an accepted part of his world before he'd moved to Alstone, but there was more to it. I knew about the scars that he hid from everyone. The scars that were now tattooed over, hidden unless you looked closely and knew exactly where to look.

I didn't want to notice. I didn't want to notice *anything* about him.

It felt like I was betraying my brother's memory.

"It was an accident," he rasped. "I tried to save him, but I couldn't get to him in time."

"No, it wasn't!" My voice rose. "I was there—I saw what happened! And if you hadn't been arguing with him right by the window, he would never have fallen!"

"Fallon. *Fuck*. I'm so fucking sorry."

"Sorry isn't going to bring him back." A part of me registered the tears that were spilling over, running hot down my cheeks, but they were secondary to the agonising pain that was like a knife to my chest.

His fists clenched at his sides, his lashes sweeping down

as he closed his eyes. "I know. I know there's nothing I can say or do to make it right."

"So that's it, then?"

"What do you want me to say, angel?"

"Don't *ever* call me that again," I hissed, digging my nails into my palms in an effort to hang on to the final threads of my composure. A part of me hated myself for the way I was speaking to him right now. How could something that had once been so pure become so tainted? But that was what we were now. Tainted. Ruined. Broken.

"Why are you here?" he said eventually, after the silence between us grew too heavy to ignore, the sounds of the party unable to penetrate the darkness surrounding us.

I shook my head, at a loss. How could I explain what I barely understood myself? Why was I here, and why had I followed him into this shadowy place where we were all alone? "I don't know."

His eyes met mine again, and he took a step towards me. Then another, and another. I should have moved. Should have turned on my heel and run away. But instead, I remained where I was, my breath catching in my throat as he came to a stop right in front of me, so close that I could feel his warm breath on my skin. "I think you do know."

"Shut up," I whispered as his head lowered.

"I—"

I didn't wait to hear the rest of his words. Instead, I did what I should have done before I let him get so close to me.

I ran from him.

9

fallon

Wiping away my tears with a shaky hand, I stumbled back up to the house, disappearing into the anonymity of the crowd, another face amongst many. I'd never been a big drinker—drinking had been discouraged during my time in Switzerland, and the tiny stipend my parents had sent over for me hadn't allowed for luxuries like alcohol, so I'd only had it on the odd occasion when I'd socialised with the few others I'd come to know during my time there. But now, all I wanted to do was to lose myself in alcohol, to blank out the memory of Zayde's hard, strong body right in front of me, the way his eyes had flashed with pain when I'd thrown those accusations at him, the way that, even now, I wanted him. It felt like I was being torn in two.

"Where are the drinks?" I mumbled to myself, going up on my tiptoes to see over the bodies blocking my view.

"Drinks? What're you in the mood for?"

I spun around to see a beautiful girl studying me with interest. She was probably a little older than me, maybe Zayde's age, with long dark hair that fell in tumbling waves down her back, wide blue eyes, and a warm smile that widened as our gazes connected.

"Oh. Um. I don't know. What is there?"

The girl took a step closer, lightly touching my arm. "First time? It can be a bit overwhelming. I remember the first time I ever came to one of the Four's parties..." She blew out a breath, shaking her head. "That's a night I'd rather put behind me."

"Why?" I asked, interested despite the fact that I was on a mission to forget. But there was something about the girl —something so warm and open that it immediately put me at ease.

"Well. *That* is a conversation that needs alcohol. Come on, I know where the good stuff is hidden." She shot me a wink as her hand moved to loosely clasp my wrist. "Because I hid it."

I let her lead me through the kitchen to the huge fridge, where she rummaged around behind several large bags of various vegetables. It was clear that she knew her way around the house, and that made me wonder just how well she knew the Four. I'd never seen her before; maybe she was a student at Alstone College.

"Here it is!" Pulling out a bottle, she waved it in the air. "Let's find somewhere a bit quieter. Outside?"

No. That was where Zayde was. I shook my head violently. "I'd rather stay inside."

"Okay. The games room should be quieter. We had everything in the lounge before, but someone broke the PlayStation and managed to crack the TV at our last party. So this week, we've been clearing out a junk room to turn it into a games room. You should've seen the shit the boys had in there—so much crap that needed to be taken to the tip. It looked like one of those hoarders' houses. At the moment, most of it's in a skip on the driveway..."

She was still talking, but all I could concentrate on was the fact that she'd said *we*.

The question burst from my lips. "Do you live here?"

Her head swung to mine, and her eyes widened as she pushed open the door to the games room. "Shit, I haven't even introduced myself yet, have I? I'm Winter."

Winter Huntington. The girl Jessa had told me about. The estranged daughter of Christine Cavendish, who Joseph had blackmailed James into hurting. Not only that, but he'd also *hit* her, and he'd been involved in the plot to take over Alstone Holdings. She was going to hate me when she found out who I was.

"To answer your question, I do live here. My boyfriend's Caiden Cavendish. Do you know who he is?"

I didn't trust myself to speak, but I managed to nod.

"Alright, that makes it easier to tell you the story of my first party here." She tugged me over to a huge squashy leather sofa against one wall that was miraculously unoccupied—the other occupants of the room were either crowded around the TV, intent on whatever game they were playing, or circling a small, low table where a large bong sat, along with various other related paraphernalia. Sinking down into the chair, she carefully opened the bottle, taking a swig before handing it to me. "Mmm. I love this stuff. It's strong, though."

I took a cautious sip, and then another. Light, bubbling liquid trickled down my throat, a taste of champagne and something fruity but with a sharpness...possibly raspberries. "Oh, this is good. What is it?"

"I think it's pink gin, Chambord, and Prosecco. Jessa made some at our last party, and I fell in love. It goes down way too easily, though." Kicking her shoes off and curling her legs up on the sofa, she turned sideways to face me. "First things first. We need proper introductions. What's your name?"

I swallowed hard, staring down at my hands. "F-Fallon."

"Fallon? That's a pretty name."

Chancing a glance back at her, I noticed that her expression hadn't changed, and I relaxed a little. That had to mean she wasn't aware of who I was. I knew I'd have to tell her eventually, but for now, I could sit here and pretend that I was normal.

The thought suddenly hit me. I'd never had this before. Never been to a party, not one my parents hadn't forced me to go to, to be on show and expected to act a certain way and speak to certain people.

It was so nice to be anonymous, even though it couldn't last.

"Thanks." Passing the bottle back to Winter, I gave her a tentative smile as I mirrored her position, toeing off my own shoes and bringing my legs up onto the sofa. "So, what's the story? Why would you rather put it behind you?"

"I'd just moved here. I transferred to Alstone College in my second year. My housemate at the time—my friend Kinslee—told me about a party that was happening here. It was a 'welcome back to uni' party, and she persuaded me to go with her. I remember standing outside the house and feeling so nervous, seeing how huge it was and so different to anything else I'd experienced in my life up until that point. And that was coupled with the knowledge that, um... certain people might be there."

"Certain people?"

She bit down on her lip. “Yeah. Caiden and Weston. They’re my stepbrothers.”

I stared at her, trying to remember what Jessa had told me. Of course—Winter’s mother had married Arlo Cavendish, their dad.

“We hadn’t met each other before our parents got married,” she added, “So it was the first time I’d seen them outside of a photo. All of the Four were there together, and well, you know how intimidating they can be.” She paused, and her gaze flicked to mine. “You know who they are?”

“Yes.” My voice came out croaky. Taking the bottle from her, I tipped it to my lips, letting the bubbling liquid slide down my throat, soothing me.

“Okay, well, Caiden was there staring at me like he wanted to murder me or something. He was so hostile. I hated it because he was so fucking sexy, you know? I really didn’t want to be attracted to him.”

I knew all too well what that was like, especially after what had happened earlier. Why had I let Zayde get so close to me? What would have happened if I hadn’t managed to gather the strength to leave?

“What happened then?”

She grimaced. “I went home with someone I shouldn’t have. Someone I regretted sleeping with afterwards. My head wasn’t in a good place after seeing Cade, and he and I had a bit of a hostile encounter before I left, too.” A sigh fell from her lips. “It seems so weird to look back on it now, especially because I’m living here, and Cade is just...I love him so much. It’s funny how life can change in ways you never expected.”

“You’re right.” Handing the bottle back to her, I rested my head against the soft leather of the sofa backrest. “How did you get over that and end up together?” It was something I didn't know because Jessa hadn't touched on their relationship outside of what she'd told me relating to my family members.

There was a long silence, her gaze becoming faraway. Eventually, she said, "We just couldn't stay away from each other. It was...it was rocky to begin with. Really rocky. We had a lot of things to work out." Her voice softened. "But we fell in love. And I would do anything for him, and I know he would for me. He...he took a bullet for me."

"He *what*?" My mouth fell open.

She clapped her hand over her mouth. "Fuck! I didn't mean to say that. It's not common knowledge."

"I won't say anything, I promise." There was no way I'd ever take advantage. Even if she hadn't meant to confide in me, it already felt like there was a level of trust she was placing in me, openly discussing her first experiences with the Four, wanting to put me at ease.

"I don't even know why I said that. But thank you." Slumping down further, she took a long drink from the bottle. "So...please, can we change the subject? What's your story? What brought you here tonight?"

It was time for me to confess. I steeled myself. "Um... before we start, can I have a bit more of that drink, please?"

She laughed as she gave me the bottle. "I'm already intrigued."

After taking another bolstering swig of the fizzing drink, I cleared my throat. "I'm actually here because Jessa invited me."

"You're a friend of Jessa's?"

I shook my head. "Not exactly. We used to, uh, mix in the same social circles when I was younger, so we knew of each other. I've been away...I went to a boarding school."

"Oh, okay. Are you going to Alstone College now?"

"No." My voice dropped to just above a whisper. "The reason I reconnected with Jessa is because I'm actually staying in her building at the moment. I'm staying in my cousin's flat."

"Who's—"

"My cousin is James Granville."

A smile spread across her face. "Oh! James." Then her smile suddenly fell. "Wait...I saw a photo once..." She scanned my face intently, and I *knew*.

It was time for me to tell her the truth about who I was. "I'm Fallon Hyde. Joseph's sister."

Wariness appeared in her eyes, but there was no sudden hostility, not like I was expecting. Before she could say anything, I rushed to explain. "Jessa told me a bit about the things that Joe and my dad did. I want you to know that to me, it was unforgivable, and I would never, ever condone a single thing that they did to you all." My lip trembled, and I inhaled shakily. "I'm so sorry. I wish...I wish that the whole stupid rivalry never existed in the first place."

"You and me both."

She was still holding her body in a tense position, as if she was ready to move away at any second, so I carried on speaking quietly. "My dad...he's not a nice man. The only reason I felt it was okay to come back was because he's in prison and can't touch me anymore."

Her shoulders loosened a little. "I can appreciate that. I...I don't want to be the kind of person who judges someone by their family members. I've had it happen to me, and it wasn't a nice experience. I guess I'm just finding it a bit difficult to get my head around because of everything we went through with the Hydes. It's different for me, too, because I didn't grow up around the rivalry. I'm a bit worried about how the boys will take it...do they know you're here?"

Before I could come up with a reply, Jessa appeared in the doorway, her hand lifted in a wave. She quickly crossed the room towards us, perching on the arm of the sofa. "I've been looking for you. I just wanted to make sure you were okay. I saw how you looked when you saw Zayde—" She cut herself off, her mouth twisting as she glanced over at Winter, clearly unsure how to finish the sentence.

"It's okay," I murmured. "It was just a bit of a shock seeing someone from my past after being away for so long." Turning to Winter, I added, "In answer to your question, one of them knows I'm here, at least. I don't know about the others." I doubted Zayde would have said anything.

Jessa gave me a reassuring smile as she held out her hand to Winter, Winter passing her the bottle. "I'm sure they won't have a problem. Although..." She cocked her head. "It took a while for the Four to come around to me, didn't it?"

Winter laughed. "We all know why that was. I don't think Cassius had the same trouble, though, did he?" Smirking at Jessa's sudden blush, she shifted closer to me on the sofa. "Cassius. The biggest flirt and the biggest player, and he fell the hardest."

"That's debatable. Cade practically worships the ground you walk on. I've never seen someone so obsessed."

"What about the others? Weston? Z-Zayde? Are they still working their way through the available gorgeous, single women in Alstone?" I didn't want to hear the answer, but at the same time, I needed to know.

"Not really." Winter tapped her lip. "West is in a relationship with Lena, Cass' sister. Totally in love. Do you know her?"

I stared at her in surprise. "I do, but I never thought I'd see that happen. Wow. I can see it, though. They suit each other."

She nodded. "Yeah. They're a perfect match. But here's a tip...don't start talking to them about computers. You'll never hear the end of it. Both of them are technology obsessed. Not that I'm complaining, I doubt we would've been able to accomplish half of what we have without them."

"I'll try to remember that. So...that just leaves Zayde."

Both Winter and Jessa sighed. Winter shook her head. "Our resident broody bad boy—"

"—with his serial killer stare," Jessa interjected.

"He keeps to himself most of the time. I think if there was anyone, we probably wouldn't find out about it unless he really wanted us to know. He's a vault of secrets. But he's Cade's best friend, and one of my best friends, too, as it stands, and I just hope that one day he can find someone who can get through his walls." She gave me a small smile. "Not that I think someone has to be in a relationship to be happy. But there's something about knowing that you have someone who's got your back, who knows you better than anyone else, and who you can share things with that neither of you can share with your other friends."

"She means epic sex on tap," Jessa stage-whispered with a smirk, and they both started laughing. Something inside me ached. I'd give anything for this easy friendship. I'd never experienced anything like it before. It hit me all over again just how lonely I truly was. But these girls, no matter how welcoming and genuinely friendly they were, could never be an option for me. I'd never be able to become close to them because it would mean being around Zayde.

"Are you both students at Alstone College?" I asked to

change the subject. They nodded, falling into an easy conversation about student life and the Guy Fawkes event that would take place in November, Winter sharing her experiences of the previous year's event. They avoided mentioning Halloween, which I was grateful for. Jessa would have been aware of when Tim had died, and I was sure Winter would know something about it, too, if she was that close to the Four.

When the drink was gone and we were all relaxed back against the sofa while I told them some of my experiences of attending Hatherley Hall, my former boarding school—which they both seemed fascinated by—I'd almost forgotten where I was.

Until everything came crashing down.

"What the fuck?"

The three of us glanced up to see Caiden Cavendish standing there with his arms folded across his chest and a scowl on his handsome face. He was just as good-looking as I remembered, if not more so, and that glare was so familiar. I'd seen it directed at my brothers so many times, whenever our families were forced to interact at social functions. He'd been good at hiding it when parents were present, but whenever they weren't around, the gloves came off.

The memory came to me, as clear as day.

"Straighten up. You're a lady, act like it." My father's brows pulled together as he pursed his lips. "Better," he said when I obediently straightened my shoulders, the picture of a demure, well-mannered member of society. "Make sure you make a point of talking to the Parkinson-Joneses and the Walkers."

I gave a single nod, which was enough to make him leave. As soon as he'd gone, my shoulders slumped again. Scanning the room, my gaze focused on my brother, and I made my way towards him as quickly as I could in kitten heels that were painfully tight. He didn't even see me coming, too busy glaring at Caiden Cavendish, and when I reached him, he stepped away.

"Tim! Where are you going?" I grabbed his wrist, stopping him from moving.

He turned to me, his eyes going wide as he shook his head. "Fal, I have to do this. Do you see the way Caiden's looking at me? I know he wants payback for last week."

"Yeah, but you were looking at him the same way. What happened last week? You never told me." We both stared across the crowded room in the Cavendish mansion, where another one of the dull parties was taking place. Members of Alstone's elite rubbed shoulders, all fake smiles, and I was glad that being at boarding school meant that I didn't have to suffer through so many of these events. I was only here because it was the Easter holidays, and I was back at home for two short weeks.

From the far side of the room, Caiden lounged against the wall, his arms folded and a sneer on his face. Cassius was with him, every now and then giving Tim warning looks, but he was more interested in flirting with Imelda Tomlinson, who was at least two years older than him and wearing a dress that my father would deem highly inappropriate. Thankfully, Zayde was nowhere to be seen. I wanted to see him, but not in front of the others. It was too hard.

Tim cleared his throat. "Uh...Joe glued their lockers shut at school, and they thought it was me. They got me put in detention, so I stole some of Mum's cigarettes and planted them in their school bags. Then I got Eli to tip off the teacher, and they had a random bag inspection, and Caiden, Cassius, and Zayde all got detention, and I think their parents got a phone call."

"Tim! This is so childish!" I shook my head at him. Wasn't

he supposed to be the older brother I looked up to? And Joe should definitely know better.

"We're fourteen, Fal. What do you expect?"

"Boys," I huffed. Gripping his arm more tightly, I leaned in. "Don't go over there. Don't make it any worse than it is, Tim."

"Yeah, Joe would never accept that. He's always on at me to do more, to keep the rivalry alive." He glanced over at me. "Okay, how about this? You come with me, and that way, nothing bad will happen. I just want to warn him not to try anything stupid."

"I cannot believe you're making me do this." Gritting my teeth, I let him lead me across the room. As we drew closer, Caiden's stare grew darker, and even Cassius had abandoned his attempts at flirting to puff out his chest and give my brother an intimidating stare.

"Cavendish. Drummond," Tim said when we reached them.

"Hyde." Caiden's lip curled. His gaze flicked to mine briefly, and he gave me a small nod before returning his attention to my brother. "What are you doing here?"

"I wanted to tell you that if you try to retaliate when we get back to school, you'll regret it."

Caiden and Cassius both laughed. Caiden pushed off the wall, taking a step forwards. "You'll be the one regretting it, if anything."

"Tim, please." I tugged at his arm, turning my own glare on Caiden. "Leave my brother alone."

Cassius cleared his throat as Caiden opened his mouth to reply. "Cade. Wanna get some air?"

Without a reply, Caiden spun away to the side, heading for the door. When he was gone, I breathed out a sigh of relief, and from the corner of my eye, I saw Tim's shoulders slump. "I don't like the rivalry, you know."

"I know. I'm not sure if they do, either."

. . .

"Can someone tell me what the fuck is happening here?"

I was dragged back to the present to see Caiden still looking hostile, although his glare had softened somewhat with Winter jumping up to place a hand on his arm.

"Do you remember Fallon?" she said way too innocently, batting her lashes at him. I almost smiled.

"Yes. Now I'm gonna ask nicely. Can someone tell me what the fuck is happening here, please?"

Before the other girls could reply, I addressed Caiden directly. He'd always been an unofficial leader of the Four, and it was best if I could explain things to him here and now and deal with whatever fallout came from it. "Can we speak without being overheard?"

His gaze swept the room, and he seemed to notice that his little outburst had drawn the attention of the other occupants in the room. With a growl, he spun away from me. "C'mon."

Winter, Jessa, and I followed him through the house. He stopped in front of a door with a keypad on the wall next to it. Shielding it with his hand, he punched in a code, and when the door unlocked, he poked his head inside, speaking in a low voice.

Turning back to me, he jerked his head at the door. "In here. Don't touch anything."

I followed the others into the room, which looked like a hacker's dream den, if I could describe it that way. Computer monitors and computery things everywhere. The monitors were all blank, and there was a guy with his back to me, his finger on the power button of one of the monitors, suggesting that they'd been quickly turned off.

Paranoid, I guessed, although I couldn't blame them. I

was a Hyde, after all, and here I was in the Four's inner sanctum.

"We need Cass and Z." The person with his back to me turned around, and I realised I was looking at Weston Cavendish. His eyes widened when they met mine, and a soft gasp came from his left.

Lena Drummond. She stared at me with unconcealed interest, and I stared right back. The last time I'd seen her, I think she'd been around fifteen or sixteen. She'd always had a kind of "don't give a fuck" attitude that I envied, and she still had it, based on her posture and challenging expression. She'd changed, though. Her formerly blonde hair was now a soft pastel pink, and the way she carried herself now...it was hard to describe, but she'd grown up.

Weston's arm slid around her waist as he gave me his own perusal, and I returned my attention to him.

We'd been in the same school year as children, until I'd been sent away to boarding school, but we were never in the same classes. Even so, he was the person that I'd seen the most often out of the Four. In school assemblies, at various school functions, and passing each other in the hallways. We'd always stayed out of each other's way by unspoken agreement. I knew that Caiden had always tried to shield him from the family rivalry, anyway.

"Fallon?" Weston's voice was soft, careful. "Uh. Hi."

I tried for a smile and failed.

The tension in the room stretched to breaking point.

And then the door opened, and suddenly, everything was a hundred times worse.

10

zayde

The first thing I saw when I walked into the room was Fallon, surrounded by my friends, her eyes huge, scared but determined. The ice around my heart cracked almost imperceptibly as I struggled with the urge to go over to her, to wrap my arms around her and hide her away from the entire fucking world. No one should be allowed to hurt her. Not after I had. We'd all known loss, but the pain of hers had been so sudden and so fucking brutal, and it had come from the man who was supposed to protect her, to look out for her, to make sure that no harm ever came to her.

Cassius stopped dead, and I gave him a push, earning me a half-hearted glare as he stepped aside so I could get all the way into the room and close the door behind us.

"Bloody hell," he whistled, as unsubtle as a ton of bricks dropping on someone's head. "I wasn't expecting this blast from the past. Feels like I've seen a ghost."

I could see the moment he realised what he'd said when we all winced, and Fallon let out a quiet gasp.

"Shit. Sorry." His tone softened. "It was a surprise to see you, that was all."

Fallon nodded, accepting his words, but she was hugging herself, her shoulders hunching over. Her gaze flicked to mine, just for a second, and she bit down on her lip. Her eyes fell closed, and she sighed before opening them. "Caiden asked me what I was doing here. I'm back in Alstone because my father has been locked up, at last. I don't owe any of you an explanation, but I'll give you one anyway. We never got on with each other. He's never been interested in me, other than..." Her voice cracked. "Other than to ensure the future of the Hyde name, to marry me off to someone who could benefit the family." Her words were bitter but resigned, and from her left, I saw Jessa step forwards and place a hand on her arm.

"We know what the world of the elite is like," she said softly. "You don't need to explain it."

"Thank you." Fallon gave her a small, genuine smile and then met Cade's eyes again. "I've said this to Winter and Jessa, and I'll say it again. I know what my dad and Joseph did to you all, and I want you to know that it makes me sick, to be honest. There's no justification for anything they did, and I'm so sorry that—" Tears pooled in her eyes, and she sniffed. "Fuck. Sorry."

Winter was instantly there, putting her arms around Fallon and murmuring something I couldn't catch, and I had to grit my teeth because I should have been the one to comfort her. Fuck.

"She's staying with James at the moment, but he's away for the weekend," Jessa spoke up.

"Fucking Granville, again," Caiden muttered, and Winter glanced up, treating him to an eye roll.

She shouldn't be alone, she mouthed to Caiden, and he

shook his head. Winter frowned at him until he sighed. "She can crash here if she wants, but no trying anything."

"What, are you planning to lock her in, like you did with me?" Winter raised a brow, and he smirked at her.

"No, because I don't think she has the same purpose for being here as you did that night."

"Which was?"

"To drive me completely fucking insane." His smirk widened into a shark-like smile, and Winter's pupils visibly dilated. He crooked a finger at her, and she stepped up to him, winding her arms around his neck while he slanted his mouth across hers.

"Get a room," West muttered. "I don't wanna see my siblings kissing."

"That sentence sounded so wrong, mate." Cassius elbowed him, grinning.

"Fuck off." He elbowed Cassius back, and I watched in bemusement as they began mock fighting with each other. There was a time and a place for pissing around, and now was not one.

Caiden disentangled himself from Winter for long enough to lock eyes with me. "Z. You're on duty tonight. I need you to keep an eye on things." He then turned to Fallon, almost apologetic. "I'm not trying to be an asshole about it. I'm just being cautious, yeah? This is my house, and this is my family. I'm looking out for them, and while I trust my girl's judgement and I don't think you're up to anything suspicious, I wanna be sure. After all the shit that's gone down—"

"It's okay. I understand." Fallon studied him from beneath her lashes. "You have no reason to trust me. We don't know each other, after all. I'm not counting those times we saw each other at social events as kids. But for what it's worth, I have no ulterior motives for being here. I heard about the party—"

"I invited her," Jessa interjected with a smile, which Fallon returned.

"Yeah, and I thought...I guess I was curious. I haven't been back in Alstone since..."

She trailed off, and we all heard her unspoken words. *Since Tim's death.*

This was fucking excruciating. We shouldn't be here interrogating her; we should be fucking begging her for forgiveness. If we hadn't gone to the abandoned house that night...

"I appreciate the offer, but I'm fine on my own, honestly. I've been fending for myself for long enough already."

"You're staying here, and I'll be watching you." My words were directed at her, but I couldn't look at her. I looked at Cade instead, feeling her eyes boring into the side of my head.

Cade gave me a nod. "It's settled, then. The guest room's available." He turned back to Fallon. "If you want to stay, that is. You'll be making my life easier if you do. Winter won't let me hear the end of it otherwise."

"Neither will I," Jessa said. "When I... When I was going through all of that shit with Petr, being here... It helped me, more than you could know. I know it's a different situation, but the thought of leaving someone alone...I mean, it has to be difficult coming back here after all this time—"

"That's enough," I growled. Fallon's lip was trembling, and she looked like she was struggling to hold it together. "Back to the party, otherwise people will be asking where we are. I'll show Fallon to her room."

"Yes, sir." Cassius saluted me, and I gave him a hard stare. "Cade! He's giving me his serial killer look again!"

Caiden cuffed him around the head as they fucking finally began filing out of the room until I was left with Fallon, West, and Lena.

West cleared his throat. "We're not going anywhere. And unless you want an eyeful in the next five minutes, I suggest you get out of here. Now."

"Come with me." I tipped my head to Fallon, still not meeting her gaze, and then turned on my heel to leave the room.

I was far too aware of Fallon's footsteps behind me as we walked through the house. When we reached the bottom of the stairs, the sound stopped, and then she spoke from behind me.

"You know I'm not staying here. I didn't want to cause a scene back there, but I can't do it. I can't sleep under the same roof—"

"I get it." Clenching my jaw, I turned to her, seeing the way her arms were folded across her chest defensively, her eyes daring me to challenge her. "I'll take you back to James' flat."

"No. I'll get a taxi."

"I'm taking you back. No arguments."

"I'm not going on your bike."

"Fine. We'll take a car." Stalking towards the door, I swiped the nearest set of keys from the drawer of the console table. Cassius' SUV. Jerking my head at her, I yanked the door open. "Move, or I'll move you."

She made a soft gasp, and I should've felt bad for the way I was speaking to her, but I really didn't. Seeing that she made it back in one piece was all I was concerned with.

She slid into the back seat of the SUV, stubborn to the

end, but at least she wasn't fighting me on driving her back anymore. I needed her safe.

When we reached the apartment building, I came to a stop at the edge of the kerb. "I'm walking you up."

"No."

Gripping her arm with one hand, I hit the button to lock the car with the other and then began moving towards the building. She huffed but seemed to realise that I wasn't going to take no for an answer, and I loosened my grip a little so my fingers were lightly curled around her. Just touching her, even in this way, after so long...it was too much and not enough. Torture. All I wanted to do was to hold her and never let her go.

The silence was fucking excruciating, but it was better than anything I'd experienced in almost two years because she was back here with me. And although she didn't know it yet, I wasn't letting her go again. I'd known it from the second I'd laid eyes on her at the party. I'd work on getting her to forgive me, to give us a second chance, and if it meant I had to play dirty, then I'd do whatever it took. She was back here, and she was mine.

"You can leave now." She paused at the bottom of the stairs.

"Nice try." I went to move, but she remained where she was, glaring at me.

We were doing this the hard way, then. I raised a brow, letting my mouth curve into a smirk. "If that's the way you want to play this, angel."

Then I released my grip on her wrist and scooped her up into a fireman's carry.

She screeched, flailing against me, but I started up the stairs and didn't stop moving until we were outside

Granville's door. Knowing exactly where he lived came in handy.

When I lowered her to the floor, she shoved against my chest, hard. "Leave me alone."

I took a step back, allowing her the space I knew she was craving. She wasted no time in unlocking the door and pushing inside the flat. But before I left her alone, I had one thing I wanted to say.

"You and I both know you're not like your dad and brother. I know you don't need me here to watch you, so I'll leave you alone." *For now*. As she took another step into the flat, I moved towards the door, closing my fingers around the handle. "Goodnight, Fallon."

11

fallon

Even though I told myself to look away, I couldn't take my eyes off him. No matter how conflicted I was, no matter how much I wanted to hate him, the indisputable fact remained that he was a beautiful man. A man that had been my first love.

"Zayde." His name fell from my mouth in a whisper full of longing, even though I didn't want it to be.

He paused in the doorway, his arms coming up to grip the top of the door frame, his biceps standing out in sharp relief, his tattoos covering almost every inch of bare skin. I swallowed hard, wishing once again that he didn't affect me so much. It wasn't only that he was so gorgeous, but it was also the memory of the way he had always been so soft with me, when he was so hard with everyone else.

He filled the door frame, his icy gaze trained on mine. "Why are you here, Fallon?"

"Because...I want to get closure. I need to. I need to be able to reconcile my past with my present, to deal with the fact that Tim's gone, so I can move on with my life. That's what he would have wanted."

The words I'd spilled unintentionally came from the heart, and they were whispered into the space between us, honest and raw. Maybe this was what I needed. The first step towards healing now I was back in Alstone.

He inclined his head, not speaking but acknowledging what I'd said.

Maybe I had a masochistic streak. It felt as if I was being torn apart by what I *should* feel and what I *did* feel.

"Zayde."

"Angel."

That low rumble did me in. I closed the remaining distance between us, and he was there to catch me. Strong arms banded around my body, his voice murmuring in my ear as his fingers stroked through my hair. Blood rushed in my ears, drowning out whatever he was saying, but he was so warm and so solid against me I understood what he was trying to tell me.

He was here for me.

Even though everything between us had crashed and burned in the most horrific way.

Even though I was betraying Tim's memory by being here with him—

A tortured sob escaped my throat, and he froze against me.

"Time for me to go." He gently released me, and before I had time to react, he left me alone, closing the door behind him. I slumped to the floor. I'd thought that when I next saw him, the only thing I'd feel was anger and betrayal. I hadn't expected any of this. This tide of feelings was so powerful, and it was pulling me under.

When I got to the bedroom and slid between the freshly washed sheets, I picked up my new phone. It only had five numbers programmed into it. Joseph, James, my friend

Hailey, my therapist Nina, and as of earlier today, Jessa. There was another number that I knew off by heart, unless it had been changed, and my fingers hovered over the Add Contact button for far too long before I dropped my head back with a sigh, letting my phone slip from my hand. Going down that path was a bad, bad idea. It wasn't an option. I was here for closure, and first thing tomorrow, I was going to go and visit Tim's grave.

It was early when I awoke after a night of tossing and turning. My eyes were gritty, and I had a headache, but despite that, I couldn't help feeling positive. I'd survived my first day and night in Alstone. I'd faced my mother, and most importantly, I'd faced Zayde, and I'd managed to get through it. I could face whatever was coming my way.

After a shower and a change of clothes, I grabbed a small bag, shoving my phone and purse inside. The sun was shining, so I scooped up my sunglasses, placing them on top of my head, and opened the door.

I stopped dead as a large body unfurled itself from the floor. Zayde drew himself to his full height, stretching out his muscles. His T-shirt was riding up, and I caught a glimpse of a dark trail of hair dipping into his jeans. My mouth went dry.

"What are you doing here?"

He stared down at me, icy and impenetrable as usual, but something flickered in his gaze. A hidden softness, and it made butterflies take flight in my stomach. I worked so hard to hold on to my anger and blame, but it was so hard when I could feel the heat of his body in front of me, and my brain was reminding me of how good we'd been together.

"I'm taking you to breakfast," he said, his voice raspy from sleep. "Back at the house."

My eyes widened. "No way."

"Do you want an interrogation from the girls about why you didn't stay? We go back to the house now, and no one will have to know you didn't stay the night there."

Oh. On the one hand, it wasn't anyone's business what I did. But on the other hand, they'd been nothing but nice to me.

"Fine. But as soon as breakfast is over, I'm leaving."

He didn't reply to that, just turned towards the stairs, and with a sigh, I followed him. "Zayde?"

"Yeah?"

"Did you stay here all night, or did you come back here early this morning?"

His shoulders lifted. "Which answer do you want to hear?"

I knew what the answer was. I'd known it the second I'd seen him outside my door. Something inside me warmed at the thought he'd stayed there all night.

He didn't try to make conversation on the way back to the Four's house, which I appreciated. That was one of the things I'd always loved about him—how he never felt like he needed to fill the silence.

When we were inside the house, he led me into the kitchen. I took a seat at the large island, taking my phone from my bag while he disappeared from the room. I needed to speak to Hailey. She was the only one who knew about Zayde, even though her finding out had been an accident, and maybe she could give me some perspective on my conflicted feelings. I sent her a quick text and then replied to Joseph's message asking how I was getting on.

"Oh, hi, Fallon. I hope you slept well?"

I looked up from my phone to see Jessa, followed by a yawning Cassius, who was only dressed in a pair of navy boxer briefs. Jessa caught my glance.

"You get used to all the boys walking around like this. Actually, Cass prefers to be naked—"

"But apparently, it's too traumatic for my sister. Not like I'm showing my dick off, anyway. I wear an apron."

"Do you remember that time you got burned by the bacon fat?" Winter appeared in the doorway with a smirking, shirtless Caiden as Cassius moved to the fridge. Cassius shot her a wounded look over his shoulder as he began pulling out ingredients.

"That *hurt*. Bloody bacon." He dumped the food he was carrying next to the oven and then grabbed an apron, tugging it over his head. When he turned around, I got a clear view of the words written across the front—*If you like my meatballs, you'll love my sausage.*

"Nice one, mate. I'm starving." Weston strolled into the kitchen, shooting Cassius a grin as he made a beeline for the fridge. I instantly averted my gaze. What was it with these guys hanging around in just their underwear? This was something I'd never experienced before, and yet everyone here seemed to be treating it like it was a normal, everyday occurrence.

Grabbing a bottle of orange juice from the fridge, Weston passed it to Lena, who had entered the kitchen and taken a seat at the island across from me at some point while I'd been distracted by Cassius' apron. Her pink hair fell in a curtain across her face as she bent her head over her phone, tapping at the screen.

Caiden moved into my line of sight, and suddenly, there was way too much tattooed, toned flesh on display wherever I looked. None of it interested me.

Until.

A throat cleared, and I lifted my gaze from the safety of the island countertop.

Fuuuuck.

Zayde was standing in the doorway, gripping the frame, his lips curved into a smirk as he watched me take him in. I was helpless to resist dragging my gaze across every inch of him, all those tattoos that covered his arms and torso. I could feel my cheeks heating, and I knew that the flush would be obvious to anyone looking at me.

And then he pushed off the doorway, turning towards the oven, and I clamped my hand over my mouth to stifle a gasp, shock thrumming through my system.

His back was covered in tattoos, as his front was. But across his shoulder blades was a pair of angel wings. The exact same wings that were on the necklace he'd given me so long ago. The necklace that was in the box of possessions I'd asked the receptionist at the sanctuary to throw away.

Tears blurred my vision, and I blinked rapidly, wrenching my gaze away from his back to the safety of the kitchen island. With the best timing, my phone chimed softly with an incoming message alert, but as soon as I read the words on the screen, bile rose in my throat, the shock of Zayde's inked acknowledgement of me almost forgotten as I was pulled straight back into the present.

Joe: Visiting Dad today before they move him to the new prison. I won't force you to come, but he might appreciate a message. I won't excuse him, and I know it's been hard for you, but it's been hard for

him too. He's lost everything Fal. No pressure
though. I know he did a lot of wrong things
especially to you x

How could he even ask me to send a message? There was no way that was happening. Eventually, I would face my father because I needed to do so to get some closure, but in the meantime, I wouldn't be initiating any contact with him.

"Fallon?"

I raised my head to find Winter studying me, her gaze too sharp and knowing. I had to be careful. I didn't want to end up in a situation where I'd be asked questions that I didn't want to answer. But maybe it was okay to share this.

"Sorry. I had a message from my brother. He's going to visit my dad today."

Silence instantly fell, only broken by a loud crack as Cassius dropped an egg into the saucepan from a height. My words were temporarily forgotten as everyone stared at him.

"Mate, what are you doing?" Caiden cocked his head, eyeing the second egg that Cassius was now holding over the pan.

"It's a hack. You get perfectly cracked eggs if you do this." Shooting me a wink, he opened his fist, and the second egg dropped, cracking into the saucepan. Cassius immediately scooped out the shell, giving Caiden a smug smile. "See?"

Caiden shook his head, the corner of his mouth pulling into a smile, and I marvelled at how different the Four actually were when they were in their own territory, at ease with one another. There was a lightness to them that I would have never imagined would exist if I hadn't seen it with my own eyes.

Winter leaned into me. "Are you okay?" she asked softly as the others began to talk amongst themselves, working together to set the island with plates and cutlery, making mugs of tea and coffee as Cassius fried eggs and bacon.

I nodded. "I don't really want to talk about it, but I wanted to tell you in the interest of transparency."

She squeezed my arm. "I understand." Her voice lowered. "But for what it's worth, I know something about bad parents. My mother...she was awful. I told you about Cade taking a bullet for me last night by accident, so you might as well hear the rest. She was the one to pull the trigger."

"What?"

"Yeah. So while I won't presume to know anything you've been through, and I'm not trying to make comparisons, I just wanted to let you know you're not alone. Cade and West, too—she was their stepmother, and they had more reason to resent her than most."

"Thanks for telling me." I met her open, honest gaze. "It means a lot."

"Good." She gave me a quick smile before raising her voice again. "Tea or coffee or something else?"

"She'll have a latte with one sugar."

Both Winter and I turned to Zayde, Winter's brows flying up as she studied him.

Shit.

"Good guess. You almost got it right. I'll have it without the sugar, though." Thankfully, the sentence came out steady, my voice deciding not to betray me. Zayde was right, except for the fact that in my time away, I'd learned to take my coffee without sugar. But the fact that he'd remembered how I used to have it...

"You're on coffee duty, then, Z." Winter gave him a bright smile and then bounded over to Caiden, planting a kiss on his cheek as he very unsubtly felt up her ass.

My gaze returned to Zayde, watching as he made my latte. When he brought the cup over to me, he leaned in, speaking too low for anyone else to hear. "I remembered."

"I remember how you have yours. Black."

"Like my soul," he said, his lips kicking up, and I found my own answering smile pulling at my mouth before I remembered myself. But when he leaned in even closer and his hot breath fanned across my cheek, goosebumps erupted all along my arms. His tongue came out, sliding across his lips, and the glint of his piercing was enough to make my knees weak.

Somehow, I made it through the rest of breakfast by steadfastly refusing to look at him, although I felt his gaze boring into me. The conversation flowed around me, no one expecting me to contribute, which I was grateful for, and bit by bit, I began to relax.

When everyone had finished eating, I stood. "Um. Thank you for breakfast. I'm going now."

"Do you need a lift?" Winter asked immediately, but I shook my head. After Zayde's insistence on taking me back last night, I'd pre-empted their actions, and I'd ordered myself an Uber, which was due outside at any minute.

"Thanks, but I've already sorted out a lift." I paused, glancing around the room again. "Thank you all. Really. You didn't have to welcome me, but you did, and just...thank you." With a small wave, I backed out of the kitchen and made my escape.

Footsteps followed me, so I increased my pace. As I

reached the front door, a hand closed around my arm, but I shook it free, pulling open the door at the same time. The Uber was waiting right outside, idling on the driveway, and I dived into the back with a sigh of relief.

As I left the house behind, the last thing I saw in the rear-view mirror was Zayde, his fists clenched at his sides and his icy eyes burning with fire.

12

fallon

The graveyard was quiet, with just a few other people meandering between the headstones, flowers clasped in their hands, and the respectful silence in the air only broken by the sound of the trees rustling in the autumn breeze and the birds chirping softly. Leaves crunched under my feet as I followed James' instructions, making my way to the family plot that I'd never visited before now. I hadn't even been able to attend Tim's funeral because I'd been shipped off to Switzerland so soon after he'd gone.

It was easy to spot the headstone, still shiny and new, black marble with my brother's name etched into the surface, the dates underneath. Below that was a short inscription, followed by a Thomas Campbell quote.

Beloved son and brother.

To live in the hearts of those we love is not to die.

I sank to the ground, tracing my fingers across his name.

Timothy Lewis Hyde.

"Why did you have to leave, Tim?" I pressed my

forehead to the cold headstone. "We were supposed to get away from here together. You're my brother, and I miss you so much."

Tears slipped down my face as I lost myself in memories of my brother. A soft breeze blew through the cemetery, caressing my hair, and for a moment, I felt it. A presence, like Tim was really there.

"What do I do, Tim? I feel so lost and confused. Everything seemed easier when I was away. My therapist worked so hard, and I thought I was okay. But being back here...I feel like I'm being pulled in a million different directions. You died, and I'm still in love with the person who—" I cut myself off, not ready to relive that moment. I'd blanked most of it out for a long time. It was a normal reaction, or so I'd been told, a way for my mind to protect itself. I hadn't wanted to remember because doing so would be exposing the raw feeling inside of me, and I knew the pain would be indescribable. I'd already had enough pain to last for a lifetime.

"I hope wherever you are, you're at peace," I whispered. The breeze caressed me again, and I smiled through my tears. "If that's you, I want you to know that I love you. And I'll stay strong for you. Make you proud of me.

"It's so hard. I feel so alone. You're not here, and the boy I loved—" With a gasp, I suddenly remembered something. I'd planned to tell Tim about Zayde. I'd never had the chance. "Tim? I need to tell you something. I fell in love with a boy that I don't think you would approve of. I definitely don't think that Joe would approve, and he'd have a lot to say on the matter, but the chances are, you would have understood. Eventually. If you could have seen how happy he made me. Did you know that he was my first kiss, and I was his? You probably don't want to know that, huh?"

"Zayde?" We were sitting on my bed. The sun was streaming through the window, sending rainbow patterns dancing across the carpet where it was shining on my crystal bedside lamp.

"Yeah?" He turned to face me, staring into my eyes. Lately, the way he looked at me had changed, and I couldn't help hoping that he was beginning to feel the same way I did.

I gathered all my courage and let the words tumble out.

"IthinkIwanttokissyou."

He stared at me, open-mouthed. When the silence went on for too long, I turned away, my cheeks flaming. Stupid. *Of course he didn't feel the same way about me. "Never mind. Forget I said anything."*

He made a noise in the back of his throat and lunged forwards, his lips crashing down on mine. Our teeth clashed, and I pulled away, trying to stifle my cry of shock.

"Sorry," he mumbled, staring down at my duvet. He was biting down on his lip, and all I could think about was that I wanted to try kissing him again. So I swallowed hard, clasping my hands together to hide the way they were shaking, and asked, "D-do you want to try again?"

His eyes flew to mine, and he gave a jerky nod, shuffling closer on the bed. This time, he angled his head carefully, pressing his lips against mine.

When he pulled away this time, I caught a glimpse of myself in my dressing table mirror. My cheeks were all pink, and my eyes were shining as a huge smile spread across my face.

"I've been wanting to kiss you for so long," I whispered.

"You have?"

I was taken aback by the shock in his voice, and I nodded

adamantly. Didn't he know how much I liked him?

He shook his head. "But—but you're way out of my league." His cheeks flushed, but he kept going. "You—you're beautiful and rich, with everything you could ever want, and I'm just a boy from the wrong side of the tracks."

How could I make him see that none of that mattered to me? "I don't care about any of the money stuff. That's not important to me. You're my best friend, Zayde, and I like you more than I've ever liked anyone. I've never met anyone I wanted to kiss until you."

"What do you mean?"

"That was my first kiss."

He carefully slipped his arm around the back of my neck, drawing me closer to him. "Mine too," he said, and then he kissed me again.

Almost every time he saw me after that, we'd end up kissing, taking care to stay hidden. As well as kissing, we'd talk about anything and everything, until I felt closer to him than I ever had to anyone.

Then one day, I woke up and realised that I'd fallen in love with him.

Shifting into a more comfortable position, I drew my knees up, resting my head on my arms. "We met by accident, really. His mum was one of our cleaners, did you know that? She brought him with her to work, and that was how I met him. He fascinated me from the first moment I saw him. I was alone a lot, and so was he, and we...we grew closer. He became my best friend. At first, I didn't tell anyone because I didn't want him to get into trouble. And then something happened that neither of us saw coming. Do you want to know what it was?"

A small gust of wind lifted the ends of my hair, and my smile widened. "I'll take that as a yes, then. You'll never guess what it was. His mum...as well as being a cleaner, she had a few other jobs. Um. One of them...she met a man. He gave her a fake name, so she didn't know who he really was, and she never saw him again. But it led to a baby. Zayde Smith. That used to be his name. Until she saw a newspaper with the man's picture and found out that Zayde's dad was, in fact, Michael Lowry."

Another gust of wind buffeted me, sending scattered golden-brown leaves into the air. "I know. It was a shock to everyone. When she got in touch with Mr. Lowry and told him about his son, he of course didn't believe her to begin with. But after a paternity test, he decided that he wanted custody of Zayde because he'd never married and didn't have an heir of his own to continue the family name. He paid her off, and Zayde never really liked to speak about it, but I got the impression that she was happy to take the money and relinquish her responsibilities." My voice hardened. "Not that she took much responsibility for him. Did you know he was constantly left to his own devices? Sometimes she kicked him out of their flat, and he'd have to crash with friends. She didn't even care about his birthdays, can you believe that? The only time he could remember ever getting a present from her was after he'd already left—" A sob escaped my throat as I remembered the battered copy of *To Kill a Mockingbird* with the inscription inside. The book that he'd gifted to me, and I'd asked the sanctuary staff to get rid of it.

"S-sometimes I feel so broken." I sobbed. "I do and say things that I regret so much, Timmy. I just—I just wish you were here. I feel so guilty. I don't know what I'm supposed to do. I miss you so much."

When I eventually stopped crying enough to be able to catch my breath, tears still dripping down my cheeks, I reached out again with a trembling hand to touch the letters of his name. "We stayed together, Zayde and me. It was hard for us to spend a lot of time together after I went away to boarding school and he moved in with his dad. But we managed to get moments together. We kept in touch by texts and emails. He was always there for me, until that day. Tim, that day...I can't talk about it yet. I don't think I'm ready to face it."

A soft breeze stirred the grass around me, drying the tears on my cheeks. "Thank you," I whispered. "I love you, and I know that a part of you will always be here with me." Lifting a hand to my heart, I leaned forwards and placed a kiss on the headstone, right on his name. "I'll come back and visit you. I promise."

Climbing to my feet, I turned around.

I gasped, feeling the colour drain from my face.

Joseph stood there, a bunch of flowers clasped in his hands. His mouth was set in a hard line, and he was gripping the stems so hard they'd bent.

"H-how long have you been here?" I managed to say, my voice shaking.

Instead of answering my question, he stepped forwards, laying the flowers in front of the headstone. When he straightened up, he spoke, his back to me. "Dad asked me to bring flowers to the grave on his and Mum's behalf before I go to visit him later."

"Oh. Okay. How long were you there?"

"I'll be in touch soon, Fallon," he said. "You should leave now."

I left, setting off the chain of events that sent us all tumbling from one hell into another.

13

fallon

"Dad's changed."

Unlikely. I gritted my teeth as I clenched my phone tightly, staring unseeingly out of the window of James' apartment. "How, exactly?"

Joseph's sigh was heavy enough to be audible through my phone speaker. "We had a long talk when I went to visit him. It really feels like he's different now, Fal. It seems like being sentenced has made him re-evaluate his life. I think... he thought he was going to get out of it, right up until the end. But now he's being moved to a proper prison, and...it's hit home for him. He wants to try and make things up to us, for our family."

There was no way on earth that it was true. My father would have had to have an entire personality transplant for that to even be a possibility, and even then, I doubted that it would have been enough.

When the silence stretched, he sighed again. "Will you consider seeing him?"

"*No*. Never."

"You're being unfair. Don't you understand how hard

this is for him? I know he did a lot of unforgivable things, but he's trying now. He wants what's best for our family. He wants to make it right, to preserve our legacy."

"I'm sorry, but as far as I'm concerned, he deserves prison." Leaning my forehead against the cool pane of glass, I closed my eyes. "I'm sorry you don't understand, but you can't ask me to do this."

"Right. If that's your final decision, then I need to go." There was something weird in his tone, but I couldn't work out what it was. "Bye, Fallon."

He ended the call before I could reply.

I had to get out of James' flat. Although it was cold outside, the sun was shining, and all I wanted to do was to walk somewhere and forget about my problems for a while. Shrugging on the thick padded navy jacket that I'd brought back from Switzerland with me, I made my way out of the building and set off down the road with no fixed destination in mind.

I could breathe more easily, being out here. Those first months I'd spent in Switzerland inside the sanctuary, I'd grown to hate seeing the same scenery over and over. Now I appreciated the freedom to be able to go where I wanted, to have that choice.

The salty tang of the sea air filled my nostrils, and I breathed in deeply. That was something I'd missed out on while I'd been gone—being in a landlocked country had meant that I hadn't seen the sea for a long time. Of course, Switzerland had absolutely breathtaking scenery, but I'd grown up on the coast, and it was something I had always taken for granted until it was gone.

It struck me then. I needed to see the sea. I hadn't actually seen it since I'd been back.

Pulling up the maps app on my phone, because I wasn't exactly sure where I'd ended up, I set a route to the coast. According to the navigation, it was only a seven-minute walk away.

I was cresting a hill with a smile on my lips because I knew the sea was on the other side, when a low rumble of an engine cut through the quiet.

A shiver went down my spine.

That sound...

My steps slowed until I was at a standstill, poised at the top of the hill.

The engine cut out. Other sounds filtered back in—the cries of the gulls, the sound of the waves breaking against the rocks, the whistle of the wind across the clifftops.

Then I heard the heavy tread of boots behind me. My body remained frozen, torn between wanting to flee and wanting to melt into *him*.

"Fallon."

Zayde's low rumble vibrated through me, his body heat palpable even through the downy thickness of my coat. I felt his breath hit my skin as I turned, so slowly, unable to resist this pull between us.

"Zayde." I waited for that familiar hate to rise up in me, the hate I'd been holding on to for so long.

He moved even closer. "What are you doing here?"

"I wanted to see the sea. What are *you* doing here?" My eyes connected with his, and it suddenly felt like all the layers had been stripped away. For one moment, it was just us. Zayde and Fallon.

It only lasted for a moment before reality intruded and I remembered why I needed to keep my distance. When I stumbled backwards, his eyes flashed with something I couldn't identify, his jaw tightening, but he remained where he was.

He studied me, his tension fading away, and that annoyingly sexy smirk curved over his lips. "I wanted to go for a ride." Butterflies fluttered inside of me as amusement danced in his gaze. Fuck him. I couldn't help the way my body reacted to his presence. I was only human, and he was a god. Despite my brain screaming at me, reminding me of what he'd done, I wanted nothing more than to close the distance between us, to feel his body against mine, to kiss that smirk from his lips. Somehow, I resisted, turning away from him, back towards my original destination.

"Goodbye," I murmured.

I kept walking, and I didn't look back.

There was no one around to witness the hitch in my breath when I heard him ride away.

"I'm not going to be the one to throw the first punch." Zayde dodged to the side, and Tim's fist swung at him. I shouted, desperate and panicked, and they both twisted towards the noise, even though they were already in motion. The momentum of their movements meant that Tim carried on lunging towards Zayde. Zayde's foot came out, and then Tim was gone.

I sat bolt upright in bed, gasping for breath, the vivid nightmare so fresh in my mind that I was shaking all over.

Tim had died because Zayde had tried to bring him down, right by the gap in the wall.

That was something I couldn't forget.

14

zayde

My phone rang, instantly jarring me out of my sleep. I swept it up, hitting the Answer button. "Yes?"

A disembodied, robotic voice spoke. THIS IS PROMETHIUM. CODE BLUE ALERT.

The call cut off, leaving my phone blinking the time. 3:40 a.m. on Sunday morning.

Fuck.

Launching myself out of the bed, I yanked my bedroom door open and ran to Caiden's room, hammering on his door. Weston's door was already open, and he flew out of his room with his phone in his hand and a wild look in his eyes. He was closely followed by Lena. He hammered on Cassius' door, shouting through the wood.

"Code fucking blue! Downstairs now!"

When we were all assembled in the computer room and all the monitors were on, Weston typed madly on the keyboard while Lena scrolled through windows on her laptop browser, hooked up to one of the monitors.

The tension was at an all-time high. A code blue alert could only mean one thing.

Caiden paced up and down, muttering under his breath, his fists clenching and unclenching at his sides. Every now and then, he'd stop to drag a hand through his hair, tugging at the strands.

Weston was in the secure chat, typing as Nitro to his hacker boss, Promethium. West still had no idea who he was. I had suspicions, but I knew that whoever it was, they wouldn't disclose their identity without good reason. What was surprising was that it was Promethium who had sent the code blue alert since that was usually used by the Alstone Holdings members to warn others within the company that something big was going down. And what was even more surprising was that I'd received a personal call. Usually, a code blue would come up as an alert on our phones.

I took a seat next to West, scanning the screen in front of him.

Nitro: What's happening?
Promethium: This affects all of the AH board but particularly Lowry x2

West shot me a startled glance before spinning back to the screen.

Nitro: Zayde and his dad?
Promethium: Correct. Link below

A link appeared, along with a countdown that informed us it would expire within fifteen seconds. West hit it, typing in a password on the screen that appeared. When we were inside, he swore under his breath, clicking through folders so quickly that I didn't even have a chance to read the names. He typed in another password when a box appeared, and as soon as he hit Enter, an image filled the screen.

"Oh, *fuck*," he breathed. "Fuck. What. The. Fuck."

He spun around in his chair, blocking the screen. "Everyone out except for Z. *Now*."

The commanding, harsh tone was one I'd never heard from him, and from the collective sharp intakes of breath, everyone else was just as shocked as I was, but I couldn't even pay them attention as I took in the image in front of me. I vaguely registered Weston squeezing my shoulder and the door closing softly as I read, bile rising in my throat.

It was the front page of the Sunday edition of one of the biggest tabloid newspapers in the country. Right across the top, the splash proclaimed in huge block letters:

FROM RAGS TO RICHES

Then underneath, in smaller letters:

EXPOSED: THE SHOCKING INSIDE STORY OF THE ELITE HEIR

Below the headlines, there was an image of my dad and me from one of the events we'd been to, and following that was an "exclusive" tell-all from "an inside source."

The ice around my heart squeezed, tightening, but underneath it was a river of blood. Betrayal hit me so fucking hard my head was spinning as I read the article.

It told everything. Details about my life in the council flat on the housing estate, my mum, the "seedy" underbelly of Alstone Holdings, painting my dad as a man who slept with hookers and meth addicts, and me as a poor, abused, easily manipulated child, "a pawn in his father's sick games." It detailed how my dad had paid my mum off, speculating that losing me had driven her to her death. They even had details of how she'd died, so they must've somehow managed to get hold of a copy of her death certificate. The second part of the article detailed the feud between Alstone Holdings and Hyde Consultings, speculating that I'd manipulated Fallon into what they called a "short-lived relationship" with me, preying on her "young, malleable mind" in order to gain advantages for Alstone Holdings. There was even a carefully worded insinuation that perhaps Roland Hyde was behind bars because he'd been framed. It didn't say it in so many words—the paper wouldn't risk getting sued, but it was heavily implied.

There was nothing about Tim's death or the parts of my life that didn't pertain to my dad and the connection with Fallon—which they'd reduced to me manipulating her for the sake of Alstone Holdings—but other than that, the rest of my fucking life was there, laid bare for the world to see. By tomorrow, everyone would know.

Fuck. What the fuck was I supposed to do?

And there was only one person that knew all the details and therefore only one person that could have been behind it.

How could she have done it? How could she have betrayed me like that? Why? Why would she want to draw attention to herself like that? The only thing that made any sense was that she'd done it as a form of payback for Tim. And maybe I deserved it, but this wouldn't only affect me.

I couldn't even swallow around the fucking lump in my throat. This betrayal hurt so fucking much. I needed...

I needed to make the pain go away.

Throwing open the desk drawers, I fumbled for

something, anything. There was nothing except pens and papers.

"Fuck!" I slammed my hands down on the table. "Fuck!"

A hand clasped my shoulder firmly. I hadn't even heard the door opening.

"Z." Cade sank down into Weston's vacated seat. He waited, keeping his grip on me until I lifted my head to meet his eyes. When I finally did, he blew out a heavy breath. "Can I read it?"

I closed my eyes. "Yeah." There was no point in stopping him anyway—tomorrow, everyone would be able to read it.

"Fucking hell," he whispered when he'd finished reading. "I don't even know what to say."

"That makes two of us."

"Fuck, mate. Fuck." He scrubbed his hand across his face. "We need to give the rest of the board a heads-up. Especially your dad—he's gonna need to see this before the papers go live. It's gonna blindside him otherwise."

"I know."

"Want me to take care of it?" His voice lowered. "I'll take care of it for you, Z. You're my best mate. I wish you could've told me about Fallon before, but I get why you didn't. You know I'm always on your side, though, right?"

"Yeah." The knot of pain untwisted, just a bit. I knew he was there.

"Okay. I'll sort it. It might be too late for the headline, but I won't let you deal with the fallout alone. You can count on me."

Fuck. I was so fucking bad at dealing with emotion, and he knew it. My childhood hadn't been filled with love, certainly not from my mum, and my dad had always been closed off, never the type to show physical affection, although I knew he cared about me in his own way—as long as I didn't get in the way of his work. "Uh, thanks. Same," I said hoarsely, and he squeezed my shoulder again before standing.

"I'm gonna go and make a few calls." There was a weighted pause, and then he added, "Z? Don't— If it gets too much, get hold of Mack, yeah? Get his tattoo kit set up, get him to give you some more ink. Whatever you need. Fuck it, I'll drive you there."

Well, shit. How much did he know? I stared up at him, lost for words, and he shook his head. "We don't have to talk about it. But I notice things. That's all I'm saying. And I —" He cleared his throat. "Look, I fucking care about you, mate."

I nodded because I couldn't fucking speak. He stepped away from me, and I sucked in a breath, willing myself to hold it together for just a bit longer. He'd reached the door when I was finally able to rasp out the words. "Get Mack."

"Consider it done."

He closed the door behind him, and I let my head fall forwards, resting on the table. He knew me, didn't he? Trusted me without question. He could read me, and he knew what I needed.

It didn't make the pain of Fallon's betrayal any easier, but it was something that I was going to hold on to.

15

zayde

Time passed, and I found myself reading and rereading the article, sick to my stomach and lost in memories. The first time I'd met my dad. I'd also met Caiden that day.

The first time I saw Michael Lowry, something weird happened. I looked at him, and it was like I knew him. Maybe because I could see something of me in his face. The same thick, dark brown hair and the same pale blue-grey eyes. I didn't look anything like my mum, and it was strange seeing features I recognised on someone else's face.

He was standing upright next to a very flashy, very shiny black Jaguar, wearing a black suit. His arms were folded across his chest, and he wasn't smiling. We were meeting in the car park of a supermarket because he hadn't wanted to leave his car anywhere on my housing estate—something that had made me apprehensive until I realised how much attention it would most likely get. And not attention of the good kind, either. There was at least a fifty percent chance that the car would be stripped of anything valuable before he'd even climbed out.

My mum hadn't even been there to say goodbye. She'd gone out last night and hadn't returned before I had to leave. The last thing she'd said to me was "See you in the morning," and then this morning, I'd had a text to say she wouldn't be home in time before I left, and I should leave my key with Mrs. Jenkins in apartment 17b.

She didn't even tell me that she'd miss me.

I swallowed down that stupid fucking useless lump in my throat and faced the man I'd now be living with. Dropping my duffel bag, I straightened my shoulders and folded my arms, mimicking his posture. A flicker of approval appeared in his eyes, his mouth turning up a tiny bit on one side.

"Zayde. I'm Michael. You can call me..." For a second, his polished veneer fell away, and he seemed unsure. "Uh, Michael. I don't expect you to feel comfortable enough to call me Dad yet. This whole thing is going to take a lot of getting used to." He held out his hand for a formal handshake like I'd seen people do on TV. Nothing like the people I knew in real life, that was for sure.

His grip was strong as he shook my hand, and I tried to match his strength, which made him almost smile again. It was awkward between us, but for the first time since my mum had told me of my dad's existence, I could almost comfort myself knowing that he was probably as out of his depth as I was.

The house was bigger than any house I'd ever seen. It looked like something from a film. It felt like I would get lost inside. The outside was painted grey, with big, black-framed windows, a shiny black double garage, and a huge black front door. When I walked inside, everything was all open, shiny blacks and greys.

"I prefer to live simply. Wasted space is wasted space, as far as I'm concerned." Once Mr. Lowry had spoken those words, his mouth twisted as if he remembered who he was speaking to. "My apologies. I didn't mean... This house isn't... Well, it's not as big as some of the others in Alstone."

When I didn't reply, he led me through the house, stopping outside an open door. "This will be your room. If you want to change the decor, let me know."

"It's fine," I managed, stepping inside and dropping my duffel bag at my feet.

He gave a quick nod. "I'll leave you to unpack. When you're finished, come and find me. We'll go through everything you need to know."

When he'd disappeared, I let myself look around the room. It was all grey and decorated like a hotel room or something, not that I'd ever been in one, but it looked like Mr. Lowry had tried to prepare it for me. Over on the dresser, there was a shiny TV and a PlayStation, still in its box with a stack of games next to it, with another small box with a phone inside it on top. To my left, on the desk, I saw a laptop and pens and notepads, still in their packaging.

My phone beeped in my pocket, and I dug it out to see a message from Creed.

***Creed:** Got a job for you. 6pm by the kebab shop*

Everything rushed back to me again. I hadn't even told him that I was going away.

***Me:** I can't. I moved in with my dad today*
***Creed:** WTF? Where?*
***Me:** Alstone. I only found out about my dad on Thursday. I didn't want to go but I had no choice*

Creed: *Alstone?! That sounds like a story I need to hear. If it makes you feel better I'll be sorry to lose you. You'd better stay in touch. Meet up soon so you can give me the details. And I've always got a job for you if you need it*
Me: *Thanks. Will do*

With a heavy sigh, I shoved my phone back in my pocket. As I was doing so, it beeped again.

Fallon.

I read through the series of texts that had come through. Her parents had sprung a last-minute family holiday on her, and they were going to be somewhere in the south of France, and her phone was blocked from making international calls. She'd only be getting back the day before she was due to go to boarding school. So I wouldn't even have a chance to see her before she went away.

With an effort, I swallowed down yet another fucking lump in my throat and then went to find Mr. Lowry.

"Now you're living in my house, there are a few things you need to be aware of."

Seated on the edge of an uncomfortably hard black leather sofa, I stared down at my hands as Mr. Lowry continued to speak.

"First of all, part of the agreement with your mother was that you'd cease all contact with any persons involved in your previous life. Think of it as a fresh start. The opportunities that you'll have here are endless."

"I don't get to see my mum again? Or my friends?"

His lips thinned, and he frowned at me. "Your mother is an alcoholic and a prostitute. I know she was your mother, but no child of mine will be allowed anywhere near that environment. The same goes for your friends. You're young; you'll make new friends easily enough."

I opened my mouth to reply, but he held up his hand. "This is non-negotiable. Besides, your mother has already agreed." The hardness faded from his expression as he sighed. "You'll thank me for this later, Zayde. I know you can't see it now, but I'm only doing what's best for you. And me. I...I'd given up hope of having a legacy, a son who could follow in my footsteps and one day join the board of Alstone Holdings. But now I have you, and I'm going to do everything in my power to give you as many advantages as I can. On that note..."

He began to reel off a list of things while I sat frozen on the sofa, my head spinning. There was something about a tutor to get me up to speed before the school year began, something about someone teaching me how to behave in a "proper" way, a whole list of staff members and trainers and chefs who would all be in and out of the house each day. I was given codes for the doors, information about where I could and couldn't go, and strict instructions not to have any friends over unless they were pre-approved by Mr. Lowry himself. The same with going out—it could only be to pre-approved places, at times that we'd agreed to in advance. On Monday, he was opening a bank account for me, and I'd be given a generous allowance, as long as I toed the line. He finished up with a reminder that my surname was now Lowry, the same as his, and he was taking care of updating all my records. I was no longer a Smith.

It was like my past identity had been wiped away. I no longer existed.

While I sat there, unable to bring myself to even speak, Mr. Lowry glanced down at his shiny Rolex.

"Ah. My business colleague will be here shortly. He's got a son the same age as you, so I asked him to come. Get to know him before the new school year."

Great. Forced friendships. Another thing to add to everything else that I still couldn't get my head around. I didn't *want new friends. And I definitely didn't want to be subject to all these rules that he'd given me. I'd been independent all my life; I was used to taking care of myself and hanging out with my friends wherever and whenever we wanted. But Fallon...*she lived in Alstone. *Maybe I could get to see her when she was home from boarding school. Maybe there was one thing in my life that didn't have to change.*

The doorbell rang, right on cue, and I followed my dad through the house just in time to see a short lady with light brown hair and a grey uniform answer the door. A maid? We had a maid? I felt like I'd been dropped in someone else's life.

A tall, muscular guy who looked to be around the same age as my dad walked in, followed by a boy with messy black hair and a sullen expression on his face. Yeah, he wanted to be here just about as much as I did.

"You boys go into Zayde's room." My dad was already striding away, followed by the other man, leaving me standing in the hallway, staring awkwardly at the boy. I shifted on my feet as he glanced everywhere but at me. Better get this over with. Clearing my throat, I took a step forward.

"Hi. I'm Zayde Smith—uh, no. I mean, Zayde Lowry."

He finally looked at me, interest sparking in his eyes. "Zayde? Cool name. I'm Caiden Cavendish."

One of the best things my dad had done for me was to introduce me to Caiden, and I knew he'd be out there right now working to fix what he could. The tabloid newspaper had dragged my dad's name through the mud, but I knew that Michael Lowry would never sit back and let them tear his reputation to shreds. The article had done a good job at attempting to discredit him, and Alstone Holdings by extension, but we wouldn't go down without a fight.

My mum, though... Fuck. The way the article painted her...the problem was, so much of it was true. Her death hadn't been due to the pain of losing me, though. I knew that deep down, but as much as I fucking hated to admit it, the article had planted a seed of doubt in my mind. Had my leaving contributed to her downward spiral?

No. She'd always been the same, prioritising drugs and alcohol over essentials like fucking food and electricity. If it hadn't been for Creed and the jobs he'd given me, I'd have gone hungry way more than I had.

The day my dad had informed me of her death was still burned into my mind.

A tragic accident. *The words echoed over and over in my head as I lay on my unmade bed, curled into a ball, my chest aching with a suffocating, heavy throb that refused to go away. Yeah, it was tragic, alright. My mum, who I hadn't seen since I'd left my previous home behind, was gone. My dad didn't believe in sugar-coating the truth, so I'd heard the full story. She'd been celebrating her thirtieth birthday by going on a massive bender, using the money my dad had given her, and at 3:25 a.m., she'd been coming out of a club, drunk and high, and had run into the road and been hit by a van. She'd died on impact.*

Despite the fact that she hadn't cared enough to say goodbye to me the day I'd left for good, despite the fact that she'd never been warm or loving towards me, despite the fact that I'd mostly been left to my own devices ever since I could remember, she was still my mum.

The ache wouldn't go away, so I put my nail to my arm. I knew by now that I shouldn't, that it was wrong to do this, but it was the only way I knew to make it better, even though it didn't last. Three days after I'd heard the news, everything was a dull haze, like I was living in a fog, and the bursts of sudden, bright pain were the only things that could penetrate it. The only thing that would quiet my mind, just for a moment.

There was a knock at my door, and I yanked my sleeve down, hiding the evidence of what I'd done to myself. Rubbing my hand across my face, I rolled over on my bed. "Come in," I croaked.

A dark head of hair appeared, followed by a body, and then Caiden was in my room, looking everywhere but at me. Leaning against my desk, he shoved his hands into his pockets. "Uh. Do you wanna go for a bike ride?"

"I don't—"

"I cleared it with your dad. I've got a surprise for you."

"Okay." It was probably better than another day of lying here staring at nothing. My dad had been in to check on me a couple of times, and some of the staff members had left me food, which mostly remained untouched. But other than that, I hadn't seen or spoken to anyone. As I swung my legs over the side of my bed, pulling up into a seated position, the mark on my arm rubbed against my jumper, and I scratched at the itch through the fabric. Caiden's eyes darted down to my arm. His jaw tensed, but he didn't say anything. He turned to head out of the door, and I followed him.

A while later, we pulled up at a car park outside some warehouses. I was confused—why had Caiden stopped here? It wasn't like there was anything around.

"They should be here," he was mumbling to himself.

"Who should be?" I dropped my bike to the ground, standing and stretching out my aching legs. Caiden didn't reply, scanning the area. The next minute, a black car with a large spoiler, huge wheels, and blacked-out windows turned into the mostly empty car park, and Caiden jogged towards it.

As I went to follow after Caiden, the car doors opened, and two people I hadn't seen in almost a year stepped out.

Creed and Mack.

We exchanged fist bumps, and then I dropped back, my gaze going between them both. "What are you two doing here?"

Mack grinned. "You can thank rich boy for that."

"What? Who's rich boy?"

Caiden stuck his hand up and pointed his thumb at himself. "That would be me. Your friend thinks he's so funny with his nicknames."

"I do." Mack shrugged. Dropping his grin, he turned back to me. "We heard about your mum. Um. Sorry. We'll be at the funeral. A lot of the estate'll be there, probably. We, uh, heard that you weren't allowed to come, but we'll make sure she has a good send-off."

I stared down at the ground, scuffing the toe of my trainer against the gritty tarmac. I'd been able to suppress it for a minute, but now the ache deep inside me had returned again. It felt like I couldn't breathe. "Thanks," I managed.

"Whatever we can do." Creed stepped around Mack, and for the first time, I noticed he had a small plastic bag in his hands. "I got one of my boys to check through her stuff before it got taken away, and we found this. Thought you might want it."

When I took the bag from him, I noticed my hand was shaking. Tugging the sleeve of my jumper lower to hide it, I cleared my throat. "Thanks." That seemed to be the only word I could manage to say.

Creed nodded. "It's no problem. Like I said, whatever we can do. And you know you've always got a job with me if you want it."

I nodded, choking down the lump in my throat. No one would ever see me cry. I'd worked hard on perfecting my mask of ice, and it wasn't going to crack now.

The boys attempted to make conversation for a bit longer,

but the atmosphere was strained, and I was almost relieved when they left. I was too raw to deal with all this.

"Was it okay that I did that? I thought...thought you might wanna see your friends. Have a connection to your mum, y'know." Caiden shot me a sideways look as he straddled his bike, biting down on his lip.

"Yeah. Yeah, it was okay."

Back at home, I shut myself in my room and emptied the bag onto my bed. Two crumpled photos fell out, plus a rectangular package wrapped in Marvel superhero wrapping paper. I studied the photos. One was a picture of me as a baby in the hospital, not long after I'd been born. I recognised it from our flat—it had been stuck to the fridge with a magnet from Brighton Beach. The other, I hadn't seen before. My mum sat on the sofa, holding me on her lap. I must've been around two or something, maybe even younger. Smoke curled in the air from a cigarette she was holding, and she had a smile on her face that I'd never seen before. She actually looked happy.

I carefully placed the photos inside my bedside drawer, then turned my attention to the wrapped package. There was no tag, but my name was scrawled on it in biro. I pulled away the Sellotape and opened it up. A battered, creased book fell out, and I turned it over. To Kill a Mockingbird, *by Harper Lee.*

My brow furrowed as I stared down at the book. Why would my mum give me this? It had obviously seen better days, and I didn't even read books.

Flipping open the first page, I immediately saw the writing inside. Biting down on my fist with one hand, I held the book open with the other and read my mum's final words to me.

Zayde,

Happy 13th birthday. This book was my dad's and it's the only thing left of mine that hasn't been sold, so I wanted you to have it. I hope it finds its way to you.

I know I wasn't a good mum. I know I should have tried harder. You were unexpected and I was only 17 and didn't know how to deal with you. For what it's worth, I'm sorry for everything I got wrong.

I'm glad I sent you away, because being around me and my life wasn't good for you.

One day I hope you'll understand and forgive me.

Mum

xx

My walls of ice cracked, and the pain rushed in.

I dropped my head to the desk again, my eyes stinging. I let my lids fall shut as the tide swept me away. Maybe when I opened my eyes again, it would turn out that this whole weekend had just been a fucked-up dream.

But I knew I was only kidding myself.

16

fallon

I'd only just blinked away the last vestiges of my nightmare when the buzzer sounded. Padding into the lounge, I pressed the key button to let James in, seeing him on the video screen. His expression was grim, and it set alarm bells ringing.

The second I'd opened the apartment door, he thrust a folded newspaper at me. "I saw this at the petrol station on the way home while my dad was filling up the car. What the fuck, Fal?"

With trembling hands, I unfolded the paper, only to see the headline, accompanied by a large image of Zayde and his dad.

"What *is* this?" My eyes widened as I turned to James, hoping he could make sense of what I was looking at.

"That's what I'm hoping you can explain to me. Because this here—" He stabbed at the paper with the tip of his finger. "—says that it's an exclusive interview about Zayde and *you*."

My legs gave way, and I crumpled to the floor, frantically scanning the words. Nausea rose in my stomach, and by the time I reached the "continued on page 12..." part, my hands were shaking too badly to turn the pages.

"You don't think *I* was behind this, do you? I didn't do this, James. How could you think I would?"

He lowered himself to the floor next to me with a sigh. "I don't think you would, but ever since I saw the article, I've been asking myself: is it true? The story?"

I stared down at the images on page 12. The tower block, with an inset image of the inside of someone's apartment, and next to it, a large mansion and inset of an opulent room, which I knew for a fact wasn't Zayde's dad's house. Nausea warred with rage at the thought that someone had laid his private life bare like this. It was vindictive and cruel, and to insinuate that he had manipulated *me*?

"Parts of it are true," I admitted. "But our relationship... it wasn't like that. Not at all. He— We— I loved him once."

"This is fucked up," James murmured. He paused and then added, "And once? What happened?"

"Tim."

"Fallon," he said softly, placing a hand on my arm. "I know how much that tore you apart. I still miss him with everything I have, and I can't even pretend to know how hard it's been for you. But...you know that was an accident, right?"

"How can you say that? You weren't even there! I saw what happened. Zayde...he...it was his fault."

His mouth twisted. "Fal...are you positive that you saw what you thought you saw? Everyone agreed that it was an accident. The police interviewed everyone there. There was an investigation into the building. There was a reason it was condemned. That room...they said that you had a lucky escape. Zayde, too. Did you know that the whole level caved in that night? The flooring was ready to collapse. It was rotten all the way through and full of woodworm, and the fire easily decimated it. They said that it could have collapsed at any time, with or without the fire. We could have lost you all and whoever was in the rooms below."

I took a deep, shuddering breath. *What?* "I-I don't understand."

"Do you want to talk me through what happened that night? It might help make things clearer," he offered.

Could I? No. Not yet. This...what he was saying...it was too much to get my head around right now. "No. I can't. I'm not ready."

"Okay. It's okay, really. I get it. Let's focus on the article for now. We need to know who was behind it. Who else has this information and would drag your name into it?"

The pieces suddenly fell into place, and my blood went cold. "No. It *couldn't* be." I stared at James, seeing the dawning horror I felt reflected in his expression.

"He wouldn't sell out his own sister, would he?" Even as James spoke, I knew that he didn't believe his own words.

"I know how he got the information. Yesterday, I was at the graveyard to visit Tim." Quickly, I detailed how I'd found Joseph standing behind me, and when I'd asked him how long he'd been there, he'd ignored my question.

"But why would he do this? I can understand him wanting to hurt Alstone Holdings—not that I agree with him in any way—but I've seen a different side of him this past year or so, and he's capable of a lot of things that I never thought he'd do. But to throw you under the bus in the process?"

I shook my head, my eyes filling with tears. Fuck. It felt like I'd been constantly crying since I'd been back in Alstone, and this was only my third day here. "I don't know.

I know he was visiting our father in prison after he'd been to the grave, so maybe..." Trailing off, I threw up my hands. "I don't know. James, I feel so alone. And the Four...the girls especially have been so kind and welcoming, and now they're going to hate me, and with good reason."

James made a surprised noise in his throat, cocking his brow at me. "Wait, when did you meet them?"

"Oh. I met Jessa here, actually. I ran into her at the main door to the building, and she invited me to a party at the Four's house."

He eyed me with curiosity. "Did any of them know about your relationship with Zayde? How did that even start? The article didn't go into much detail."

Groaning, I buried my face in my hands. "I guess I have to tell you now that the whole world knows. No one else knew we were together, but we were in a relationship for a lot longer than the paper made out. I'm not sure if there was ever a point where we specifically changed from friends to boyfriend and girlfriend—the whole thing just happened so naturally. You know how the article mentioned that his mum was a cleaner for us? That's how we met."

"I have to say, I'm having a hard time getting my head around Zayde Lowry being in a relationship with anyone, let alone you." He huffed out a laugh. "That man is as cold as ice, and he never lets anyone close."

My heart ached. "I know. But he was different with me."

James was quiet for a while, digesting everything. Eventually, he climbed to his feet, holding out his hand to pull me up. "Right. The first thing we need to do is to make sure everyone knows that you didn't have anything to do with the article. I hate to say it, but I think you're going to have to start with Zayde because it affects him the most."

"He won't listen to me, James. And I don't even know if I can be in the same room as him without... I feel so confused. My head feels so messed up."

"You have to try."

I knew he was right, although I wished he wasn't. It was time for me to face things head-on.

"Okay. Let's go."

17

zayde

I paced the Alstone Holdings boardroom. It was a hive of activity—the Cavendishes, Drummonds, and my dad were all here, plus Winter and Jessa. At one end of the huge conference table, a screen was showing a larger version of the video call that the board members were currently on via their laptops, the faces of our lawyers drawn and serious. Taylor, Paul Drummond's assistant, was running around with a panicked look on her face like she was personally responsible for this shitshow. It was giving me a headache, and I dropped my gaze to the table. It made no difference. Coffee cups, biscuits, pens, and papers cluttered the surface, and the atmosphere was so fucking oppressive it made me want to scream.

I needed a break. To get out of here. To clear my head before I did something I knew I'd regret.

"Cade." Dipping down, I spoke in a low voice. "I'm going for a ride. Text me if anything comes up, okay?"

He nodded. "I'll cover for you. Do what you need to."

Wasting no more time, I headed out of the room and took the lift down to the ground floor. Once I was in the car park, helmet on and straddling my bike, I felt like I could breathe again for the first time in hours. Twisting the throttle, I pressed down the Start button, and the bike roared to life, thrumming powerfully beneath me. Then I took off.

My body worked on autopilot, leaning into the road curves, taking me away from the town centre as my mind emptied of everything but the feel of my bike's wheels flying across the tarmac. This was what I'd needed—had needed ever since I found out about Fallon's return. Slipping back into old habits wasn't what I wanted, not after I'd crawled out of the dark place I'd been in since Tim had died and Fallon had gone. My coping mechanisms now were better. The temporary sting of the tattoo or piercing needles. The open road where I was free of everything, just me and my bike.

When I came to a stop, I realised that I was at the ruins of Alstone Castle. The day was cool and overcast, meaning it was even colder up on the clifftops above the sea, and in the sudden silence, I could hear the waves battering harshly at the cliffs.

Removing my helmet, I headed for the edge of the cliff. I'd been in a very fucking dark place after Tim had died. About four or five days after it had happened, I'd been standing here in this spot, in the dead of night.

The rain was a deluge, and the wind was howling, and I was so fucking empty and broken. I stared down at the blackness of the sea, churning far below. The rocks were jagged, with lethal edges, and the wind buffeted my body, making me stumble. Bolts of lightning split the sky, followed by the low rumble of thunder.

It would be so easy to let go. To take one step forwards.

My final step. And then the darkness would pull me under, and I'd finally be at peace.

No one would miss me. My own mother hadn't wanted me. My dad wanted what I represented—a legacy. My friends would soon forget about me. And the only person who'd ever captured my heart was gone. She hated me with every fibre of her being, and for good reason.

I gasped in a breath, the icy air stinging my lungs.

My mind was at war, torn in two.

I wanted the pain to stop.

I wanted everything to go away.

Inhaling another lungful of the sea air, I screamed at the sky, pouring every bit of rage and despair I felt into the sound.

Then I lifted my foot and took a step.

Back.

Away from the edge.

I fell to the stony ground, slippery with mud, tearing my jeans on a serrated edge. My head cracked against a rock, making me see stars.

The sudden pain was a welcome relief.

I lay there, the storm raging all around me until I was numb. Until I'd locked everything away. Every single feeling that had the power to break me.

Then I climbed to my feet, slipping in the mud, and wiped the rain away from my face. I was soaked through, frozen, bruised and bleeding, but I was still here.

I was alive.

To this day, I wasn't sure what had stopped me from going over the cliff. Looking back, I knew now that some of the things I'd thought that night had been distorted by my own grief and pain. My dad did care about me in his own way.

The Four were my closest friends, and I knew they'd be fucking horrified if they knew what I'd almost done, not least because Cade and West had lost their own mum to suicide.

But that's the thing with the darkness in your mind. It's like a suffocating, insidious fog, spreading into your blackest corners, whispering that everyone would be better off without you. Telling you that everything would stop hurting if you just gave in and let go.

"Fuck," I whispered, sinking down onto a large flat rock and burying my face in my arms.

"Zayde?"

My whole body froze at the sound of the soft, tentative voice. Slowly, I raised my head.

"I need to explain. Please will you listen?"

The shake in Fallon's voice did me in. There was no way I could ever refuse her anything. Ever. I'd give her the whole fucking world if I could.

Taking my silence as assent, she picked her way across the rocky ground to where I was sitting, her red Converse sending small clouds of dust into the air as she scuffed her feet over the dirt. When she reached me, she sank down onto one of the rocks next to me. Something crinkled in her hand, and it was only then that I realised she was carrying a copy of that fucking newspaper.

"How did you find me?"

She shook her head. "Luck. We went to your house first, but there was no one there, and then James drove this way. I saw your bike at the side of the road."

I stiffened at the mention of Granville, but she was quick to speak up. "James isn't here. I asked him to leave. This is a conversation that I need to have with you."

"What do you want? Haven't you done enough?"

She visibly recoiled at the venom in my voice, but she took several deep breaths, squaring her shoulders. “Do you really think I’d do something like that?”

“I don’t know. I don’t even know you anymore.”

Her lip trembled, and she bit down on it, the fingers of her free hand squeezing her thigh. “I didn’t do it. But I know who did.”

18

fallon

Zayde listened in silence as I gave him a rundown of everything I'd said out loud at Tim's grave, his face a blank, impassive mask. When I'd finished speaking, he let his face drop into his arms again, the same way I'd found him when I arrived at the castle ruins.

The sight of him made me ache. Even though he was hiding his true feelings behind his impenetrable walls of ice, I knew that the article would have hurt him deeply. But it wasn't my place to comfort him, was it?

Except...after my conversation with Tim and then with James earlier, it was getting harder and harder to hang on to the hate. The day would soon come when I'd have to properly face what had happened that night, to examine it with fresh eyes, and to acknowledge that maybe I'd been blinded by my own agony.

Before I knew what I was doing, I was placing the newspaper on the ground, slipping off the rock, and closing the distance between us. "Zayde." I tentatively placed a hand on his shoulder.

His head lifted, and his eyes met mine, almost

colourless in this light. He swallowed hard, and I saw the exact moment when he let me in, just a little. Just enough to see the raw pain in his gaze, making the breath catch in my throat as my heart twisted for this man with a broken boy inside him that just needed someone to be in his corner. Someone who'd hold him tight so he knew he didn't have to face the world alone.

"Oh, *Zayde*." I gave in, sliding my hand into his soft hair and allowing him to wind his arms around my waist. I stroked my fingers across his scalp, my other hand going to his nape, cupping it and holding him gently in place.

It was a long time before he drew back from me. Keeping his gaze averted, he pulled his phone from his pocket and got to his feet. I could see him talking into it, but he'd walked away from me, so I couldn't hear what he was saying. When he finished the call, he stayed where he was, running a hand through his hair, already mussed from the wind.

The wind rustled the discarded newspaper, and I had a sudden thought. It would only be symbolic, but maybe it would help. I scooped it up. "Zayde? Do you have a lighter?"

His gaze arrowed to mine and then to the paper. The corners of his lips curved up a little as he crossed back over to me. Kneeling down, I began balling up the pages as best as I could, throwing them into the ashy remains of what looked to be a firepit.

He knelt down next to me, holding out a shiny black lighter engraved with a grinning skull. Flipping open the top, he lit the flame and held it to the edge of the closest page.

It immediately caught light, the words disappearing as the fire devoured the paper. It was a relief watching it burn, watching those hateful words go up in smoke.

When the other pages began to light up, he got to his feet. “Come on.”

I followed him back to the place he’d parked his bike, next to the side of the road. He leaned back against his bike, his arms folded across his chest. Just when I was about to ask what he was doing, I heard the sound of a car engine, and a silver VW Polo appeared over the crest of the hill. Zayde straightened up as the car came to a stop. The driver’s door opened, and a pretty girl stepped out, holding a red motorbike helmet. She smiled at Zayde and eyed me with curiosity. “Good thing I kept forgetting to give you this helmet back, wasn’t it?”

Zayde took the helmet from her. “I owe you one.”

She shook her head, her smile brightening. “If anything, I owe you for giving me a lift home that night. If I hadn’t been back in time to turn in that essay, I would’ve failed my module.” Turning to me, she said, “Since I doubt Zayde will introduce us, I’ll introduce myself. I’m Kinslee.”

“Hi. I’m Fallon.” I returned her smile automatically. More words came spilling out of my mouth, unchecked. “Why have all the girls I’ve met recently been so nice? This isn’t how I remember Alstone.”

Kinslee laughed. “Oh, there’s plenty of that around, so I guess you’ve been lucky. Thankfully, I’m not part of the elite, so I’ve escaped the worst of it, although hanging around with this lot over the past year has meant I’ve had my share of run-ins with the less friendly part of Alstone’s population. I’m sure Zayde can tell you about it.”

I filed that information away for later. “It’s nice to meet you.”

“You too.” She stepped back towards her car. “I don’t want to seem rude, but I was about to go and visit my brother when Zayde called me, so I’d better get going before

I'm ridiculously late. I'm sure I'll see you around. I've never caught Zayde alone with a girl before, and he's definitely never asked a favour for one, so you must be special." Her smile turned into a huge grin at Zayde's warning growl. Diving back into her car, she shouted, "Bye," out of the window and drove away.

You must be special.

The words kept replaying in my mind.

"Helmet on. You can hold the bar if you don't want to hold on to me," Zayde instructed gruffly, shoving the helmet into my arms.

You must be special.

I let the helmet fall to the ground.

"What are you—"

Launching myself up onto my toes, I cut him off with a kiss.

It was so wrong yet so right.

It felt inevitable.

It felt like coming home.

The way his strong arms instantly wrapped around me, holding me in place as his lips slanted across mine, made my entire body shiver. My mouth opened for his, and the warm metal of his barbell glided over my skin as his tongue slid against mine. His kiss was so familiar and so new at the same time.

I wanted it to stop, and I never wanted it to end.

I tasted salt, and I realised that I was crying. Breaking away from his kiss, I gasped for breath, speaking in a broken whisper. "I can't help wanting you. But I don't want to want you. I hated you so much, Zayde, for so long. I hate you for what you did." *But I think I still love you.*

He inhaled sharply, his arms tightening around me. His

voice was so low and raw, his words pressed into my skin as he buried his head in my neck.

"Sometimes I hate me, too."

Fuck. My stomach churned at his defeated tone, that raw honesty that let me know that he truly believed what he was saying. And I hated myself for the words I'd flung at him, despite the fact that I meant them, yet didn't mean them, all at the same time.

"I'm sorry. I-I shouldn't have done that. I just wish...I wish that things could have been different." Drawing back from him was a struggle because it felt so right to be in his arms, but how could I get over the past? How could I even contemplate it when my brother was dead because of him?

With a sigh, I picked up the helmet, brushing the dirt from it.

Zayde rubbed his hand across his face, turning away from me. Swinging his leg over the bike, he mounted it, tugging his own helmet over his head. I fought the shiver that raced through my body at the sight of him sitting astride the powerful machine, all dressed in black and sexy as fuck. No one else had ever caught and held my attention the way he had. He was beautiful, and dangerous, and everything I'd ever wanted, once upon a time.

When I climbed on behind him and wrapped my arms around his waist, not even entertaining thoughts of holding the handlebar, I knew I had to stop lying to myself.

He wasn't only everything I'd wanted once upon a time.

He was everything I still wanted.

When we entered the Alstone Holdings offices, I steeled myself for the backlash that my presence would bring. I couldn't even blame anyone for it because if I'd been in their situation, I would have been the same.

What felt like a hundred pairs of eyes swung to me when I entered the boardroom right on Zayde's heels. The room erupted with noise, but Zayde held up a hand, effectively silencing it.

"Fallon has something to tell you all. Before she does, I want to make one thing crystal fucking clear. Any discussion about our relationship is off limits. You don't mention it, you don't even fucking think about it. If you don't agree to those terms, we both walk out of here, right now. Do I make myself clear?"

Several people gaped at him in shock, myself included. I hadn't expected that, not in a million years. But I appreciated it, more than he could ever know. I knew he was protecting himself, but he was also protecting me.

Arlo Cavendish was the first to recover. After glancing over at Zayde's dad, who had pursed his lips but remained silent, he met Zayde's gaze. "Understood." He turned his attention to me, his tone softening. "Ms. Hyde. What would you like to tell us?"

I faltered. I'd never had so many eyes on me at once. But then I felt the heat of Zayde's body against my side.

"Breathe," he murmured, too softly for anyone else to hear.

It was enough. Sucking in a breath, I stepped right into the room, grasping the back of the empty chair in front of me as a bolster.

And then I threw my brother under the bus. "I need you all to know that I had no knowledge of the article. I believe that my brother Joseph was behind it."

19

fallon

I hadn't been allowed to stay while the negotiations happened. I'd relayed everything I knew to everyone gathered in the boardroom, but it still didn't give anyone a reason to trust me. Alstone Holdings was caught up in damage control, and the last thing they needed was to have me around. James had picked me up and taken me back to his apartment, which suddenly seemed claustrophobic with the two of us there and only one bedroom. Once again, he insisted he was fine with sleeping on the floor, but I couldn't kick him out of his own bedroom. In the end, after we'd had a stand-off, both of us stubborn to the end, he'd eventually relented. Or so he said.

We spent a long time talking about everything. About Hyde Consultings and how my dad had been the sole person in charge for a long time. Unlike Alstone Holdings, which was run by a board comprised of three separate family groups, the Hydes had always entrusted their business to one immediate family. Which meant that there was an obligation for each company head to pass it on to their children, primarily their firstborn sons. In my family's case, that meant Joseph. I'd always had an awareness of the fact, of the way that he seemed to both hate our father for the way he treated us but simultaneously looked up to him and wanted to please him. And Roland Hyde had invested years in grooming his eldest son to be his successor. Did it make me a bad person for feeling some sympathy for my brother? Would he have made the decisions he had without my father speaking in his ear, tainting his perceptions?

I guess it was a question I'd never really know the answer to, but I hoped that deep down, Joe was a good person.

Or I had always hoped, up until now. With everything that had happened today, I hadn't really had time to process my brother's part in this whole thing, but now all the pieces had fallen into place.

"Why did he do it?" I spoke out loud, interrupting James. He blinked and then turned his gaze on me, instant understanding in his eyes.

"He's been too heavily influenced by your dad," he said at last. "I know it's not what you want to hear."

Picking up the cup of peppermint tea James had brewed for me, I blew across it, dispersing the steam curling through the air while I thought about my answer. "It's not what I want to hear, but I know what you're saying is the truth."

He nodded. "For what it's worth, my parents never agreed with yours. I don't think my dad ever got on with your dad, even as kids. That's why he only ever got involved in the superficial levels of the business, and then he diversified, branching out into other industries on his own. You can trust my family to be impartial. I hope."

"I know." My cousin had always been a bit of an outlier.

He'd never been one to get involved in conflict, not if he could help it, preferring to stay neutral.

Before James could reply, my phone chimed, and a message preview popped up. It was Jessa.

I swiped my thumb across my screen to unlock it, and the full message popped up.

Jessa: Pleeease don't hate me but I gave Z your number. I've never seen him look like that before

Like what?

Me: ???
Jessa: This is Cass. He looked like someone had run over a puppy *crying emoji*
Jessa: Sorry about Cass. He's not wrong though

My heart skipped a beat.

I needed to know what they meant by that, but before I could reply, my phone started buzzing in my hand, telling me that I had an incoming video call.

Hailey.

My friend who'd been there that night. She'd been at school with Tim while I was away at Hatherley Hall, but we'd always been close. And she was the only person who knew about Zayde, until now.

"Hailey."

"Fal, are you okay? I got your text, and I'd planned to call you tonight anyway, but then I saw the papers online. Those bastards. I just knew everyone would jump to conclusions, but I know for a fact that you'd never have anything to do with a story like that." On the screen, I could see her face pulling into a frown. Behind her, through a sash window, I could see the cobbled street she lived on gleaming in the rain, thrown into sharp relief by the glow of the lamp posts.

I glanced over at James. He coughed, climbing to his feet. "I'm going to check out some stuff on my laptop in my bedroom."

Glad that he could sense that I needed a bit of space, I settled back into the sofa cushions, angling my phone so that my face filled the screen. "I'm not really okay."

By the time I'd finished giving her all the details, her brows were pulled together in an even deeper frown, and her bottom lip was red from where she'd been biting down on it. "Disregarding the paper for just a minute, exactly what happened that night? Because I remember Zayde's face, Fallon, and I've never, ever seen anyone so utterly devastated as he was."

Fuck.

"I-it hurts too much to think about it," I whispered. "I don't want to remember."

"I know it hurts. But you have to. Please. Listen to me. It's the only way you'll be able to move on."

"I can't."

"You can." Her voice was firm, and her eyes were brimming with empathy. "I know you can."

I took a deep, shuddering breath. "I know you're right. I've just...I've been holding on to the hate for so long. What happens if it's gone? What if it turns out it was my fault?"

"Fallon. Listen to me very carefully. Tim's death is not *anyone's* fault. It was a horrible, horrible accident."

"You don't...I don't...I can't..."

"Hey. It's alright. Take some time. You don't have to have all the answers straight away. I know you can get through this, but if you need moral support, I'm only a phone call away, and I can come back to Alstone if you need me. You don't have to face this alone."

"Th-thank you." I hoped she could see just how sincere I was. "I need time to think about everything. Can I phone you again when my head's not all over the place?"

She gave me a soft smile. "Whatever you need."

We said our goodbyes, and when she was gone, I felt like a tiny bit of the weight had been lifted.

I had about ninety seconds of respite before my phone chimed with another message.

Unknown: Outside. We need to talk

Racing to the nearest window, I lifted the blinds, scanning the street below.

A matte-black motorbike was parked in the glow of a street lamp, the rider dressed all in black, their head tilted upwards, towards my window, their face obscured by the visor of their helmet.

My heart stuttered, then kicked into high gear.

"James?" I called. "I'm going out. Don't wait up for me."

The sound of the blinds being yanked up, followed by a muffled curse, rang in my ears as I closed the door behind me and raced down the stairs and out of the building. I didn't stop running until I was right in front of Zayde's beast of a motorbike, its owner holding it upright between his powerful thighs.

He handed me a shiny red helmet, and I wasted no time in jamming it on my head and straddling the bike behind him. When I'd wrapped my arms around his waist, he twisted the throttle, and then we shot off down the street. A smile of pure joy spread across my face, unexpected and bright. Just being here in this moment, forgetting everything else, I was free. Untouchable, flying along the open roads, protected by the warm body in front of me. It was a heady rush that I didn't think I'd ever tire of.

We reached the Four's driveway, and he pulled up next to a row of cars. Every single one was matte black, as was Zayde's bike.

Lifting my visor, I climbed off the bike. Stretching out my arms and legs, I glanced over at Zayde, who had lifted his own visor and was pulling off his thick leather gloves.

"I'm beginning to sense a trend." A teasing smile curled over my lips as I indicated the row of black-on-black vehicles.

"Yeah?" He followed my gaze, his own lips kicking up. When his gaze returned to mine, there was something in his eyes. Hope? Whatever it was, it made my heart beat just a little bit faster.

Entering the house, he dropped both our helmets on the table and led me into the kitchen. "Drink?"

I nodded. "Please." At least holding a drink would give me something to do. Without asking me to elaborate further, he began pulling mugs from the cupboard and stuck a pod in the coffee machine. A couple of minutes later, I was handed a delicious-smelling hot chocolate laced with Baileys. Perfect.

After making himself a black coffee, he walked to the doors that led onto the covered decking area outside. He flipped a switch on the panel next to the wall, which activated a string of fairy lights. A press of another button dimmed the lights to a soft, barely-there glow.

"I asked everyone to give us space," he told me when I was seated across from him in a large wooden chair with padded cushions, wrapped in a thick, fluffy grey blanket. A small gas firepit-slash-coffee table was between us, taking off the chill of the October evening.

We were so close to the second anniversary of Tim's death. I sipped my hot chocolate to ease the sudden lump in my throat. "What did you want to talk about?"

"There's a lot of things we need to discuss. But tonight, we need to focus on this tabloid shitstorm. We tracked down the source of the article, and as we suspected, Joseph was the one behind it. Alstone Holdings' lawyers are putting out a statement, and the newspaper has been threatened into printing a public apology. It was that, or we sued them for all they were worth."

"But a lot of that article was true."

"They can't prove most of it. They had my mum's death certificate, and I guess they'd done enough digging to get the details of where I used to live, but most of the rest of it was our word against theirs." His jaw clenched. "Not that it helps because other reporters are going to be sniffing around for a scoop now. It's big news since we're so well connected, especially because we have connections with influential government figures. The prime minister was at the Alstone winter ball, and even if that hadn't been the case, you know how the fucking tabloid vultures like to drag anyone successful through the mud."

"So what does this mean?"

"It means that you need to lay low because those fuckers will probably be camped outside our houses for the next few days."

"*James.* I need to warn him in case he gets caught up in it. They'll come after him, won't they? They know that he's my cousin."

Zayde's expression grew icy. "Yeah. Winter has a plan."

"I take it you don't like the plan?"

"No," he bit out, "but even I can see that it makes sense. He's coming to stay here, with us. We're all gonna lay low here for a few days." His gaze dropped to his coffee mug, and he licked his lips. "We were hoping you'd stay here, too."

"Wait, James knows about this already?" I focused on the first part of what he'd just told me because my brain needed time to process.

"He will by now. Winter was gonna speak to him. I wanted you here first because I...fuck, I just wanted to talk to you alone before everyone sits down and starts planning shit like they always do."

My heart beat faster. Making a decision, I stood, tugging my blanket up with me, and rounded the firepit to him. Without either of us needing to say a word, he shifted over in his seat, making a space for me. I sank down next to him, my side pressed against his side. Taking a sip of hot chocolate, I willed my hands to stop trembling. "What are you going to do about Joseph?"

"What do you mean?"

Placing my mug down carefully, I stared into the dancing flames of the firepit. "You're not going to let this go. I know you."

He shook his head. "I want to fucking kill him for what he did. But it's up to you, baby. What do you want to do?"

"You're really leaving that up to me? Why?"

"He's your brother. Fuck, angel, I've had to hold myself back from doing so much shit to him. When he sucked Granville into his games and fucked with Cade and Winter. When he hit Winter. When we captured him after we found him plotting with Christine Cavendish and your dad at the castle. So many fucking times, I wanted to make him pay, to break him, to make him beg for mercy, but I held back. Went easy on him. Because he was your brother. I knew what he'd done for you. Taking those beatings from your dad on your behalf." His lashes swept down as his eyes closed, and his voice dropped lower. "But it wasn't just that. I couldn't…I couldn't risk you losing another brother because of me."

"Zayde." There were so many things I wanted to say. "*Zayde*."

"Yeah?" he rasped.

"I don't— I can't…I'm not ready to think about what happened yet. But I think I might…we might be able to…"

He exhaled sharply, his eyes flying open and connecting with mine. His gaze was so intense. "You don't have to explain. I'm not going anywhere, and if there's even a one fucking percent chance that we can get past everything that's happened, I'm taking it." He reached down to grip my chin. "You know why?"

"N-no." My lip trembled.

"Because you're fucking *mine*."

He covered my mouth with his, and I let myself get swept away by his claiming kiss. I lost myself in his touch, letting him pull me closer, pushing the blankets aside so I could straddle his muscular thighs while I wound my arms around his neck.

No one else could ever make me feel the way he made me feel.

"You're. Fucking. Mine," he ground out between kisses, pulling me closer, winding his hand into my hair and giving it a tug that sent delicious shivers all down my spine. I let my fingers slide around to the front of his throat, pressing my index finger to his pulse point, just so I could feel how hard his heart was pounding. My own heart was going crazy, and my body was on fire, nerve endings alight with a million sensations.

Curving my hand around his throat, I pulled back from him so I could see his face, both of us breathing hard. "Would you let me do this?" I squeezed lightly, unable to believe that I had this powerful man beneath me and he was letting me hold him vulnerable like this.

"Baby, I'd let you do anything you fucking wanted. *Anything*." He surged forwards again, capturing my mouth in a fierce, biting kiss that made me moan into his mouth, and my grip on his throat dropped in favour of cupping the back of his head with both hands, willing him to kiss me even harder. I could feel the steel length of his big cock between my legs, trapped within the confines of his jeans, and my hand went down between us, rubbing over the denim.

"Fuck," he groaned, moving his mouth to my throat, biting down. "Do you want my dick?"

"Y-yes," I panted, undone. How had I managed to hold back for so long? How could I have denied the chemistry between us, always pulling us together?

"I bet you're so fucking wet for me, aren't you?" His hand covered mine, guiding it back towards me. My knuckles brushed across my clit, so sensitive even through the double layers of my underwear and leggings, and I moaned again.

"Zayde. *Please*."

Real life intruded when both of our phones went off at the same time. With effort, I scooted back, enough to put an inch or two of space between us. My chest was heaving, and all I could do was look at Zayde, the iciness of those thickly lashed eyes almost fully hidden by black. He was so gorgeous it took my breath away.

All the obstacles in our relationship that had once seemed insurmountable—the secret we were keeping from our families and friends, my father's plan for my life—all of that was gone now.

But... But what remained was the fact that Tim was also gone, and nothing that either of us said or did would bring him back.

Zayde adjusted the thick bulge in his jeans as I shifted off his lap and reached for my phone, sending my thoughts spiralling down a path that I shouldn't let them go down until I'd had time to process everything. I shouldn't have even kissed him, not really, but I'd been starving for him for so long, and I wanted him so, so badly.

Thankfully...or not...the messages waiting for us both derailed my train of thought and sent me down an entirely different track. I'd been added to a group chat titled *OPERATION ANNIHILATION.*

My brows lifted at the title and rose higher as I began scrolling through the chat.

Cassius: Operation Annihilation is ONNNNNN
Weston: FFS
Cassius: Don't pretend you didn't already pick a theme tune. I heard you blasting it earlier
Weston: That was my Spotify playlist, dickhead
Cassius: Lies. The song's too embarrassing to share isn't it?
Weston: *middle finger emoji*
Winter: DEJA VU. Why does this happen every time?!!!!!
Lena: Jessa, take his phone away
Cassius: She wouldn't dare!
Jessa: I could be tempted

Cassius: Traitor!!! *shocked face emoji*
Caiden: Can someone explain why fucking GRANVILLE has to stay under our roof???
James: Hello to you too Cavendish. Thanks for making me feel welcome. So kind of you!
Caiden: Who added Granville to this fucking chat?!!
Cassius: Moi. He's involved remember?
Cassius: Moving on. Tell us our theme tune West. I wanna listen to it
Lena: Just tell him. He'll never shut up otherwise *eyeroll emoji*
Cassius: Love you too sis *kiss emoji*
Weston: FINE. https://alstoneholdings.co.uk/westons-secret-page/
Cassius: You made a whole playlist *heart eyes emoji*
Caiden: OK back to business. Lawyer statements are done, extra security will be in place by 6am at AH offices, AMC, all houses. The uni has been informed that none of us will be there for lectures in the next couple of days. Poss even a week
Weston: Does that mean we get out of doing coursework?
Caiden: I fucking wish. No they're gonna email us everything
James: What time should I head over?
Caiden: Does never o'clock work for you?
James: Hahaha. You should be a comedian
Caiden: I'll keep that in mind
Cassius: Could you imagine Cade doing stand-up? *yawn emoji*
Weston: Or Z!
Cassius: *crying laugh emoji*

Zayde: *middle finger emoji*
Winter: There you are Z! Is Fallon there with you?

Zayde glanced at me over the top of his coffee mug, his phone balanced on his thigh as he scrolled through the messages. "Those fuckers," he muttered, but there was a half-smile tugging at his lips.

"I guess that's my cue to reply," I said.

Fallon: I'm here. Hi

My message was followed by a flurry of replies saying hi and welcome, and I found myself smiling, too. Winter messaged to say that James should head over now, and I added a comment to ask him to bring my bags, seeing Zayde's gaze boring into me as he read the words.

"You decided to stay?"

I nodded. "If there's enough space. I think...if it is going to be a media circus, then I'd rather be here than trapped in James' apartment."

"Yeah, there's space." He eyed me from beneath his lashes. "We have a spare guest bedroom. The other room upstairs got turned into a dressing room, but James can crash in our games room. Or you can sleep in my room, and James can have the guest room. I spent the first twelve years of my life sleeping on a lumpy mattress on a broken bed; the games room isn't a problem for me to sleep in. It doesn't matter to me. I can sleep anywhere. "

Both our phones sounded again, and I found a message from Caiden in the group chat, summoning us all to the kitchen table to go through our plan of action for the next couple of days.

"C'mon, let's go inside." Clambering to his feet, he

offered me his hand, and I took it, letting him pull me upright. He released his grip when I was standing, picking up his coffee mug, and I immediately missed the warmth of his palm against mine.

When we reached the door, he stopped. “Think about what you want to do about Joseph, okay?”

“I think...I’d like to talk to him first. Alone. I’d like some answers from him. And then maybe we can talk about it again after that?”

“Alright, but I’m not letting you meet him alone. But I’ll give you space.”

“If you have to.”

He gave me a hard look as we entered the kitchen, letting me know he wouldn’t compromise, and I didn’t mind that because after everything Joe had done, I knew I’d feel safer with him close by.

“Is there another option for sleeping arrangements?” I asked softly, moving closer to him as the others began filing into the room, taking seats around the large kitchen table.

There was an almost imperceptible hitch in his breathing, but he didn’t reply. As I slid into one of the free seats, my phone chimed.

I glanced down at the screen, hiding my phone beneath the table.

There was a single text from the same number as earlier. I quickly saved it to my contacts, making his name appear on the message.

Zayde: There could be another option. Your decision, angel

20

fallon

Zayde paused just inside his bedroom door, giving me time to look my fill. The room was lit by a single lamp, but the glow was enough for me to see that it was minimally decorated, mostly in black, with the odd grey accent to break it up. And quite a few skulls... In fact...I took in the black flocked wallpaper. The ebony flock pattern was actually made up of skulls.

It was all very Zayde. The only decoration on the walls was a framed picture over the head of the bed. It was a simple image. Lines of words in plain black text, with a sketch of a pair of angel wings underneath, identical to the tattoo that Zayde had across his shoulders. A lump came into my throat as I stepped closer to study it.

The words above the wings were from Sonnet XVII by Pablo Neruda. And as for the sketch itself...

"Is that...?"

"Yeah. It's the original sketch I did. The same one I based your necklace on."

Guilt arrowed through me again, remembering how

callously I'd discarded the precious things he'd given me. How could I have been so cruel?

I took a deep breath. "Zayde? I want to sleep in here tonight."

He inclined his head. "Okay, yeah. Granville—*James* is already in the guest room. I'll grab my shit, and then I'll get out of your way."

Very deliberately, I crossed the room, stopping close to where he was standing, and I shut the door. "What was the other option for sleeping arrangements?"

His eyes darkened, his gaze raking over me. "Are you sure you want to go down that path? I need you to be sure."

Lifting my hand, I placed it over his heart. The firm muscle of his pec flexed, and I could feel his steady heartbeat under my palm. James' and Hailey's words and my own uncertain recollection spun through my mind, and it only took me a second to decide. "All I know is I'm finished with denying you. I want you, Zayde." *I think I still love you.* "Ever since I saw you again, I've felt like I'm being torn in two."

He exhaled harshly and pressed into me, walking us towards the bed. When the backs of my knees hit the mattress, I threw out my hands, curling them into the duvet so I could keep my balance. His hands came down on either side of mine, making the mattress dip under his weight, and he lowered his head so his face was level with mine.

"Do you still blame me? Do you think you might be able to forgive me for not being able to save your brother?"

I took a deep breath, all too aware of how shaky it came out. "I...I don't...I can't answer that yet. But please...give me time."

His head dipped even lower, his nose brushing against

mine. "If you can't answer that, then what do you want from me?"

I brought one of my hands up to curl around his nape, inhaling his addictive scent of leather, motorbikes, and something that was uniquely him. "I want you to touch me, Zayde. But I need it to hurt."

A choked sound came from his throat. "*What*?"

Oh, fuck. *No*. Why had I let those words come out? I'd unthinkingly said them because there was a huge part of me that felt guilty, like I shouldn't take any pleasure from anything or anyone that might have caused my brother pain. That I should hurt in his stead. But the second I'd said them, I wished more than anything that I could take them back. As much as my head was conflicted with the fact that I was here with the love of my life, who may or may not have caused my brother's death—

No. Regardless of what had happened before or since, it was now starting to become clear to me that my viewpoint had been skewed. I'd been blaming Zayde for such a long time, but it *wasn't* his fault, was it? My mind had been in such a dark place for so long, holding on to the pain and anger because the thought of reliving that night again, of facing up to it—it had been utterly unbearable. But now, after everything that had happened since I'd come back to Alstone, I was starting to realise that it had been an accident. A horrible, horrible accident, and although thinking about the night I'd lost my brother was almost too much to bear, I thought that maybe I might be beginning to come to terms with that.

And I knew Zayde's coping mechanisms. I could *never* ask him to punish me for being with him.

"I didn't mean that," I breathed. "I'm sorry. I'm so sorry. Please forget I said anything. We don't have to make it hurt.

I don't want you to make it hurt, ever. I just...I want you." My eyes met his, and I let him see everything that I was feeling. "Zayde. I want you. However I can have you."

After studying me for a long, long time, he dipped his head. His lips trailed a line of fire up the side of my throat, soft kisses that burned my skin all the way to my ear. I could feel his mouth searing the words into my flesh as he spoke, so low and resolute. "This isn't a good idea. We have so much between us to deal with. But fuck, I want you, too. I've wanted you for so fucking long." Skimming his lips over mine, he whispered hoarsely, "If you're sure you want this, I can hurt enough for the both of us."

A tear slipped down my cheek. "Okay."

I moved back on the bed, my head cradled by his soft pillows. Straightening back up, he stared down at me, his gaze drinking me in for the longest time. "Fuck." His hand came up to scrub over his face, and he turned away from me, speaking in a low voice. "Fuck. I never thought I'd get to see you in my bed."

"Did anyone else—"

He spun back around, yanking off his black hoodie, leaving him in a deep grey T-shirt that stretched across his torso. His eyes were blazing. "No one else has ever slept in here. No one else has ever been in my bed. No other girl has *ever* been in here at my invitation. I keep my room locked when we have parties."

"*Oh*," I breathed, arching my back up off the bed as I pulled my cornflower-blue cashmere jumper over my head. Zayde's eyes darkened as he took in the tiny, lacy top I had on underneath, a pale cream silk that matched my underwear. His tongue came out to slide across his lips, and I pressed my thighs together, aching.

Some masochistic part of me made me ask another question. "Other girls...after—"

"They meant fucking nothing." He ripped off his T-shirt, his gorgeous, inked body bared to me. There was a metal barbell in one of his nipples, and I needed my mouth on it so badly. I whimpered, reaching for the hem of my top, but he stopped me with a shake of his head. "No. Wait. I need you to know that when you left, I was in a really fucking dark place. I lost myself for a while. There were some girls. But none of them got to have *me*." His words were raw and honest, scraped from the depths of his soul.

When his hands went to the button of his jeans, I forgot about my arousal because I knew what he was trying to tell me. As he unbuttoned them and let them fall to the floor, leaving him in tight black boxer briefs, the outline of his large erection tenting the fabric, he pointed to the top of his right inner thigh, his skin hidden beneath the fabric. "They never got to see this. Those girls—they were one-offs, meaningless, never face to face. It was a phase of my life that was over so fucking quickly it barely even began. Because none of them were *you*."

This man. I didn't care about the reasons why we shouldn't be together. That could come later. The only thing I cared about right now was him. Kicking off my leggings and socks, I held out my hand. "Zayde. Oh, *Zayde*. Come here. Please."

He climbed onto the bed, bracketing me with his body, his gaze open and imploring me to understand, and how could I have ever thought I could get over this incredible man? Lowering his head, he brushed his nose against mine. "You're the only person who's ever seen all my scars. You're the only person I've ever let in."

"There's never been anyone but you," I whispered, the

truth spilling from my lips. I needed him to know just what he meant to me, how I couldn't even stomach the thought of being with anyone else if it wasn't him. But as much as it hurt, I didn't blame him for sleeping with anyone else. How could I, when I'd left him, and neither of us had known whether I'd come back?

"Fuck," he muttered against my lips. "Come here, baby. I need to make you mine."

I wound my arms around him, losing myself in the slide of his mouth against mine and the hot, heavy grind of his body as we moved against one another. His cock was so hard, rubbing against my aching core in a delicious, frustrating tease, and I needed more.

"Zayde. *Please.*"

"You want more, baby?"

"Yes. I need you."

He dropped his head down to softly bite at my throat, grinding his hard length against my pussy. "I'm going to take you apart. Do you think you can stay still for me?"

I arched up, and he growled into my neck. "No, angel. Stay still." His hand encircled my wrists, pulling them up above my head so they were resting against the black iron bars of his headboard. "Hold," he instructed, and I curled my fingers around the smooth metal cylinders.

Pushing himself up, he slid his gaze over my body, so hot and hungry. "Good girl," he murmured, and *fuck*. I shamelessly widened my legs, thrusting my breasts up, suddenly desperate to feel his hands on me. But he didn't take the hint. Instead, he planted his hands on either side of my body, kissing across my collarbone. "You're so fucking beautiful. My angel."

I moaned, raking my nails down his back. The words falling from his mouth had me so wet and ready for him.

He'd never been vocal before, inside or outside of the bedroom. But tonight, it felt like all of the pent-up feelings between us were being released, and neither of us could stay quiet. "Zayde. This is...you feel so good."

He hummed against my skin, kissing lower until his head was poised over my breasts. My nipples were so hard, obvious through the thin silk of my top, and I arched up again, needing his mouth on them.

"What do you want?" His eyes met mine, and he slowly, deliberately ran his tongue across his teeth and lips, playing with the gleaming barbell that I needed to feel against my bare skin. I hooked my ankles around him, trying to drive his erection down onto my aching pussy, but he smirked down at me, all fucking sexy and sinful. "Use your words, baby."

"I want you," I moaned. "Please."

Lowering his head, he closed his mouth around one of my nipples through the fabric, and I cried out at the sensation. His hand came up to cup my breast, and he kissed, licked, and sucked the silk covering me until it was translucent and I was bucking up against him. The slide of the soaked material against my sensitive breast was like nothing I'd experienced before. When he moved his attention to my other breast, my hands came down to the muscles of his ass, tugging him into me, my fingers digging into his skin.

"I can't fucking get enough of you," he rasped, finally, finally, pulling up my top. When it was gone and all that was left between us was a drenched triangle of silk and his boxer briefs, wet from my arousal and his precum, we fell together, kissing and kissing and kissing, until I was shaking against him, right on the precipice.

"Zayde, I, I—" I gasped into his mouth, rolling my hips up.

He wrenched his head away from mine, dragging his face down my throat, his teeth and stubble scratching at my skin. "Don't you dare fucking come until I've put my mouth on you." Biting kisses trailed down my body, over my breasts, and lower still, until he stopped right above my most sensitive area. He pushed my thighs apart, holding me open for his gaze, his eyes so dark. His thumb came down, rubbing across the soaked material. "You're so ready for me, aren't you?"

"*Please*."

That sinful smirk curved over his full lips again as he peeled my underwear from my body, and I shuddered against him. At the first flick of his tongue across my clit, the barbell sliding over my exposed skin, I cried out, my hands finding his head and gripping handfuls of his hair. He actually laughed against me, a low rumble that sparked sensations through my nerve endings. Then he moved his head lower, his pierced tongue working magic, stripping all coherent thought from my brain, leaving only spiralling pleasure behind.

My entire body arched up, and then I let go, stars bursting across my vision as my orgasm blew me away.

I eventually became aware again. I was cradling Zayde's head on my stomach, my fingers still threaded through his hair, and he was stroking lazy patterns over my leg. A small tug of his hair was enough for his gaze to turn to mine, his expression satisfied, but lust still burned underneath.

"Can I?" I whispered. Instead of replying, he moved up the bed, falling onto the pillow next to mine, shifting his body onto his side.

"I still can't believe you're here."

I smiled. I couldn't, either, but right now, there was nowhere else I'd rather be. As I pressed my hand to his chest so that he took the hint and moved onto his back, I savoured the feel of his warm skin underneath my palm, the shift of his powerful muscles, the black ink that decorated his skin. Nothing else mattered right now. It was just me and him.

Giving in to what I'd wanted to do ever since he'd taken his T-shirt off, I leaned down to close my mouth around his nipple piercing.

A low groan fell from his throat, and I felt his cock jerk against my thigh. Experimentally, I lightly tugged the piercing between my teeth. "Do you like that?"

"Fuck, yeah," he growled.

Releasing his nipple, I ran my hand down his body, over the bumps and ridges of his abs flexing beneath my touch. My fingers closed around the band of his underwear, and his groan vibrated through me as I removed it, allowing me the first look at his dick.

Oh. My. Fucking. Days. *He was pierced there, too,* on the head of his cock, a shiny, smooth, curved barbell glistening with his precum.

My throat went dry.

I lifted a finger, tracing it across the barbell and over his exposed shaft, smearing his precum across the metal. This was the sexiest thing I'd ever seen.

"When did you get this?" I asked, although I didn't really need to know the answer. It had been while I was gone. He didn't get a chance to reply, anyway, because I closed my mouth over his dick, swirling my tongue around his thick length, taking care with his piercing because I wasn't sure how sensitive it would be. His body jerked, his hips thrusting up, and I fought back the sudden tears that came to my eyes when he filled my throat. I pulled off to catch my breath, rolling his balls in my hand, the noises falling from his mouth spurring me on.

It was then that I noticed what he'd been referring to earlier. At the top of his inner thigh, there was a jagged cut, a darker slash bisecting the small, silvery scars that were normally hidden by his underwear. Without missing a beat, I closed my hand around his erection and bent down to kiss the scar. His body tensed beneath me, but I didn't make a big deal of it, returning my attention to his dick and taking him as far down my throat as I could.

His hot, hard length throbbed on my tongue, filling my mouth. I'd missed this...making him feel good, the way he'd always made me feel. He cradled my head, his fingers flexing in my hair, and I knew he was holding himself back. We'd been each other's firsts, and he'd always taken care of me, but there was a hesitance in his movements that I knew stemmed from the delicate balance of our relationship. But I didn't want him to hold back. I wanted him to be free, to let his darkness out to play, to use me because I trusted him to never take it too far, to never give me more than I could handle.

Pulling back, I released his cock from my mouth, replacing it with my hand. I stared up at him, licking my lips, and his eyes flashed with fire as he stared right back at me.

"Don't hold back. I want all of you."

His fingers twisted in the strands of my hair. "Fuck. Are you sure that's what you want?"

"*Yes.*" I dipped down, swirling my tongue around the head of his cock, running it over his piercing, and a low, warning rumble fell from his throat.

"You'd better be completely fucking sure."

I hummed in reply, and he growled, thrusting his hips up, his dick filling my throat in a matter of seconds. Tears came to my eyes as he held my head exactly where he wanted it, choking me on his thick length. I managed to get one of my hands on his balls, tugging lightly as he fucked my mouth, and as I moaned around his dick, he pushed my head down, holding me in place while he came down my throat.

His hands released their grip on me, and he threw his head back with a groan, his eyes falling shut as I swallowed around him. When I lifted my head, slowly drawing my mouth from him, he opened his eyes, watching me with a glassy, heavy-lidded gaze, sated and spent.

I did that.

"Come here," he murmured, low, and I crawled up the bed, collapsing down next to him. His arms wrapped around me, and I laid my head on his chest, his heartbeat steady beneath my ear. He ran his hand up and down my bare back, and then his fingers began to stroke through my hair.

I wished we could stay like this forever.

21

zayde

"Zayde?" Fallon's voice was hushed, like she didn't want to disturb the peaceful silence between us.

"Yeah?"

Her hand slid down my torso, and *fuck*, I'd missed this. She was the only person to ever touch me this way. I hadn't been lying when I'd told her that the only other girls I'd been with had been meaningless quick fucks. There was no one I trusted with my body. Only her. There was no one else I'd ever been able to properly open up to.

There had always been something different about her, and I'd known it from the moment we'd met. Something that called to the deepest parts of me, bringing light to the darkest corners of my soul.

She stopped at the top of my thigh. Her words were hesitant, her lashes lowering as she moved her index finger in small circles on my skin. "Um. Would you tell me? You don't have to—"

"I'll tell you." Burying my face in her silky blonde hair and tightening my arms around her, I forced the next words out. "You might not want to hear it because it happened that night."

She trembled against me but pressed a kiss to my chest. "I want to hear it. Please, Zayde." Her hand dipped lower until her finger was tracing across my scar, so fucking carefully.

"The night it happened...fuck...this is—" I had to pause, squeezing my eyes shut. Talking about anything deep went against my nature, but she was the one person that I'd do this for. And fuck it, she deserved to know. "You need to know that I'm not blaming you for any of this, baby. My actions were my responsibility, okay? No one else. Just me."

When she nodded, I resumed stroking her hair, my fingers sifting through the long, silky strands. The action calmed me enough that I could tell her the rest. "After everything, and when I was confronted with what I'd done to you and how much you hated me—with good reason—I was in so much fucking pain. I'm not comparing it to yours, but I'm...*fuck*." Why was it so fucking difficult to get the words out? Saying how I was feeling out loud went against every single one of my instincts. "I'm telling you how I felt. I...I fucking broke that night."

"Oh, Zayde." She exhaled against my chest. "I want you to tell me, and I know you're not comparing. Just tell me."

"Cade took me home after everything had happened. He didn't know about you and me, obviously, but we were all shaken up and left fucking reeling by what had happened, and he thought I was falling apart for the same reason he was. It was true, but I knew I'd lost you that night, too. He kept telling me over and over that it was an accident, but I blamed myself, and...fuck, I was in a really bad place."

Fallon's fingers continued tracing across the jagged scar, a physical reminder of what I'd done to myself.

"When everyone had fallen asleep, I went back there. Everything was covered in tape, and the house was a charred, wrecked ruin. I couldn't get anywhere near it because they had police everywhere. But even seeing it from a distance...it really hit home. I'd have done anything to turn back time, but I couldn't, and it was too fucking late.

"I rode my bike for a while, and I ended up back at the waste ground behind the block of flats I used to live in. I sat there until the sun came up, thinking of how everything had gone to shit because of me. I should never have been born. Then maybe my mum wouldn't have died so young, maybe Tim would still be alive, and maybe you would've found someone good to be with, someone that was the complete fucking opposite of me. Someone who was nice, and kind, and fucking treated you like the queen you are."

Her fingers stilled, and her gaze flew to mine, wide and horrified. "*No*. No. No. No. How can you say that? You're... please tell me you don't still feel that way."

Telling her all of this was so fucking hard, but she needed to know every single ugly, twisted part of me. "I don't...most of the time. I wish I could go back and change things, and I wish you were happy. The selfish part of me always wished it could be with me, but I know that you deserve so much better than a man as fucked up as I am inside."

Fallon shook her head, her eyes filling with tears. "Zayde. I've *never* wanted anyone else. I know that our situation is all messed up right now, but I need you to know that you...you're amazing. You're loyal, and you'd do anything for the people you care about. Your experiences have made you who you are—made you into the man lying here with me right now, and there's nothing I would change about you." She paused, her hand coming up to stroke through my hair. "Nina, my therapist, always tells me that we can't change the past, and we're not responsible for how other people perceive us. What we need to do is to learn to accept ourselves and the things we can't change and to learn to love ourselves."

I was silent for a long time before I managed to reply. "I don't hate myself...but I'm not sure I can ever love myself." Taking her hand, I placed it back on the scar. "By the time I got back to the house, I was so fucking overwhelmed by everything that had happened and what my fucking brain was telling me. All my usual coping mechanisms had turned to ash. The only thing I could think was that I needed to hurt, and it had to be somewhere no one would see. The others would've noticed if I started covering up all the time inside the house. I took one of my knives into my bathroom—one with a serrated blade—stripped down, sat on the floor, and sliced."

Fallon's lip trembled, and a tear tracked its way down her cheek. "You don't have to deal with feeling this way alone. Ever." Her voice was so fucking quiet and shaky. "Can I give you Nina's details, or will you at least think about it? Please? She'll see you, Zayde."

Catching her tear with my thumb, I cupped her chin. "Yeah, baby, I'll think about it."

"Thank you." She leaned forwards to press her lips against mine. Then she shifted down the bed until her mouth was hovering right above my scar. "I know kissing it better doesn't really work, but I'm going to do it anyway. I-if that's okay."

"It's okay."

Softly, carefully, she kissed across my scar, from one end

to the other, and then up onto my IV tattoo, which was just above it. When she raised her head, she was smiling through her tears. "This feels right. You and me, taking care of each other. I know we have a lot of things to get through, but I feel like I might finally be ready to face it. Ready to let go of the things I've been holding on to for so long."

"Come here," I said gruffly. This was so fucking monumental. I'd opened up to her, and she had accepted everything, and she was giving us a chance. I couldn't get my head around it. What had I done to deserve a second chance with this incredible girl?

She curled into my arms, resting her head back on my chest. "Z? I want to tell you something. In case you still had any doubts about my loyalty—"

"I don't." There wasn't one single doubt in my mind.

"That's good, but I still want to tell you. Do you know why I was at the abandoned house that night? I wanted to get out of my house before my parents got home, but I was too late. I ran into them in the kitchen, and they weren't happy with me. I guess I'd ruined their plans for the evening, and my dad said something about me ducking out of school on a whim. He said that my brothers were of age, and he couldn't punish them for my actions, so he—he hit me with the buckle of his belt." Her voice cracked, and I wanted to kill that bastard for daring to lay his hands on my angel. "He hit me quite a few times, and I was b-bleeding, and I had to get out, to come and find you and T-Tim."

"I. Am. Going. To. Kill. Him."

Inhaling a deep, shuddering breath, she pressed her body into mine. "The medical staff...they said I was lucky that it only left a few little scars."

"Scars?" I spoke through gritted teeth.

"Yes." Sitting up, she turned around so her back was to me. "See them? At the bottom of my back."

Leaning forwards, I traced a finger across the small, silvery lines. My fingers were fucking shaking with rage. How *dare* he mark her?

I moved to kiss the scars, like she'd done for me. When I lifted my head, she turned back around, and I tugged her back into my arms, holding her tight while I attempted to calm myself enough to speak. "You're beautiful, every bit of you. And he will pay for what he did."

"He's in prison now. The next part...after the, um, the accident. I don't remember much. Just flashes. Um. I'd never seen him so angry before. I suppose I couldn't blame him after what happened to-to Tim, but do you know what? He blamed *me*. Said if I hadn't been there that night, if I'd just stayed at school like I was supposed to, Tim would be alive."

That fucking piece of scum. How fucking dare he? "It wasn't your fault. Not *any* of it."

"I know. Well, there's still a tiny part of me that blames myself. But Nina helped me to see that I wasn't at fault for it or for what he did before and after."

My jaw was clenched so hard that my head was pounding. "After?" I ground out through gritted teeth.

Her voice dropped to a whisper. "He beat me. With his bare hands. I...um, like I said, I don't remember much. I blacked out after a while. They, um, they said I broke three ribs. I think he might have used his feet, too."

Fucking *fuck*. He was going to die for what he'd done to my girl. "That motherfucking sick fucking *bastard*. I'm going to fucking kill him and take my time doing it."

"He can't touch me now, Zayde. It's okay. I'm safe. I'm

here with you." Her hand stroked across my racing heart. "After that, he had me shipped off to Switzerland because he couldn't stand to look at me anymore. And I, well, I wasn't in the best mental state at the time, either. It was thanks to Joe that they even paid for my treatment. He fed them some lines about it reflecting badly on them if it ever got out."

"He needs to pay. He needs to pay so fucking badly for hurting my girl. Death isn't good enough for him."

"Your girl?" There was a hint of a smile in her voice, and it calmed the rage burning inside me, just a bit. Enough that I could take a breath. She pressed a kiss to my jaw. "I know this is a lot for you to hear. I've had almost two years to come to terms with it, and you're only just hearing about it now. But he's behind bars, where he belongs, and I finally felt safe enough to come back because he's gone. I'm here. I'm okay. I'm with you."

"Yes, you're my fucking girl. But he needs to pay. I need to have a word with Creed. Accidents happen in prison—" I cut myself off. What if she wanted him to live, despite everything he'd done? I couldn't be responsible for another death of someone in her family.

It seemed like she could read my mind because she moved to lie on top of me, looking down into my eyes. "I know you want to kill him. But he's locked away, and just knowing that he's paying for his crimes...it makes me feel that I can move on. I got the courage to face my past because I know he can't hurt me anymore. It's...it's enough. I don't want anyone else to die."

Fuck. It would have to be enough. If that was what she wanted.

She lifted my wrist, kissing the underside, her lips tracing across the faded scar that ran part way up the inside of my arm, hidden by my tattoos. "Will you tell me? Only if you want to."

"I'll tell you whatever you want. I don't want to hide anything from you." I'd lay myself bare for her, give her all my secrets, so she knew just how important she was to me.

We'd discussed my scars in the past, but I hadn't told her the story of this one yet. I forced myself to remain detached as I shared the story.

"It was my ninth birthday. Birthdays didn't mean much to me, as you know. You were the only one that ever gave me anything that meant something." Her parents held her on a tight leash when it came to money, but material goods weren't important to me, and every year, she'd given me another part of herself. Another secret. A small token of her love, like an interestingly shaped pebble or a poem she'd read at school that reminded her of me, and she'd copied it out on notepaper. When we were older, she'd given me her body, as well as her heart, and I cherished it.

"You deserve so much more than that, Z." Lowering my hand, she tilted her head up for another kiss, her lips so fucking soft against mine.

"Yeah." I cleared my throat. "The point was, I wasn't expecting anything, but at the same time, I was hoping that my mum might remember. Stupid, huh?" A soft noise of distress escaped her, and I stroked my fingers through her hair, soothing her. "I walked into the kitchen...it must've been around seven in the morning or something. My mum was in there, bending over the table with this bearded man right behind her. I wasn't really aware of what was happening at the time, but looking back on it, I think they'd probably been on an all-night bender. Both of them were high as fuck, and I can remember my toe catching on the edge of an empty vodka bottle that was lying on the floor.

There were needles in front of the fridge, and the fridge door was wide open. All that was in there was an open carton of orange juice, lying on its side, and the juice was running down the shelves and onto the floor."

I paused. Even staying detached, it was so fucking hard to talk about this. I tightened my arms around Fallon, reminding myself that that part of my life was behind me, and I had my girl back where she belonged.

"My mum just gave me this bleary stare, like she wasn't focused on me. I whispered that it was my birthday, but she didn't say anything, so I said it louder. She said, 'Can't you see I'm busy? Go back to your room.'"

Fallon's breath hitched. "Zayde. How—how could she—"

"I know, baby. Let me get through the rest. For some reason, I kept standing there, staring at her, expecting her to acknowledge my birthday or something. The man she was with straightened up and came over to me. He leaned down to me, right in my face, and his breath smelled like a fucking brewery. His words were so slurred I could barely understand him, but I know he said, 'Get out of here, kid, unless you want to watch me pound your mother into next week.' Then the fucking bastard kicked me in the stomach."

"He *what*?"

"I was so unprepared I went down like a sack of bricks, smacking my head against the door, and they both laughed."

"Fucking hell, Zayde. You were *nine years old*." Fallon's voice was full of horror. She curled into me more tightly, her lips pressing against my skin.

"Yeah. I was...fuck. I shouldn't have even been shocked, but I was. I was winded, and my head was pounding, but I managed to get out of there. I thought I was going to throw up, and I knew if they heard me, I'd be in even more trouble. So I was looking around frantically for something to distract me from the nausea, to keep me quiet and fuck...my head was all over the place. I made it back to my room and curled up into a ball to make myself as small as possible, and I don't know why I did it, but I just put my nail to my arm and dug it in. And then, yeah."

"I don't even know what to say," she whispered shakily.

"You don't have to say anything. It's over now. I'm here. Yeah, I have good and bad periods, but I'm here. I'm here." I was saying the words for myself as well as for her. Reminding myself that I'd made it through.

Fallon lifted her head, and her luminous blue eyes met mine, her gaze so open and so fucking full of emotion it made my breath catch. "I know. I'm here, too. And I'll be with you through the highs *and* the lows."

The way she was looking at me.

Right then, I was one hundred percent certain that no matter what had happened in our past, everything between us was going to work out. We were in this together.

22

zayde

Fallon was still sleeping when there was a loud banging on my door, followed by a shout. Somehow, she slept through it, and after throwing on a pair of boxers, I cracked open the door, taking one last look back at my angel with her blonde hair spread out all over my pillows before I faced whatever shit was going down.

"Reporters are here." Caiden's mouth was set in a flat line. "My dad said they're outside his house, Cass' parents' house, and the offices. But there're more here and outside your dad's."

"For fuck's sake." I rubbed my hand over my face, blinking away the last vestiges of sleep. "Can we do anything?"

"They're beyond our property boundary, so no. But that means they can't do anything, either. We're not going anywhere, so they're not gonna get anything from us. The Alstone Holdings' lawyers have prepared that statement we discussed, too. They can freeze outside, waiting for a scoop that'll never come."

"Fuck. It's too early for this shit. I need coffee."

"Yeah. Does Fallon want one?" He shot me a sly look, and when I narrowed my eyes, he smirked. "That serial killer stare doesn't work on me, mate. Never has."

"Fuck off." I shoved at him as we moved towards the stairs, and he shoved me back, grinning, but then his smile dropped.

"Seriously, though, you know we won't give her shit anymore. After what happened, and the fact that you and the girls all trust her, know the rest of us have her back, too. I'm happy for you, Z. If she's the one or whatever."

"I have to hope she forgives me first," I muttered as we reached the bottom of the stairs.

"The fuck? For what?"

"She...she was there when her brother fell. She saw us together."

"*Fuck*," he breathed. "It was an accident, though, wasn't it."

The way he worded it as a statement, like it was fact, made something go warm inside of me. I gave a short nod. "Yeah. But I didn't get to him in time, and now he's gone, and I can't do anything to get him back, and she thinks that I..." Fuck. I trailed off, unwilling to put it into words. Did she still believe that I'd caused her brother's death? Yeah, I felt guilty as fuck, and I did feel responsible, but... It really had been an accident. A nightmare, but I would never have done anything to purposely hurt Tim. He was her best friend as well as her brother, and so I'd always done my best to be careful with him.

Yet that sick feeling of guilt lay heavy in my stomach.

As we entered the kitchen, Cade shook his head at me, his brows pulling together. "It wasn't your fucking fault. Okay?"

Thank fuck everyone jumping on us saved me from replying because I had no idea what to say.

"Z!" Mack bounded up to me, a grin stretching across his face. "Glad to see you took my advice and included me in this."

What? It was then that I noticed who was crowding into the kitchen. Cass, West, Cade, Winter, Lena, and Jessa were the obvious ones. But as well as them, there was Mack, our friend Obie, and Kinslee. And Granville, of course. He was making himself useful for once, brewing coffees for everyone while Cass and Jessa were cooking. I inhaled the smell of bacon, heading for the cupboards to grab plates. Piling them up next to the oven, I turned to Mack. "Alright, mate?"

"Any ideas for your next tatt? Or do you want a piercing? Cade told me to bring everything. You owe me for making me lug all my shit over here."

I glanced over at Caiden, one arm around Winter's waist, her back to his chest, while he listened to whatever Kinslee was saying to them. He caught my glance and shot me a small smile. Right after that, West slid a coffee under my nose, and Cass began plating up the bacon and eggs, giving me the first dish. I exhaled, reminding myself to breathe. Fuck. These guys were my brothers, and they were showing their support without making a big deal out of it.

It was then that I realised that I didn't need to feel the pain anymore. But I wanted to be inked. I glanced down my body, thinking. "Can you do me a lightning bolt?" Lightning was the closest description I could come to when it came to my scar, and when it eventually faded to the same silvery white as the others, I wanted to remember. How I'd been so fucking low then, and how I'd pushed through, and I was still here.

"Course." Mack smirked at me, following my gaze. "If I'm going into uncharted territory, you'd better make sure you cover your dick."

"You pierced my dick, fucker."

His grin was evil. "As if I could forget that."

"Mack," I growled.

He threw up his hands, his grin still plastered across his face. "Okay, okay. Bloody hell."

I cuffed him around the head, and after he punched me in the arm, we made arrangements to do the ink after we'd eaten. It was a good excuse to get my mind off all the other shit that was happening. With the tattoo's positioning, the top of it would end up being just below my Roman numerals Four tattoo.

Mack was about to say something to me when his gaze shot to something behind my head, and his eyes darkened. "Fucking hell," he mumbled, and I spun around to see Fallon poised in the doorway.

Fuck me. Her platinum hair framed her face, a little messy from being in bed but still dropping down her back in a silky waterfall. She didn't have any makeup on, and she didn't need it because her huge, fucking beautiful eyes, fringed by long lashes, stood out without any help. Her soft lips were a pale pink, and I wanted to fucking bite them, to redden them so everyone would see the evidence that she was mine. But it wasn't even her gorgeous face that captivated me, nor her sexy-as-fuck, perfectly proportioned body. It was what she was wearing.

One of my T-shirts—an Alstone College one in black, which hung off her body, slipping down to expose her collarbones. And just visible below it was a pair of my fucking boxers.

Fuuuuck.

My dick hardened in my underwear as I took her in. I wanted to fuck her so badly. To claim her as mine. I needed to go at her pace, but I wanted her so fucking much.

"Down, boy." Mack gave a low whistle, eyeing my obvious boner with a smirk, and I gave him my middle finger. "Can't blame you," he added in an undertone, and I glared at him. He held up his hands in mock surrender, taking a step back from me. "It's a free country. I can look. But I know she's yours."

Too fucking right. She was mine. Always had been, always would be.

Fallon's wide-eyed gaze bounced around the kitchen, and I moved towards her, needing to reassure her that everything was okay, but Winter got to her first. She whispered something in her ear, and Fallon nodded, and then they disappeared from the kitchen.

When they returned and we were all seated at the table, Fallon was wearing leggings with my T-shirt. Was she still wearing my boxers underneath?

"No boners at the table." Cassius yanked back his chair, widening his eyes dramatically as he stared down at my dick.

First Mack, now him? Was he asking to be stabbed?

It was easy to keep my mask in place, though, and I just raised a brow. "What about last week when Jessa was reading—"

"*Zayde,*" he hissed, and my lips curved upwards. It was fun to fuck with him.

"Was that the fae book?" Kinslee asked from across the table, and after that question, it was a fucking free-for-all, with way too much information about the anatomy of supposedly immortal beings that no one should ever have to hear at the breakfast table.

But no one stopped the discussion because it was our version of normality. We were reminding ourselves that those bloodhounds outside weren't worthy of our attention, and all that mattered was the people inside.

When breakfast was over and everyone had dispersed, I found myself in the garage on a reclining chair next to Mack's portable tattoo setup. Fallon was there with us, running her fingers over the surface of the tools, never quite touching, asking Mack questions about the process and which tool did what. He answered all her questions patiently, and every now and then, when Fallon's attention was diverted, he gave me a pointed look. Once, he even mouthed *go for it,* and I had to hold myself back from saying something I'd regret. It wasn't his fault that he knew fuck all about Fallon's and my situation.

When he'd shaved and prepped the area he was going to ink, I reached out my hand to Fallon. She'd never been here for this process before, but it felt right. The buzz of the needle started up, and her fingers tightened around mine. I watched her focusing on Mack's needle as the black lines appeared on my skin right alongside my scar.

It didn't take him long to finish, and after he'd cleaned me up, he sat back with a grin on his face. "Anything else I can do for you while I'm here? Want me to pierce your balls?"

"Fuck off."

"Can you pierce ears?"

We both turned at the sound of Fallon's voice. She looked between Mack and me with a tiny, hesitant smile. "My dad never let me have them done, and I'd like to."

"I can do that. Sit here." Mack tapped my thigh, and after a second's hesitation, she came and sat on me, taking care to avoid the area that had just been inked. My arms immediately wrapped around her waist, and she leaned back against my chest with a sigh.

As Mack went through the procedure, she melted into me, and it felt so fucking good to hold her in front of someone I knew. Everything between us in the past had been hidden, and to have this with her now...yeah, I could get used to this.

When he prepped her ear and positioned the needle, she curled into me, and I held on to her, savouring the moment. It was over in seconds, but even after her second lobe was pierced and Mack had explained the aftercare, she still held on to me tightly, and there was no way I was letting her go. Still curled into my body, she took the mirror Mack handed to her with a smile on her face, examining the small diamond studs in her earlobes.

"I like them. Thank you," she murmured softly.

"Anytime. I can pierce or tattoo wherever you like." He winked at her, and she huffed out an amused laugh.

"Thanks. I'll keep that in mind." She twisted on my lap, her eyes meeting mine. "Can we talk?"

More talking. This was all so fucking far out of my comfort zone.

But as we'd already established, for her, I'd do anything.

23

fallon

I was ready to face my past.

It was time.

I'd been putting it off for so long, and now it was here. I'd asked Zayde to give me some time on my own to go through everything in my head, and then I wanted to talk to him. This would be the moment when we either moved on together or went our separate ways.

Lying back on Zayde's bed, I closed my eyes and for the first time allowed the memory to play through my mind in full.

It swept over me, a technicolour tsunami, stealing the breath from my lungs.

Riding my bike there...searching for my brother and my boyfriend...finding them arguing close to the window...my presence catching them by surprise...the floorboard breaking...Tim falling and Zayde desperately trying to catch him...

I curled into a ball, sobbing, as I faced the truth. It *had* been an accident. A horrible, horrible accident. And Zayde had tried to save him. Tim was gone, and all of us would have to live with that, *but it was no one's fault*. We'd been blaming ourselves and each other, and yet...

And yet. I'd held on to the blame. Held Zayde responsible because I hadn't been able to face what had really happened. Tim would never have wanted me to hold on to this anger, this grudge, this animosity, this guilt. I was sure of it now. Coming back to Alstone had allowed me to see clearly for the first time since the accident had happened, and I *knew* that all he ever wanted for me was to be happy.

So maybe it was time I took this step and let myself accept that I'd been so, so wrong. And do my best to move on.

Wiping the tears from my eyes, I sat up. With shaking fingers, I dialled Nina's number, hoping she would answer.

She did, and we talked for a long, long time. When it was done, I felt wrung out, collapsing back onto the bed and closing my eyes. I was so drained, and it was all I could do to stay awake.

"Fallon?"

I blinked my eyes open to find Zayde watching me, his brows pulled together. He was seated on the edge of the bed, close enough that if I reached out, I could touch him, but he was keeping a distance from me. My heart jumped in my chest. Even now, he was so careful not to make me uncomfortable.

"Hi." My voice was scratchy, and I cleared my throat. "Zayde?"

"Yeah?"

"Can—can you come here?" I held out my arms.

"Fuck, baby," he breathed, and then he was holding me, and I was crying into his chest.

"I'm sorry. I'm sorry. I'm so, so sorry. You did nothing

wrong," I choked out, and he made a noise I'd never heard before, like a wounded animal.

"You have nothing to apologise for. Fucking *nothing*, okay?"

The lump in my throat was too big for me to speak, so I let him hold me and wipe away my tears until I was cleansed of every single thing that had been poisoning my mind for so long.

"Zayde. I know that there's nothing I can say to make things right. I—"

"Hey. You went through fucking unimaginable trauma, baby. You don't have anything to apologise for, okay?"

I inhaled shakily, tightening my arms around him, and pressing a kiss to his jaw. "You're the best man I know. I know I have so much to make up for, and I'm so thankful that you're here with me now."

"No. There's nothing that you need to make up for. This is our chance for a fresh start, and I'm not gonna leave you. Do you want to get out of here?" he asked softly. "Get away from everything for a while?"

"How can we?"

"You think the paps can catch us on my bike?" A grin spread across his face. "Let them try."

I returned his grin with a smile of my own. Even though it was a little wobbly, it felt so good. "I'm in."

Sneaking out hadn't been Zayde's style, not this time. He'd mounted his bike in front of everyone, and I'd climbed on behind him, wrapping my arms tightly around his waist. Then he'd started the engine with a roar and shot straight down the driveway towards the gathered paparazzi. They'd scattered when they realised that he wasn't going to swerve, and we'd ridden straight through the middle of them and out onto the open road. I laughed against Zayde's back, free and happy, the sun sparkling on the sea next to us, the road empty and stretching before us like a glimmering ribbon.

I felt Zayde's answering laugh, and I savoured it. We'd never been so carefree. Never had a moment that wasn't fraught with the possibility of someone discovering us. But now here we were, finally free to be together. My heart felt like it could burst with the love I felt for the man I was holding on to. I knew that he struggled to process his emotions, and it might be the case that he never said he loved me in words, but that didn't matter to me because I knew he felt so deeply for me. He'd proven it, over and over.

We finally came to a stop at the top of a small cove with a tiny, bumpy lane leading down to it. Zayde lifted his visor, turning to speak to me. "Hold on tight." Flipping down his visor, he turned back to the front of the bike. He carefully bumped us down the track until we were at the bottom, with a pristine, untouched beach stretching before us, hard-packed sand providing a smooth path for the bike's wheels. This time when he stopped, I pulled off my helmet and leaned down to carefully place it on the sand, needing to take in the view without any obstruction.

The setting sun touched the tips of the waves with gold, and everything was bathed in shades of pinks and oranges and reds. It was so beautiful, and it was just the two of us here.

Coming back to Alstone was the best decision I'd ever made.

"This is gorgeous," I whispered.

Zayde removed his own helmet, placing it next to mine. When he straightened up, he swung himself off the bike, coming to stand to the side of me.

"Come here, baby."

His hand landed on my thigh, his fingers flexing beneath the thick leather of his motorbike gloves. A shiver went through my body, and all thoughts of the sunset flew from my mind as I took in the sight in front of me.

Dark, tousled hair. Thick lashes surrounding those wintery eyes that could be so cold but were now full of heat. Those full lips, his tongue sliding along them sinfully, giving me a peek at his barbell as he dragged it against his teeth. That sexy, powerful body, pressing closer, rendering me helpless as he manoeuvred me around to face him.

The way he was looking at me. Like I was something he wanted to devour.

Heat pooled between my thighs, and my nipples hardened beneath my layers of clothes. "Zayde."

"Do you like your piercings?" He dipped his head, skimming his tongue across the shell of my ear, careful to avoid my newly pierced lobes. It felt so good.

"Mmmm. More."

"More?" There was a dark promise in his tone. "I'll give you more."

His mouth moved to my other ear, and at the same time, his gloved hand skimmed up my inner thigh, his touch hot even with the leather and the soft wool of my tights between us. I gasped as his index finger pressed in between my legs.

"These need to come off."

This was really happening. And after the emotions I'd been through earlier, I needed this. Needed him. And he could read me so easily—he'd known exactly what I'd needed before I even thought of it.

Bracing one arm on the seat, with his hand curved around my waist to hold me steady, I tugged down my tights and underwear, kicking them off along with my boots. The leather of the seat was warm beneath my bare skin, and I didn't even notice the chill of the autumn air because I was burning at Zayde's touch.

He let go of my waist to slide both hands up my thighs, the gloves a contrast of buttery-soft leather and the ridges of stitching on the seams. Goosebumps erupted across my skin, and I spread my legs wider, arching forwards.

"I've dreamed about this for so fucking long." His mouth met mine, and I was lost in him. That same finger pressed between my legs again, and I shuddered as the tip of his glove dipped inside my soaked pussy.

"Oh, fuck. Zayde," I moaned against his mouth as he slid his finger in farther, then out, moving slowly upwards until he was circling my clit. "More."

Lowering his head, he ran his teeth down my throat. "What do you want, baby?"

I knew exactly what I wanted.

"Y-your cock. Inside me."

"Fuck." His groan vibrated against my skin as a second finger joined the first, this one slowly running along my slit, teasing me, before dipping inside. "You're so fucking wet for me."

"Please. Please. I need you."

He withdrew his fingers, his gaze fixed on mine as he slowly, deliberately removed his gloves, flexing his hands. "Hold on." Lifting me as if I weighed nothing, he spun me so I was straddling the bike again, except this time, I was facing the back. Then he slung his leg over the seat, sitting while facing me. "Open my jeans."

Him commanding me in that raspy tone did things to me. I shivered, rocking forwards to get some friction on my pussy as I reached for the button of his jeans. His erection strained at his fly, and as I lowered the zip and my fingertips brushed over the head of his cock, over his barbell, he groaned under his breath. When I carefully pulled down his underwear, exposing his thick length, I couldn't control myself anymore. I shifted forwards, straddling his thighs. I needed him inside me.

"Fallon." His hand came up to cup my cheek. "Are you on anything? The pill?"

"Yes. The clinic. I have the implant."

A wicked grin curved across his lips. "I want to fuck you bare."

"Oh, *yes*. I want that."

As he brushed his lips across mine, his voice turned serious. "I've been tested, and there's been no one since. You're the only one I want."

You're the only one I want. Those words.

"Fuck me. Please. Now. I don't want to wait anymore."

He tugged me forwards, our bodies pressing together, his hard dick between my legs, rubbing against my wetness, and I couldn't hold back any longer. My hand slid down between us, and I shifted up, positioning myself over the head of his cock. Then I sank down in a slow, steady slide, the feeling of being completely filled, along with his piercing, sparking sensations inside me that I'd never experienced before. I was conscious of his new tattoo, although it was farther around his thigh, away from where our bodies were touching. Even so, I started up a gentle, rocking pace that he sank into with me. I wound my arms around his neck, kissing and kissing and kissing him, relishing the feel of his strong arms wrapped around me, his hips grinding slowly against mine, his solid thighs holding me up as I moved against him.

His hands lifted my dress, his tongue circling my breasts, the barbell sliding across my nipples. I moved harder against him, needing more friction, the chilly bite of the sea air at my lower back and the shocking heat at my front combining to send nerve endings firing all over my body.

"Zayde. *Zayde.*"

"Are you going to come for me?" He raised his head, kissing me hard, and at the same time, he angled his hips, and I fell over the edge, helpless, lost to the orgasm that swept through my entire body. I unconsciously tensed my legs, tightening my grip on him, and with a long, low groan, he came, pulsing inside me, filling me with his cum.

Collapsing against him, I tried to catch my breath, feeling his heart beating beneath my ear, gradually slowing as he stroked up and down my back, lowering my dress and gently tugging my jacket back into place.

His eyes met mine, so open and unguarded, and my heart skipped a beat.

I wanted him to look at me that way—always.

24

fallon

The paparazzi had backed off, bored when they found nothing to report, and that, combined with the legal threat, had been enough to suppress any further action. Five days after the story had broken, I still hadn't spoken to Joseph, and he'd made no effort to contact me. James wasn't speaking to him, either. As far as James was concerned, he'd cut Joe out of his life. They hadn't been speaking before then anyway, other than to either talk about me or for James to attempt to persuade my brother to do the right thing. It had obviously been a wasted effort.

"Cuppa?" Kinslee flipped on the kettle. I was staying with her for now since she temporarily had a spare bedroom, and it meant that James could have his own bedroom back. Zayde had offered for me to stay with him, but I knew that with our relationship only just beginning to find its footing again, we needed to take things slowly. Letting go of the past wasn't an instant thing—there was a lot that I needed to work through, but what I did know for sure was that I was completely committed to working through it. I wanted to be with Zayde, as his girlfriend and partner, out in the open, loving and supporting him.

"Please." I got up from the kitchen table, crossing to the cupboard and pulling out two mugs. "What time are your lectures today?"

Glancing at her phone, Kinslee swore under her breath. "Too soon. Shit. Where did I leave my notebook?"

"Coffee table. On top of your laptop."

"Right." She smiled, the stress disappearing from her eyes as she placed tea bags in the mugs. "Hey, want to swap? You can sit in my very boring lecture while I binge Netflix all day."

"Tempting, but no." Watching her carefully pour hot water over the tea bags, I sighed. "Actually, I thought I might look at some options for myself. I need to either find a job or possibly look at enrolling in higher education. I'm just not sure because I never really dared to plan for a future before, so I don't know what I want to do. Stupid, isn't it?"

"Not really. Can you pass me the milk?" When I handed the bottle to her, she shook her head. "I'll tell you now that half of the people on my degree course don't have a clue what they want to do afterwards. I don't, either. I'm not one of the elite, which is a good and bad thing. Good, because it means I don't have to be forced into a career I might not want to do or, worse, marry someone with a boring career while I sit at home going out of my mind with boredom. Not that all of the elite are forced into a specific career path. I suppose there's just the expectation there, you know?"

"I know." That had been my life up until recently.

Handing me my tea, she pursed her lips in thought. "And it's bad because I don't have the luxury of living off my family's money while I decide what to do. And I don't have those connections that come with certain family names. Anyway, I'm glad I don't have the pressure, to be honest. But that's enough about me. Why not look at enrolling at Alstone College? It'll give you another few years to decide what you want to do with your life."

"I have thought about it." I could probably catch up with the work I'd missed so far during the first semester, but then it would also require me to live off student loans now that family money wasn't an option. James and even Zayde would probably offer to help me out, but I didn't want to be indebted to them. "I think I'd like to get a job, though. Pay my way."

"You don't have to decide anything right now, and you're welcome to stay here for as long as you want." Her voice lowered. "It's, uh, the anniversary in a few days, isn't it? Maybe you shouldn't worry about anything else until..." Trailing off, she placed a hand on my arm. "Sorry, it's not my place to bring it up."

"No. It's fine. I'm ready to face it this year."

"That's good. I'm glad." She smiled again before sipping from her mug. "We have celebrations to look forward to as well. The Guy Fawkes celebrations at the castle."

"Oh, yes. I've been hearing about that. What happened at the last one?"

"Ask Winter." A smirk curved over her lips. "Just don't do it around Cade. I don't think he likes to be reminded of what an asshole he used to be towards her."

"I'll remember that." My phone chimed loudly from my bedroom, and I startled, making Kinslee laugh.

"I'll take that as my cue to get out of here. I don't want to be late." Gulping down the rest of her tea, she grabbed her laptop and notebook, shoving them inside her bag, and then disappeared with a wave. I headed into my bedroom to check my phone, faltering when I saw the name on the screen.

Joe.

Sinking down onto the bed, I opened the message.

Joe: We need to talk. I have things I need to discuss with you. It's the anniversary of Tim's death too, and I think we should commemorate that

No word about the article.

Me: Why should we talk after what you did? I know it was you behind the article

Joe: That's one of the things I want to discuss. I'm sorry. I had my reasons and I want to speak to you in person. Please can we meet? You're my sister Fal. Please

Me: I don't know if I can forget what you've done. You took private information and hurt someone that's really important to me. You hurt me, Joe

Joe: I'm sorry. Just five minutes of your time. Please can we meet on Halloween? And maybe we can see Tim's grave together?

Should I meet him? There was a big part of me that wanted nothing to do with him, but I was curious about his reasoning for the article. Maybe he'd tell me the truth, maybe he wouldn't, but I guessed I should at least hear what he had to say. It wouldn't make a difference, but I wanted to know how he thought he could justify doing something like that. And then there was Tim. Despite everything, Joe had been his brother, too, and they'd been close.

Me: I'll meet you at Tim's grave and we can talk then
Joe: Thank you. Is 10am ok? I took the day off
Me: Yes. I'll be there

Even though I didn't want to be. I owed it to Tim, and Joseph owed me some answers.

25

zayde

"Fucking love waking up to you in the morning." Kissing down Fallon's shoulder, I let my hard cock grind against the soft curves of her ass.

"Me too. I love that I can wake up with you." She twisted on the bed, winding her arms around me, and I lowered my head to kiss her. We'd spent all weekend together, and although she'd originally planned to leave on the Sunday, she'd asked to stay because it was Halloween. The anniversary of her brother's death.

I had serious misgivings about her meeting up with Hyde, but I understood her reasons. I'd planned to show up, staying out of sight, just in case the fucker tried anything, but she'd made me promise to stay away. It went against every single one of my instincts, and even though I'd agreed to stay away from the graveyard, I planned to be nearby. She was mine to protect, and so I'd do my fucking best to protect her.

"You've got to go to uni soon, haven't you?" She ran her hand down my back. I rolled us, pinning her underneath me.

"Not yet."

When I reached down, pushing apart her legs, she got the hint, her cheeks flushing as her eyes darkened. I slid a finger down between her legs, finding her already wet for me. My girl had been making up for lost time, and we'd fucked so much that Cass had started making comments about not getting any sleep and needing to soundproof his room. Like he wasn't the worst one of us all.

"Zayde," she moaned, and all thoughts of Cass flew out of my head, thank fuck, and then it was only me and my girl and my dick sinking inside her tight, wet heat.

When I'd come inside her, I made her come again with my fingers and mouth. I had a lot of making up to do, and seeing her fall apart for me was so fucking addictive that I never wanted to stop.

After showering together, which took longer than it should have because I couldn't resist bending her over and fucking into her again, we were both running late. Although she thought I was running late because I was late for lectures rather than the fact that I was going to put my stalking skills to good use. "I'm gonna have my phone on me at all times today, baby."

"I know. Just knowing you're at the other end of the phone is enough, Z." Scooping up her small bag, she pressed a quick kiss to my jaw. "I don't want you to worry, okay? I can handle my brother."

Of that, I had no doubt, but I didn't trust the bastard as far as I could throw him.

"I know you can. It's him that's the issue." My jaw clenched. "I don't want him to hurt you."

"He won't. It'll be okay. Please don't worry about me. Promise you'll give me the space to do this." Closing her fingers around the door handle, she shot me an imploring look, all big blue eyes and long lashes, and fuck, I was a red-blooded male who was so fucking weak when it came to her.

"Okay, baby." I pressed her up against the door, taking her mouth in a hard kiss. She gasped, opening up to me, her arms wrapping around my neck. "Fuck. It goes against all my instincts to stay away."

"I know."

My mouth went to her throat, and I bit down, making her moan. "I'm gonna mark you up so everyone knows you're mine. So your brother knows that if he fucks with you, he fucks with me."

"So territorial," she laughed breathlessly, arching her neck to give me more room as I sucked a mark into her soft skin.

"Yeah, I fucking am. I've got you back, I'm not letting you go again."

"I don't want you to let me go. Except, I really do need to leave now, otherwise, I'm going to be seriously late." With a sigh, she released me, and I stepped back to give her space to leave my bedroom.

"I'll see you after," I murmured. "Be careful."

"I will. Promise."

When she was gone, driving off in Winter's car, I closed the front door, running my hand over my face with a groan. "Fuck," I muttered under my breath.

"You're not letting her go," came a voice from behind me, a statement rather than a question.

Turning to face Caiden, I picked up my bike helmet. "I'm giving her a head start, and then I'm going. I'm giving her the space she wants, but I have to be close."

"I get it. Want some company?"

"I—"

"Code blue! We need to get down to the offices right now!" West's shout echoed down the corridor, and Caiden's eyes widened.

"What the fuck is it *now*?" he growled.

"There's some shit going down," West panted as he skidded to a stop in front of us. "Some fucking new leak. They want us to prepare for a big story being broken tomorrow. The lawyers are on it, but Dad wants us there."

"Fuck. This timing is—*fuck*. If it's Hyde again, I'm going to fucking kill him," Cade ground out.

"Get in line." I began tugging on my leather gloves. "I need to get to Fallon."

West shook his head, a grim look on his face. "It's not Hyde. They said it's an inside job. Someone sold us out."

"Z, you'd better come with us in case any shit goes down. Stop at the graveyard on the way, yeah?" Cade gripped my arm. "Tell her what's going on."

"I'm going." I grabbed the second helmet. "Meet you at the offices."

26

fallon

Ten o'clock on a Monday morning, and the cemetery was empty other than a lone figure standing next to Tim's grave. My heart clenched as I took in my brother, a serious figure in a grey wool overcoat. He had his hands in his pockets and his collar turned up to protect him from the autumn chill. A bouquet of flowers in autumnal colours lay at his feet, propped up against the headstone.

"Joe."

He turned around as I approached, giving me a wary glance. "Fallon. Thanks for coming."

I didn't reply to him straight away. Instead, I knelt down in front of the grave, carefully placing my own flowers next to Joseph's. "Hi, Tim," I whispered. "I miss you."

Joseph crouched down next to me, running his gloved finger across the letters of Tim's name. "I miss him, too."

We both stood, and he pointed down the path that wound through the cemetery to a small, circular area with benches and an ornamental pond. "Can we talk?"

I nodded, and he set off down the path. When we reached the benches, he came to a stop but remained standing, turning to face me. "Okay. I need to explain the article. You have to understand that I was so angry when I heard about your relationship with Zayde Lowry. You'd betrayed us all by sneaking around with the very worst person imaginable."

A burning anger filled me. How dare he? "Joseph!"

He held up a hand. "Please, just let me finish, then you can have your say. I called him the worst person imaginable for two reasons. The first reason is obvious. He's one of our rivals. Every single one of us accepted the fact that we can play nice in public while we stab each other in the back, except for you. And him. It's just—" He shook his head in disbelief. "—I couldn't believe what I was hearing, Fallon. Of all the people, of all the fucking options open to you with your status, you had to pick him?" His voice rose, and he clenched and unclenched his fists. Breathing out heavily, he made a visible effort to calm himself before continuing. "The second reason is that even if we didn't have this rivalry, he still wouldn't be a suitable match, and deep down, you know that. He grew up on a housing estate, in a council flat. His mother was a whore and a drug addict. He's not worthy of being with someone like you. He came from nothing, and despite Michael Lowry's status, he'll never be one of the elite, not like us."

My blood was boiling. I couldn't stay silent any longer. "I. Don't. Care. I don't care that he's part of some stupid rivalry, which, by the way, only you and Dad seem to be holding on to, and I don't give a single fuck where he grew up or what his status is or isn't. I feel beyond lucky that he's chosen me. I love him, and that's never going to change. *Never*. Do you hear me?"

He recoiled at the rage in my tone, his jaw dropping. "You...you've changed. I remember a time when you'd actually listen to me, but I don't...you're like a different person. Do you even understand the consequences of your choices? You actually *love* this person?"

"I *have* changed. I'm not a naive child, Joe. I'm capable of making my own decisions, of understanding them, and I will always choose him. Every. Single. Time."

"Fuck." His shoulders slumped. "Please, Fal. Don't do this. Our family's falling apart. We need to pull together. Otherwise, we risk losing everything that the Hydes have worked for, for generations."

"My decision is final." I stepped closer to him, waiting until he met my gaze again. "So that was why you decided to release the article? Because of my relationship with a man that you don't approve of?"

He couldn't hold my gaze, and alarm bells started ringing. Shaking his head, he ground a fallen leaf under the toe of his shoe. "The article wasn't my decision. I was just...I was so angry and betrayed, like I said. I went to visit Dad—remember I told you I was going to see him after I'd been to the grave—and the whole thing came out. He was... incensed was probably the word. He told me about a contact he had at that sleazy tabloid and made me agree to speak to him and get the paper to run the story. The guy owed Dad a favour or something, I guess."

"You didn't *have* to do anything, Joe. He's in prison! What's he going to do from there?"

"No. I spoke to you before him. Remember our phone call? You weren't willing to budge. And Dad...he's not—He's got contacts in a lot of places, Fal. You can't underestimate just how far he'd go to save our family."

"Save his money, more like."

Joseph stared at me in disbelief. "I don't understand why you're being like this. Do you want to be broke? I know he did things wrong. A lot of things. There's no excusing what he's done, and that's why he was sentenced. But—"

"Do you know what happened to me the night Tim died? Did you know that our father, the man who should have been there for us, beat me so badly I ended up unconscious with three broken ribs?" I hissed. "He could have *killed* me. So forgive me if I don't have any sympathy for that monster."

"W-what?" Joseph's face drained of colour, and he swayed on his feet. "*What*?"

"You heard me. Then I was shipped off to Switzerland, and I was out of sight, out of mind. Problem dealt with."

"Oh, fuck. Fuck. What have I done?" Joseph shook his head, his eyes widening in horror. "I'm so sorry. I-I didn't know."

"It's in the past. I've dealt with it. But I hope you can understand why I don't have any sympathy for his situation."

"It's not that. It's—"

Leaves crunched behind us, and we both startled. Joseph's head bowed, and I could hear him mumbling, "Oh, fuck," over and over again.

An icy chill trickled down my spine as I slowly turned around.

I clapped a shaking hand over my mouth, bile rising in my throat.

When my eyes met his harsh gaze, his lips pulled up into a cold smile, devoid of any amusement. "Hello, Fallon."

27

zayde

The car park was empty other than Winter's matte-black Fiat 500, which Fallon had borrowed. Yanking my helmet off, I took off for the graveyard at a run. I'd promised not to interfere, but Fallon needed to know what was happening. Except she wasn't fucking *there*. Where was she? I yanked my phone from my pocket, scrolling to her name as fast as I could. Fuck. Fuck. Fuck. I shouldn't have let her go alone.

My phone started buzzing in my hand, Creed's name appearing on the screen, and I swiped it open. "Now's not a good time," I barked out. "Fallon's missing."

"Roland Hyde's on the loose," he said, and my fucking world fell apart. "According to my intel, he had help, both inside and out. He was being transferred from one minimum-security facility to another in the early hours of this morning, and he somehow managed to give them the slip. Probably bribed whoever was involved. He got picked up by what we think was one of his business associates. Possibly even Joseph Hyde."

"Fuck. I— Fallon was supposed to meet Joseph Hyde

this morning at the graveyard. I'm here now, and her car's here, but there's no fucking sign of either of them."

"Have you tried calling her? Can you track her phone?"

"I'm on it."

"Good. I'm on my way. We think he'll be heading to Alstone. Obie's with me, and he's on the phone to Mack right now. I'm not staying out of it this time, Z. That fucking asshole has burned every fucking bridge going. He's a cockroach that needs to be destroyed."

"I'm gonna find Fallon. Let Cade know what's happening." Ending the call, I ran for my bike, dialling Fallon's number as I did so. It rang and rang until the generic voicemail kicked in, and I swore, hitting Granville's number next.

He answered after two rings, and I didn't give him a chance to speak. "Granville. Hyde Senior's on the loose and heading this way. Do you have Joseph's number? He was supposed to meet Fallon today at Tim's grave, but neither of them are here."

"*Shit.*" His voice shook. "Yeah. I'll call him. Anything I can do?"

"Call Cade. He's on his way to the Alstone Holdings offices. We had a tip-off about a new story that's going to be printed. I can't help feeling like it has to be connected."

"It can't be a coincidence," he agreed. "I'm on it."

Ending the call, I launched the map on my phone. Why the fuck hadn't I got West to add our tracking app to her phone? At least she'd turned on her location sharing on her maps app, so it gave me somewhere to start. I clipped my phone into the holder and started up the engine.

I'm coming for you, baby.

PART THREE

fallon

"How are you out of prison?" I whispered, staring at the stranger who had once been my father. *Roland.*

"Money can achieve many things. Why do you think I've been working so hard? I'm trying to better our lives, Fallon. I'm trying to get back everything that was lost." He took three quick steps towards me, and then he lunged.

He was strong, and despite my struggles, I couldn't get free. "Joe! Please," I begged, desperately trying to free myself. "Don't let him do this."

Roland began dragging me down the path as I kicked out, thrashing in his iron grip. Joseph stepped forwards.

"Don't even think about it, Joseph. I'm doing this for the family. For our legacy."

My brother's eyes filled with tears, and he shook his head. *I'm sorry,* he mouthed, his lips trembling.

"Sorry means nothing," I spat. "How can you stand by and watch this happen? You *know* what he did to me."

"He knows what's best for the family." Roland yanked me back harder as he increased his pace. "Stop struggling. You're only going to hurt yourself."

As much as I wanted to lash out, to thrash and kick and get free, he had a point. I shouldn't waste my energy struggling. I needed to be smart about this.

I allowed myself to go lax, although it went against all my survival instincts. We reached Joseph's car, and Roland shoved me inside, keeping my hands behind my back and binding them with a strip of duct tape. "I'm sorry to do this to you, Princess, but I can't risk you trying to contact anyone or, worse, getting ideas about leaving. We need to complete the second part of the plan, and I want you to see the consequences with your own eyes. Once it's over, I'll be on a private plane to a place the law will never be able to touch me, and the two of you will be able to continue my legacy."

Okay. He had an actual plan. This was worse than I thought. I needed to find out exactly what was happening here. "Why should I be interested in continuing your legacy?"

Glancing at me in the rear-view mirror while he started up the engine, Joseph in the passenger seat, his eyes narrowed. "Because it's your heritage. Because your mother deserves to return to the life that she's accustomed to. And because Alstone Holdings needs to pay. After I'm finished with them, we'll be back on a much more even footing. They won't know what hit them." That same cold smile from earlier appeared on his face, sending a chill down my spine.

"What's the plan?" I asked, keeping my voice flat like I didn't care one way or another.

He chuckled. "You'll soon see. But once it's done, I've lined up a meeting with Peter Parkinson-Jones. He's very interested in a match with you if we can bring him some of Alstone Holdings' assets, particularly the town centre land that they own."

Joseph's head shot around, his eyes widening. "Peter Parkinson-Jones? Isn't he forty-something?"

Roland spun the wheel, sending me sliding across the back seat. "He's prepared to overlook her indiscretions, and he has a peerage. She should be grateful that anyone's interested after she'd been sullied by the Lowry boy." He pointed at his neck. "Even with the mark of a whore on your skin."

A whore? Then I realised he was referring to the love bite on my neck. Too bad for him I liked being marked by the man I loved. And as for his idea, that was never, ever happening. It was laughable that he even thought it might. There was nothing that could persuade me to marry a man I didn't love, not anymore. He held nothing over me.

I bit down on my tongue in an effort to remain silent, tasting blood. The car swerved, and my head knocked against the window.

"Is that—" Joseph turned right around in his seat, staring out of the back window.

Roland slammed his foot down on the accelerator. "Pathetic. He'll never catch us. And if he does, well..." His laugh was almost maniacal. "Part of my plan will happen sooner rather than later."

Twisting as best as I could with my hands bound behind my back, I stared out of the rear windscreen.

There, visible in the distance, was a matte-black motorbike, the rider wearing dark jeans, boots, and a leather jacket, topped with a matte-black helmet. The helmet's visor was also black, hiding his face, but I'd know him anywhere.

And he was headed straight for us.

My knight didn't come for me on a stallion, wearing shining armour and waving a sword. No, he came on a metal beast with the power of two hundred horses, wrapped in leather and carrying a wickedly sharp knife.

28

michael lowry

"What is it now?" I barked at my assistant, Rachel, when she entered my office without knocking.

She flinched back, and I gave her what I hoped passed for an apologetic look. Clearing her throat, she straightened her shoulders. "Sorry, sir. Mr. Cavendish has requested everyone's presence in the conference room."

"Right." Shrugging my suit jacket back on, I stalked through the building to the conference room, pausing in the doorway when I took in the scene in front of me. Arlo Cavendish, Paul and Stella Drummond, our team of lawyers, several assistants and junior managers, and our children and their assorted collection of hangers-on. I scanned the faces...Caiden, Winter, Weston, Lena, Cassius, Jessa...even Lloyd Mackenzie was there, sitting next to Winter's friend Kinslee. I pursed my lips. Lloyd Mackenzie, or Mack, as my son referred to him, had been a bit of a thorn in my side over the years. Zayde had been friends with him when they lived on the housing estate, and I'd had my concerns that he would lead my son into trouble, so

I'd discouraged their friendship. In fact, I'd encouraged Zayde to cut all ties with his old life, something that I regretted in hindsight, especially after reflecting on the recent tabloid article. It must have been jarring for Zayde to be plucked from his old life and thrust into mine, and yet I'd never taken the time to think about how it had affected him.

I'd been young, foolish, and reckless when I'd had the one-night stand with Zayde's mother, and yet I couldn't even begin to regret it because it had brought him to me. I was proud of my son. He'd been through a lot in his life, experienced things that no one should have to face, and here he was—

Hold on a moment. Where was he?

"Where's Zayde?" I growled, cutting through the noise.

Caiden's gaze flew to mine, and he held up his phone. "I'm tracking him right now. He was going after Fallon. She was supposed to meet Hyde—uh, Joseph Hyde at their brother's grave. It's the anniversary of his death."

The mood in the room dropped even lower, if that was possible. None of us wanted a reminder of that night. Arlo, Paul, and I had privately agreed that we felt somewhat responsible for encouraging the feud between the boys. None of us had ever dreamed it would end in such tragedy.

"Get the tracker up on the screen," I instructed, and Caiden nodded at me.

"Hang—" His phone began ringing, and he swiped to answer, hitting the speaker button.

"Caiden. Roland Hyde escaped from prison in the early hours of this morning. We believe he's heading for Alstone. Stay alert. I'm on my way, bringing Obie and the van. Hyde may be desperate, so be prepared."

The call cut off, and Caiden's phone immediately began

ringing again. He swiped the screen without looking at it, too busy exchanging worried glances with his friends. "Hello?"

"Cavendish."

"What the fuck do *you* want, Granville?"

"Zayde asked me to call you. He thinks there's a link between Roland Hyde and the story—wait, did you hear he escaped?"

"Yes. Anything else?"

"He wanted me to get hold of Joseph, but I can't. I think his phone's switched off. Is there anything else I can do?"

Caiden sighed, rubbing his brow. "Fuck it. You might as well come and join us here in the offices. Everyone else has, so why not add my third least-favourite person to the mix."

"I knew you were starting to warm up to me."

"Fuck off." He ended the call, launching his phone across the table, and then groaned. "Fuck. Sorry. Uh, Dad, can you chuck my phone back? I need to get Z's tracker up on the screen."

Arlo smirked at him, sending the phone skittering back across the table. "It's so nice to see my son burying old grudges and taking steps towards friendship."

"Not another word about Granville," Caiden gritted out, but I could see the corners of his mouth turning up. Not that any of it concerned me, the only two things I was concerned about right now were where my son was and what Roland Hyde was planning.

"It's a fake." Paul lifted his head from his laptop.

"The upcoming newspaper story is a plant," Stella elaborated, peering at the screen from behind her reading glasses. "According to this email from..." She trailed off, her gaze bouncing all over the conference room until it settled on Taylor, Paul's assistant. "Taylor?"

Taylor stepped forwards, visibly shaking from head to toe. "Y-yes. I'm so, so sorry. He—he sent someone to me in the middle of the night. He said that if I didn't co-operate, Edward would die."

Stella's hand flew to her mouth, her eyes wide with shock, but I had no fucking time for dramatics. "Explain," I demanded, slamming my hands down on the table as I stared Taylor down.

"I'm sorry." She was openly crying now, but it didn't move me. The only thing I was interested in was getting answers. "I had an anonymous message to say that if I didn't get hold of some of the files containing sensitive information, I could expect to say goodbye to my son. He's my only child. My reason for living." Her sobs grew louder, and I fought back the desire to shout at her to get to the fucking point. "I-I copied some files. I felt so sick doing it. I...I couldn't...after I'd given the information to the anonymous person, I sent you an email because I felt so guilty." That comment was directed at Paul.

"My source at the paper, who, by the way, I never wished to utilise—" Paul's mouth curled down in distaste. "—said they haven't heard anything about a story."

"It's blackmail. They want to have something in case —" Arlo's brilliant mind was working faster than the rest of us could think. "In case their plan doesn't work. Fuck. They knew that the news of a breaking story would get us all here today. We need to get out. *Now*. Hit the fire alarm."

There was a scramble for the doors when everyone came to the realisation at the same time. We were sitting ducks. All gathered together in one room. And in the meantime, my son was out there, most likely being lured into danger.

I wasn't a religious man, but right then, I prayed.

29

fallon

The car was speeding so fast the scenery outside was a blur. But still, Zayde came. Little by little, he drew closer, his bike skirting around the traffic in an easy, graceful dance.

Was it wrong to be completely petrified by the situation yet so completely turned on by my man's lethal grace and skill?

"Alstone?" Joseph questioned, and it broke my concentration. Flicking my gaze to the side windows, I realised that we'd entered the outskirts of Alstone town. The roar of Zayde's bike was audible now as he gained on us, despite Roland accelerating as hard as he dared.

"I set up everything at the offices. It's ready. They should all be there." Roland spoke in gasps in between manoeuvring the car with a death grip on the steering wheel, sweat beading on his brow.

"Who should be? What's happening?" Joe's voice shook. "I never signed up to be involved in anything like this."

"It's too late for second thoughts." Roland smiled grimly as we skidded into a turn, and I recognised the road as the one that led to the Alstone Holdings offices. Zayde was so close now that I could feel the vibrations of his bike, the rear of Joseph's car reflecting in his visor.

The Alstone Holdings offices were right up ahead of us when it happened.

There was a huge boom, and what looked like a fireball shot into the air. Then, as Roland slammed on the brakes, there was a loud cracking sound, and right in front of my eyes, part of the building collapsed in on itself.

A sound tore from my throat, raw and animalistic. There was no way anyone could survive that.

"Even better than I'd imagined," Roland said, his words muffled by the ringing in my ears, and then someone yanked my door open.

I blinked again and again, the cloud of dust from the collapsed building obscuring my vision.

"Here."

Joe? When did he get here? What was he doing in the back seat with me?

He slipped something between my wrists, allowing them to separate, and I wasted no time in peeling off the duct tape. When I was free, I slid across the seats to the open door. I staggered outside, dust drifting through the air and settling on me, getting caught in my hair, my brows, my eyelashes. Frantically wiping it away from my face, I straightened up, ready to make an attempt at running towards the remains of the Alstone Holdings offices. Sirens cut through the ringing in my ears, louder and louder as they drew closer.

I couldn't breathe.

"This is even better than I'd planned."

Spinning around, my plan to run abandoned, I saw Roland slumped against Joseph's car. He was sucking in deep, gasping breaths, but there was a huge, deranged smile on his face that was at odds with his actions.

"What did you do?" Before I knew it, I was right in front of him, squaring up to the man who had once been my parent, the man that had tried to control me for so long. The man that had beaten me so badly and, even now, was still trying to roll the dice in his favour.

"I used what was left of our money to pay someone to plant a story and for someone else to rig the building with enough explosives to cause a collapse. It was laughably easy. Our finances may have taken a hit after what I've done, but there's no doubt in my mind that once people see that the mighty Alstone Holdings has fallen, they'll come crawling back to Hyde Consultings. It was a gamble that I was willing to take because I knew it would pay off."

The motorbike roared behind us, and there he was. My avenging angel, a black streak against the devastating clouds of dust, so fast and so powerful. He skidded to a stop right in front of us, jumping off the bike in one smooth movement, his knife already at Roland's throat before I even had a chance to blink.

"He needs to die," Zayde rasped, and I hated myself for hesitating. The man was a monster, I knew that. But he was my *dad*. Or had been, once. And he'd been Tim's dad, too. Ending his life...would that make me as bad as him?

"You're all so naive." Roland laughed, his Adam's apple moving against the knife. His gaze was fixed on the rubble of the offices, his finger circling the pieces of ash drifting through the air. "Look at what I did. You won't be able to get them back now."

"Baby."

I met Zayde's eyes, reading the intent in his gaze, swirling with hesitation. He wanted to act, to make Roland pay, but he wouldn't do it without my permission.

I loved him so, so much in that moment, even more than I had before.

"An eye for an eye." We both turned to Roland, who was grinning maniacally again, despite the knife digging into the underside of his chin. His gaze fixed on Zayde. "My son died because of your rivalry, and still, you took away everything that mattered to me. Christine. My reputation. My business. I had to even the scales, so I ruined Alstone Holdings. Now you're the only one left. Even if I die here today, you'll have to live with the knowledge that you've lost everything."

"No. *You* will die here today. But first, you need to pay for hurting the person that means the most to me." Zayde moved so fast that Roland's scream registered before I realised what he'd done. "You used that hand to hurt Fallon, and now you'll never be able to touch her with it again." Roland screamed again, and this time, I heard the crunch of bone as Zayde twisted his hand violently and then pinned it up against Joseph's car window, using his knife to sever the rest of the hand from his arm.

"I'm gonna throw up," Joseph mumbled, stumbling away from me, covering his mouth.

"You're going to burn for what you did." Roland was nearly incoherent with rage and pain, and as I stared at him, I couldn't find any traces of the severe, composed man he'd once been. I couldn't recognise this person as my father. He'd...well, he was clearly a desperate man driven to desperate measures, but there wasn't a single part of me that felt any sympathy for him.

I stepped into his line of sight. "You are a despicable person," I said, and my voice was steady. "And you are *not* my father."

His hate-filled gaze flicked to mine for the briefest moment before it returned to Zayde. "Didn't you hear me?" he spat, his words garbled. "An eye for an eye. You're going to *burn*!"

"Do you ever fucking *stop talking*?" Creed appeared from nowhere, his fingers flicking out, and a line of scarlet slashed across Roland's throat.

Roland gasped out a breath that sounded like he had bubbles in his chest. He staggered forwards, clutching his neck, red bleeding beneath his fingers. I took a step backwards as he fell to the floor in front of me.

"An eye for an eye makes the whole world blind," I whispered as the life drained from him. Looking down at his body, I felt nothing, only a sense of relief that he would never be able to hurt anyone again.

Creed turned to Joseph, and I watched as Joseph slowly straightened up, wiping his mouth. It was then that I realised that he'd just been sick. His whole body was trembling as he held up his hands. "I know when I'm beaten. I'll give you all the information I have on my dad. All the info on everything you want. The business. You can have it. Just let me go. *Please*. I won't take anything."

Creed and Zayde both glanced at me. Zayde was fingering his knife, and Creed was casually wiping the streaks of blood from the flying weapon he'd used to slash Roland's throat. What was I supposed to do? "You two decide."

I realised then that I trusted them to make the decision that was best for us. Taking a step back, I closed my eyes.

I heard murmured voices and Creed calling someone's name—Obie.

After that, there was a long silence, and then Zayde was wrapping me in his arms, his voice soothing in my ear. "It's over now. You're safe. I've got you."

I was safe, but at what price?

30

zayde

I couldn't fucking breathe. Right in front of me, obscured by huge clouds of dust, was a huge, gaping hole in the Alstone Holdings offices. It was only the knowledge that I needed to stay strong for my girl that was keeping me standing.

"Zayde!"

There was a shout, and Fallon gasped, letting go of me as she turned towards the sound.

Caiden. Fucking hell. I'd never been so glad to see him in my fucking life. I took a step towards him, then another, and then he was barrelling towards me, with Cassius and Weston right behind him, all of them covered in dust and bits of rubble but alive and unharmed. Then they were fucking hugging me, and shock of all shocks, I was hugging them right back.

"We were so worried," West breathed when we separated. "None of us knew what was happening outside. Dad worked out what was going on just in time, so we managed to evacuate the building. Except people got hurt." He glanced at Caiden, who placed a hand on my shoulder.

"The ambulances are there now. Your dad, uh, he was injured. But he's gonna be okay."

My heart was pounding out of my chest.

"Zayde? Do you want to go to the hospital?"

It was then that I realised that Fallon was here, listening to our conversation. I held out my hand, pulling her into me. "Yeah. We should go." Flicking my gaze back to Cade, I said, "Are you sure my dad's gonna be okay?"

Cade nodded. "Yeah. Some of the rubble hit him. I think he might have a broken arm. But he's okay. He wasn't the only one to get hurt, either. My dad's hurt, too. And Mack. But no one's badly injured. We're all alive."

"He's not."

We all turned to where Cassius was pointing. Roland Hyde's body was sprawled across the ground, the dust gradually settling over him, covering the bloodstains. Fallon curled into me, and I tightened my arm around her, dropping a kiss on top of her head. "He's gone," I said, too low for anyone else to hear. "He can't hurt anyone else again."

She looked up at me with a shaky smile. "I know. It was the right thing to do. I wish I hadn't hesitated. It was just..."

"Hey. I would never expect you not to be conflicted, baby. You're good. So good. My angel. So fucking pure, I don't know how—"

Reaching up, she covered my mouth. "I love you. You think you have a black soul, but it's not true. You're a good man, Zayde Lowry. And I love you so much."

Fucking hell. I wished more than anything that I could say the words back to her. Why was it so hard to admit it to myself? How fucking broken was I inside that I didn't truly know how to love?

Footsteps sounded, and then more people were there,

but I kept my eyes fixed on Fallon. "It's okay. I know," she whispered. "You don't have to say anything. You don't have to try and be anything you're not. I love you the way you are." She held my gaze, her arms wrapping around me, and suddenly, I could breathe again.

"Let's get out of here," I rasped around the tightness in my throat.

"Okay."

"Rich boy! You owe me a new car."

Mack's voice carried through the open door, and as I entered his hospital room, I raised my brows at the sight of Caiden standing next to Mack's bed, his arms folded over his chest, and James Granville right there next to him.

"Why do I owe you a car?"

"I'm scarred for life. Look." Mack pulled up his shirt, showing a bandaged area on his side. "That's your fault."

Caiden's brows lifted. "You wanna compare? I took a bullet for my girl, and I've got the scar to prove it. You tripped over when you were running and fell into that fucking plant pot. And that still doesn't explain why I owe you a new car."

"Compensation," he said, grinning at Cade. "My car is shit; therefore, I need a new one, and you owe me for being injured at your future place of work."

"Nice try, but no."

I cleared my throat, and the three of them turned to look at me. "Alright?"

"There you are. Where's Fallon? Is she okay? Have you seen your dad yet?" Cade stepped over to me, his eyes scanning my face with apparent concern.

"I haven't seen my dad yet. Fallon's in Lena's room with the other girls." I lowered my voice so that the others didn't overhear. "She's...it was a big shock. She had to watch her dad die right in front of her, and even though he deserved everything he had coming, I wish she hadn't had to witness it. But I know she's gonna be okay. She's been through so fucking much, but my girl's strong. It won't break her."

Caiden's brows lifted, and a smile pulled at his lips. "I never thought I'd see the day. But here it is."

"What day?" My voice was low and dangerous as I narrowed my eyes, but he just laughed.

"You love her. You're so fucking in love with her, Z. Don't even deny it. And that girl loves you, too. Fuck knows why—you're such a grumpy bastard." His smile widened into a huge grin. "Just kidding. She's lucky to have you, mate. I'm happy for you."

"You think I love her?" I was stuck on the first part of what he'd just said, his words playing in my head over and over.

"No. I don't *think* you love her, I *know* you love her." He patted me on the shoulder. "Don't look so surprised." When I stood there, frozen in place with no fucking words, his smile dropped. "Z. It's okay to let yourself love her. She's not going to leave you. And neither are the rest of us. We're in this for life, mate. And if we're still having this same argument when we're old and fucking shrivelled, I will shank you."

Fuck. I gave him a nod because I wasn't capable of words, and he shot me a smile before turning back to the others, who were studying something on Granville's phone. He clicked his fingers, and both of them looked up.

"Granville. You're coming with me. Now. We're going to

my dad, and you're gonna tell him all the shit you know about your relatives."

Granville rolled his eyes but sauntered over to us anyway. "I can't wait to spend *even more* time with you. As if today hasn't already been enough of a pleasure." His eyes were alight with humour in his failed attempt to piss off my best mate.

"Likewise." Cade didn't even bother to hide his amusement as he grinned. "You know how much I love being forced to spend time around you. Almost as much as I love having a bad case of food poisoning from Mack's undercooked burgers. Let's go."

They disappeared out of the door to the sound of Mack shouting, "That was one time! You can't hold it against me forever!" When they were gone, he dropped the theatrics and gave me an expectant look.

"What?"

"Just waiting for you to leave so when the girls pass by my room and see me in here all alone, they'll give me all the sympathy."

"Good luck with that." I rolled my eyes. "I'm going to see my dad." But before I left, I glanced back at him. "You okay?"

He nodded immediately. "Yeah. This is nothing. Just a few stitches, probably won't even scar. The boys would laugh at us if they could see how much everyone was fussing over me at this snooty private hospital. Although that one nurse was hot as fuck. Maybe I should play up my injuries a bit."

I left him hitting the button to call the nurse and strode down the corridor to my dad's room. I fucking hated this place. It brought back memories of being here after everything had gone down at the docks, when we were waiting for Cade to wake up after he'd been shot. That was when it hit home just how important the three of them were to me. Cade, Cass, and West. We were brothers. They were my family.

My dad was sitting up in bed, a glass of water held to his lips with his right hand and a splint on his other arm. When he saw me enter the room, he placed the glass down and indicated towards the seat next to him.

"What a day," he said when I was seated.

"Yeah."

"There's an upside, of course." He gave me a shark-like grin. "No more Hydes."

"That's not true."

"Ah. Yes. Fallon. She won't be a Hyde forever, though, will she?" he said carefully, and I stared at him in disbelief.

"Is this you giving me your approval?"

Drumming his fingers on the bed sheets, he smiled. A real, honest smile. "Zayde. You're my son, and I want you to be happy. She makes you happy. That's enough for me."

My eyes were wide as fuck. Since when? He'd always been about the business, always putting it above pleasure, and he'd always despised the Hydes.

A groan fell from his throat, and he pinched his brow. "I've fucked up more than I thought if you're giving me that look when I tell you that I want you to be happy. Look. I know I'm not very..." He waved his hand in the air, searching for a word, eventually settling on, "Emotional. Whatever you want to call it. I know I don't have the best work-life balance, but I want you to believe me when I say that you're more important to me than the business. Even... even if I'm incapable of showing it. And I'm proud of you. I'm not sure if I've told you before."

"Oh."

He lifted his arm, leaning forwards almost as if he was going to hug me, but seemed to think better of it. "One step at a time," he muttered. Then he held out his hand to me, and I took it. It was only a quick clasp, but it was firm, and his expression was determined. "We're going to be busy over the next few weeks. There's a lot we need to deal with, business-wise. First order of the day—Paul's working with Arlo to get a statement out to say that we'd been doing some planned demolition work. A few falsified permits, and no one will be any the wiser."

"Good idea." We needed to crush any speculation as soon as possible. Creed would've taken care of the clean-up by now, but a body was much easier to hide than a giant fucking hole in the middle of one of the more prominent buildings in Alstone.

"But that's neither here nor there," he continued. "I want you to speak to Fallon and choose an evening or even an afternoon you'd both like to meet with me next week. Perhaps for a meal, or if there's something else you'd prefer to do, I'm sure we can accommodate it. When you've decided, get in touch with my assistant. She'll make sure my calendar is blocked off. I'd like to get to know the girl that my son has fallen in love with. And I'd like to try making up for some of the time I've lost with you."

Fucking hell, who was this man? Had he hit his head when everything had gone down? I'd thought he only had a minor arm injury. "Is your head okay?"

His brows pulled together. "Yes, why? It was my arm that was injured, and it's only a hairline fracture. Nothing to be concerned about."

So he meant it, then. "Never mind. Yeah. I'll talk to Fallon." I attempted a smile, and it felt unnatural and strange, but it seemed like he appreciated the effort because he returned it with another small, genuine one of his own.

"See that you do." He leaned back, closing his eyes. "I should rest now. Go and find your girl. Do something nice with her. Goodness knows you've both earned it."

I climbed to my feet and crossed the room to the exit. "Bye, Dad," I said softly and closed the door behind me.

31

fallon

"Hi, Tim." I crouched down in front of the headstone. "I can't believe it's been two years since you've been gone. I know you're at peace now, but I miss you so much. I wanted to officially introduce you to Zayde. I know you've met before, but I want to introduce him as my...well, my boyfriend?" Glancing up at Zayde, I caught his gaze, my breath catching in my throat at the soft look he was giving me.

He nodded, his lips curving up into that small, rare smile I loved so much. "Yeah. Your boyfriend."

I smiled. "I think that if we'd managed to get over this rivalry sooner, you'd like each other. He's amazing, Tim." I decided not to mention what had happened with my dad and Joseph, not today. That was all still too raw, too big to come to terms with, and I'd wanted to come here to remember my brother. To celebrate his life. "Do you remember when I was obsessed with *To Kill a Mockingbird* and I carried that book around with me? I never told you, but Zayde gave me the book. I was having a hard time at school, being away from both of you. He sent it to me. It was his most precious possession, and he let me have it." Tears filled my eyes. "I wish I'd told you then that he was the one to give it to me. I wish I'd taken the time to show you his other side, the side that I got to see."

"Baby." Zayde crouched down next to me, brushing my hair back from my face and tucking it behind my ear. "He knows now."

"I know," I whispered. "It's just so hard. It's been two years, but sometimes it feels like it only happened yesterday."

"There's no timeline on grief. There's no one way you're supposed to feel. Or that's what Cade tells Winter when she's having a tough time, and she tells him and West the same thing. If anyone knows what they're talking about, it's those three. You know."

"You're right." Shifting closer to him, I laid my head on his shoulder. "Do you want to say anything to Tim?"

There was a long silence. I drew back from him. "You don't have to. I promise I won't be upset. I just thought—"

"No. No. I want to." Swallowing hard, he inched closer to the headstone, his icy eyes filled with so much pain and regret and sorrow. "I'm so fucking sorry I couldn't save you," he said hoarsely, his throat working. "It's the biggest regret of my life. I'm sorry I let the rivalry escalate so much. None of us were blameless, but Fallon was my girl, and I should've tried to smooth things over between us." His gaze lowered, and he blinked rapidly, and when he opened his eyes again, I saw his inky lashes were wet. *Fuck.* My heart ached for my beautiful man, who wore a mask to keep his emotions locked up so tightly but felt so, so deeply inside. He cleared his throat. "I want—I want you to know that I'm going to take care of your sister. I'm going to make sure she knows just how special she is every single day for the rest of our lives."

"Please don't blame yourself. It's not your fault, Zayde. I'm going to keep telling you that until you believe it." I threw my arms around him, burying my face in the warm skin of his neck. He sighed against me, his breath ruffling my hair.

"Keep telling me, angel. Please."

"Always."

Back at the Four's house, we gathered in the lounge. For now, it was just the eight of us. Zayde had asked me what I wanted to do as we were leaving the hospital, and other than going back to see Tim after everything that had happened this morning, I was just craving some normality. I knew that it would be good for him to be with his friends—his family—but I knew that he got drained after a while when he was around too many people. So I'd tentatively suggested that we could see if the rest of the Four wanted to order a takeaway and hang out together. His eyes had lit up at my suggestion, and I immediately knew I'd done the right thing.

"Is anyone having this last piece?" Cassius' hand hovered over the remaining slice of pepperoni pizza.

"Yeah, me." Caiden swiped the piece from under him, and his mouth fell open before he retaliated, diving for Caiden and taking a huge bite out of the slice, right out of his hand.

"What the fuck?" Caiden exclaimed, and I couldn't help it—I started laughing. There was a millisecond of silence, and then everyone else was joining in, even Caiden, who was now mashing the rest of the slice into Cassius' face while Cassius screeched for Winter to control her boyfriend. There was a levity I hadn't known existed, like the recent events had brought us all together, and now everyone felt like a sudden weight had been lifted. Everyone was genuinely happy and carefree, and despite everything that had happened today, it was rubbing off on me. I'd be dealing with the fallout for a long time, probably working through it with the help of my therapist and Zayde...and these guys, too, who had accepted me wholeheartedly because they loved Zayde and wanted him to be happy. And to think that I could be someone who could contribute to his happiness...that was a privilege I'd never, ever take for granted.

As I took in my boyfriend, who was now deep in conversation with Winter, saying something about Creed and Skirmish, I couldn't help the wide smile spreading across my face. I'd come back to Alstone for closure, but now I had so much more than I could have ever dreamed of. As I watched him, he stretched, his muscles flexing, and my heart skipped a beat. He was so gorgeous, inside and out. I was a lucky, lucky girl.

"What are you thinking about?" Cassius was suddenly in my face, his eyes sparkling with humour and a smirk tugging at his lips.

I thought fast. I hadn't had all that many interactions with Cassius yet, but I thought I had a pretty good idea about how to handle his playful personality. "Nothing much. Just thinking about how much I like Zayde's piercing."

Zayde's head whipped around to mine, one brow raised.

"What piercing?" Jessa leaned forwards, unconcealed curiosity on her face.

"Oh, I don't think I should say."

"She's talking about your dick, isn't she?" Caiden cut in, also smirking. Honestly, what was it with these boys and their constant smirks?

"You have your *dick* pierced?" Cassius clapped his hands over his crotch, wincing. "You crazy fucker." He glanced over at Caiden. "Wait. How did you know?"

Caiden shrugged. "I was there when Mack pierced it. I wanted to see what it was like. Decided against getting mine done in the end, though." Grabbing Winter and pulling her into his lap, he added, "My girl's never had any complaints about my dick, so I'm not bothered either way. Have you, Snowflake?"

Winter's cheeks flushed as she shook her head. "Seriously, Cade. Do you have to drag me into this? You know I have no complaints. At all."

"Can we talk about anything except my brother's dick, please?" West grimaced around a mouthful of meat feast pizza. "It's enough to put me off my food."

"Yeah, really looks like it." Cassius laughed at him as he wiped the remains of pizza from his face with one of the napkins the pizza place had provided.

"We propose a toast."

I hadn't even noticed Jessa and Lena disappearing from the lounge, but they were standing in the doorway. Lena was holding up a bottle of some kind of green liquid, and Jessa had a teetering pile of shot glasses balanced in her hands.

They crossed the room to the coffee table. Jessa lined up the shot glasses, and Lena poured the vibrant liquid into them. When the little glasses were all full to the brim, they handed them out to all of us.

"We should have sugar if we're doing this properly, but

we don't care about proper. Don't tell my brother," Jessa said.

Lena caught my puzzled frown. "Her brother owns a club in London. He's particular about his drinks."

"Yeah, and we'll take you there sometime very soon," Jessa promised. "You can meet JJ."

Cassius jumped to his feet, doing some kind of hip thrust that I wasn't prepared to see, not when he was standing so close to me, wearing such tight jeans. "JJ!"

"Not another word about those fucking gold shorts," Zayde ground out, and I stared between them both, intrigued.

Jessa caught my gaze and mouthed, *I'll tell you later.*

I nodded with a smile, holding up my shot glass in acknowledgement. "What are we toasting, anyway?"

Lena and Jessa exchanged glances, and then Lena held up her own glass. She took a deep breath, fixing her gaze on mine. "We thought we'd do a cheers to Tim."

A lump came into my throat. "Th-that would be really good," I whispered. Then Zayde was there, pulling me into his arms and surrounding me with his strong, safe presence.

"Breathe, baby."

I took a breath, and then another. "To Tim," I murmured, and everyone downed their drinks as one.

In that moment, I loved them all.

"Fuck me, that was strong," Lena exclaimed, wiping her hand over her mouth. "No more of those for me."

"Z. Want to play?" Caiden threw a game controller at Zayde, who caught it easily. I felt him relax against me as his hands gripped the controller in front of me, with me sitting between his legs.

"When did you move the PS5 back in here?" West questioned, grabbing one of the free controllers.

Caiden glanced over at Zayde. "As soon as we got back. Thought we might feel like playing after the food, and I didn't want us to have to worry about moving."

He'd known exactly what my boyfriend needed, and it made me so happy that he was surrounded by people who knew him and looked out for him.

I settled back in the cradle of Zayde's arms as they started to play, savouring the soft kisses he dropped on my hair every now and then as he decimated his opponents on-screen. Looking around the room, it seemed like everyone else was just as relaxed. Cassius was stretched out on the sofa with Jessa in his arms, both of their heads bent over her Kindle while he read something aloud in a low voice, making Jessa's cheeks flush with whatever he was saying. Lena was right next to Weston, both of them leaning into each other and laughing as they mashed the buttons on their controllers. Caiden was more or less losing the game at this point, too distracted by Winter, who was wriggling in his lap. One of his hands was somewhere under her top, and I quickly averted my gaze.

"What do you think?" Zayde's voice was quiet in my ear. "Could you get used to this?"

I twisted my head to look at him. There was no hesitation in my mind. "Yes."

32

zayde

I could hear the thud of the music of the Guy Fawkes celebrations way before Cade, Cass, West, and I reached the top of the cliffs. We crested the hill, the castle appearing right in front of us, a hulking black shadow against a cloudless night sky dotted with stars. Spotlights blinded me as we drew nearer, cycling through a nauseating rainbow of colours so fast it made my head spin. There was the usual bar and DJ setup, and the bonfire was piled high, ready to be lit later.

The bouncers waved us in without bothering to ask for our tickets. *Good*. As it should be. Yeah, maybe there were one or two things I liked about my elite status.

We avoided being given the strips of fabric that were being handed out, too, and as we strolled past the people tying the strips of cloth around themselves, Cade smirked at me. "We don't need that shit. We've got our targets ready."

In reply, I yanked my skull bandana up over my nose and mouth, pulling my hood lower on my head so that my eyes were the only part of my face in view. Even so, they were shadowed by my hood.

Cade gave me a savage grin, pulling up his own bandana and hood, and Cass and West followed suit. Adrenaline thrummed through my veins in time with the dark beats of the music. We were ready and on the hunt for our prey.

The klaxon sounded, signalling the start of the games, and the four of us melted into the shadows, silent and deadly.

"Remember last year?" Cass whispered loudly, instantly ruining our deadly vibe as we hugged the crumbling stone wall, moving as one, deeper into the castle ruins, ready to lie in wait. "It was just Cade with Winter, and, uh." He gave an exaggerated cough. "We all had to push that one along."

"Fuck off," Cade muttered, but he was looking at Cass with something that I thought might be gratitude. "I guess I should probably thank you for that, even though you went about it completely the wrong way. Fucking hell, the three of you..." He trailed off with a shake of his head, his jaw tightening, and I knew he was remembering how the three of us had held Winter until he'd finally seen the light. Cade was way more stubborn than the rest of us, and sometimes he needed the equivalent of a sledgehammer to the head to realise what was obvious to everyone else. This time last year had been one of those nights, but it had ended well for both him and Winter.

"You should definitely be thanking us," West whispered back but then fell silent as we heard the sound of running footsteps. We pressed against the wall, still hidden in the shadows, as shouts echoed around us. Someone must've lit the bonfire because suddenly, our hidden area shrunk, the glow of faraway flames sending shadows jumping and flickering around us.

"Stay hidden. I'm gonna catch myself a snowflake," Cade murmured, moving to the left and disappearing behind the remains of what was either a stone column or a stack of stones that had probably once held up one of the upper floors.

"I know Lena's tracking me, but she's underestimated me." West slid in the opposite direction to Cade, his eyes sparkling with the thrill of the chase. Then it was just me and Cassius left.

"Z?"

"Yeah?"

He shifted on his feet, staring down at the ground. "I'm glad you have Fallon. I like her. I'm, uh, glad you're happy."

Fuck. "Uh. Me too," I muttered. "Yeah. Same. For you and Jessa." This was so fucking awkward.

His gaze swung to mine, and I could tell he was grinning from the way his eyes creased above his bandana. "We have the best fucking taste, don't we?"

I huffed out a surprised laugh. "Yeah. We do."

"I think we should hunt our girls down. Give them the surprise of their lives. What do you say?" Without waiting for me to reply, he moved to the corner of the stone wall we were leaning against, peering around the edge.

"I say, fuck yeah. Let's do it." I held up my fist, and he bumped his against mine immediately, chuckling quietly.

We both scanned the running figures for our girls, but there was no sight of either of them. Without needing to communicate verbally, we moved farther back, hugging the walls, keeping to the shadows.

"There," Cass breathed, barely audible, inclining his head to our left. When I caught sight of our girls with their hoods up, attempting to keep to the shadows but still so obviously them, I nodded sharply.

Throwing me a quick thumbs up, he stepped forwards, keeping his gaze fixed on the two of them. "Let's go."

We moved in a diagonal line with the intention of cutting them off, but they suddenly swerved, heading towards the line of trees behind the castle. We weren't going to let them get there, though. With a wild, excited look in his eyes, Cassius looked at me and then took off at a run, abandoning all sense of caution.

That wasn't my style. I kept to the shadows, gradually drawing closer to my girl, completely silent. She was becoming twitchy, glancing all around her, shrinking into the wall. I wanted to reveal myself, to reassure her that she didn't need to be afraid, but at the same time, I fucking loved the chase.

I was almost within touching distance when the first firework went off. Fallon jumped and then huffed out a laugh at herself. More bangs echoed around us, bouncing off the walls, as the second and third fireworks were released. Fallon crept around a corner that I knew was a dead end, leading to a shadowy alcove between two walls. I took my chance, coming right up behind her and clamping my hand over her mouth, pushing her into the alcove.

Her scream was muffled by my hand as I held her in place with my body, trapped against the wall. I lowered my mouth to her ear. "Got you."

She instantly stilled, and I lowered my hand, letting her turn to face me. In the darkness, I could just about make out her features—her wide eyes, her mouth open as she gasped for breath.

"You look—scary."

"Yeah? Good or bad?"

She hummed. "Good. A sexy masked man come to hunt me down in the dark." One deep breath, and she reached up to trace my lips, covered by the fabric of the bandana. "All my monsters are gone, and I'm not afraid of the dark. I want to play."

Then my girl ducked down, spun around me, and was gone.

Fuuuck. She wanted to play. My dick was so on board with the plan. I adjusted myself in my jeans with a groan and took off after her.

I had the advantage because I knew the castle better than she did, and I knew how to remain silent. But Fallon was good—fast and light-footed, and I nearly lost her once or twice as she darted around corners, swerving past the larger, crumbling remains, always keeping to the shadows. But her speed was no match for mine, and even with her head start, I easily caught up with her.

Using the same manoeuvre as before, I clamped my hand over her mouth, pressing my chest into her back as I pressed us into another alcove. This one was narrower than before, but it had a gap in the wall at one side, up above our heads, allowing the glow from the bonfire to penetrate the gloom just enough to see.

"You thought you could run from me." My voice was a low growl right next to her ear, and I felt her shiver against me. "You made me chase you, and now you need to be punished for being a bad girl." Sliding my hand down, I gripped her throat, her pulse pounding underneath my grip.

"H-how are you going to punish me?"

I ground the thick length of my cock against the curve of her ass. "I was thinking about fucking you before you ran away, but now I don't think you deserve the pleasure."

She went lax in my grip. "I can be good. Please don't hurt me."

"No promises, angel." I'd never hurt her, and she knew it, but this little role play we had going on was making my dick so fucking hard. Lightly squeezing her throat as my other hand slipped under her hoodie, up to cup one of her gorgeous tits, I was rewarded with a throaty moan that went straight to my cock.

"I-I *can* be good." Her breath stuttered as I began to circle her nipple through the paper-thin silk of her bra. "I can."

"Prove it."

There was a second of silence, and then she lifted her hand, sliding it up under her hoodie, next to mine. A whimper fell from her throat as she began to circle her fingers. "I can touch myself for you."

Fucking hell.

"How does it feel?"

"Good. *So* good."

"Yeah?" Pinching her nipple between my thumb and forefinger, I lowered my head, dragging my nose up the side of her neck. I wanted to yank down my bandana and get my mouth on her, but I'd seen the way her pupils had dilated when she looked at me, even in the shadows.

She moaned, her head falling back to my shoulder. "More."

My hand traced a path across her soft skin, moving lower until it slipped from beneath her hoodie. "Don't stop," I commanded as my fingers closed around the handle of my knife. "You don't know how much danger you're in."

"Danger?" Her voice was so fucking breathy.

"Yeah." Lifting the knife, I brought it up in front of her

face. "This kind of danger. I need you to hold very, very still."

"Ohhh."

Fucking hell, that was the sexiest little noise I'd ever heard. She was so into this, and I couldn't wait to bury myself inside her and make her mine. I twisted the knife, placing the flat of my blade to her throat, and slowly and oh-so-fucking-carefully dragged it down her gorgeous body. Her breaths were coming faster, and I could feel her trembling, the effort of holding herself completely still almost too much for her to bear.

I was so tempted to slice into her clothes, to bare her to me, but that was something that we could save for another time when we were alone. Stopping at the bottom of her hoodie, I breathed across her ear. "Spread your legs, baby."

She instantly obeyed, panting, her chest rising and falling faster and faster.

I continued trailing the knife down and then, with the utmost care, tapped the flat of the blade lightly against her covered clit.

The sinful fucking moan that came from her made my dick throb.

"Touch yourself here. Get yourself ready for me." There was no way I was going to last when I got inside her, and I wanted her on edge and ready for me before I got my cock inside her.

"I'm ready. *Please.*"

Her begging words were so fucking sweet. I squeezed her throat lightly again as I lifted the knife away from her and stowed it safely.

"No. Not yet. Touch yourself."

Another moan spilled from her lips as her free hand went to her leggings.

"Use both hands. I want you bare and ready for me in two minutes."

"Ohhhh," she gasped, obeying instantly. She had her leggings and underwear yanked down and two fingers in her pussy before I even registered what she was fucking doing. It was so hot, being here like this, knowing that there was a possibility of someone catching us at any moment.

"Good girl." Releasing my grip on her throat, I used my knee to push her legs farther apart. "Bend over. Hands on the wall."

Her back arched, her head lowering. "Please."

I stepped back, taking in the view as I undid my jeans. So fucking gorgeous. All that platinum hair was spilling down her back and falling around her shoulders, a bright contrast against the midnight blue of her hoodie. The luscious, creamy curve of her ass was yet another contrast, arched enticingly towards me. I caught a glimpse of the wetness between her legs at the top of her thighs when she shifted on her feet, and my mouth went dry as I finished shoving my jeans down. My erection was a hard outline against my underwear, the curved barbell at the tip clearly visible where the fabric was stretched to fuck trying to keep my dick in check.

When I freed my dick, I pressed forwards, sliding my thick erection between her legs, her wetness giving it a smooth slide that felt so good it made my eyes roll back, a low groan tearing from my throat. Fuck. My girl was incomparable. No one else could ever come close to her. "Are you ready for me?"

"*Yes*. I need you."

"Bend over just a little more, baby." She immediately followed my instructions, and I wasted no time. I gripped her hips and thrust home, sinking inside her, sheathing my dick inside her hot body.

Fucking incredible.

My breathing was a little restricted, thanks to my bandana, but somehow, it added to the sensations. One of my hands slid around the front of her hip and down onto her clit. Her moans increased in both volume and frequency as I took her right to the edge before pulling back.

“You feel so good,” I rasped, thrusting all the way in again, my fingers working right alongside my dick to send her over the edge this time. She cried out, her body shuddering around my length as I buried myself balls-deep with a long, low groan, my dick pulsing, filling her with my cum. I couldn’t catch my fucking breath. It was so intense.

Slumping forwards, she leaned her forehead against the cool stone wall, breathing hard. I slowly withdrew my cock from her, my cum glistening on her thighs as it trickled out of her.

She suddenly turned around, pressing her back into the wall and tilting her head upwards. Her fingers came up to curl around the top of my bandana. Carefully, gently, she tugged it down, and I could breathe again. “Zayde. Kiss me.”

I lowered my head to hers, kissing her so fucking softly, feeling her lips move against mine. She wound her arms around my neck, the quietest moan escaping her throat, and my heart fucking flipped. I was so gone for this girl. She was everything I’d always wanted, and now she was really, properly mine.

We’d been through so much in our journey to where we were now. More than anyone should ever have to go through. But here we were, and I was holding her in my arms, and I was never going to let her go.

Pulling back just enough that I could meet her eyes, I ran my hand up and down her back. I took in her gaze, intent on mine, filled with so many feelings that I couldn't even begin to process. But maybe I didn't have to yet. There was no rush. I had forever to figure it out now.

My lips pressed against hers. "You're mine."

I felt her smile. "Yes. I am."

When we rejoined the others by the bonfire, I couldn't help the grin that overtook my face as Fallon was immediately pulled into a huddle with Winter, Lena, and Jessa. My girlfriend fit right in with our group, and even though she'd lost her family, now she got to share mine.

"You missed most of the fireworks." Caiden nudged me with a smirk as the loud booms of the finale sounded, the entire sky lit up with a rainbow of colours.

"Yeah? When did you get here, then?"

He grinned. "About a minute before you did."

I cuffed him around the head, and he ducked, laughing, punching me in the side. Cassius and Weston glanced over at us, then each other, and then made a run, attempting to tackle Cade and me.

"This is war!" Caiden shouted, grabbing his brother in a headlock, while I dodged Cassius' advance, making him stumble. With a wide grin, he spun around, aiming for me again.

I lifted my middle fingers in the air, my own grin still plastered to my face. "Come and get me, fuckers."

Then I ran.

33

fallon

There was nothing left. Just the charred remains. A shell.

Removing my helmet, I climbed off the back of Zayde's bike, adjusting the straps of the small backpack on my shoulders.

"Are you sure you want to do this?" My boyfriend took off his own helmet, revealing his gorgeous face, his brows pulled together in concern as his eyes met mine.

"I'm sure." This was something that I felt strongly about, something I needed to do in my process of moving on. Everyone had different methods to gain closure, but for me, what seemed to work best was facing my past, and that's why I was here at the site of the abandoned house today. It had been ten days since the Guy Fawkes celebrations, which was the first day I'd truly felt like I could put the past behind me, to be present in the moment. My dad was gone, and as for Joseph and my mum...I'd trusted Zayde to take care of it, and I knew that he would.

Zayde took my hand as we made our way up what was

once the driveway. I was grateful for it, his palm warm against the chill of the November air. It was the early hours of the morning, still dark, but the sky was clear, with the moon brightly illuminating our surroundings in shades of silver and grey. The trees around us were almost bare of leaves, leaving the landscape stark and featureless. Memories washed over me as I took in the scene, but for once, they didn't pull me under.

It had taken a lot of work to get to this point. Just over two years since Tim's death. Two years in which to come to terms with what had happened, to work with my therapist, to get to this moment right now, where I could actually stand here and acknowledge everything that had happened. There wasn't one recommended method for anyone, nor was there a set timeline, but for me personally? I was here.

And that was enough.

"Want to walk closer?" His fingers tightened around mine. "I want to show you something."

Surely he knew by now that I'd follow him anywhere. I let him lead me forwards until we were standing where the front wall had once been. His posture was ramrod straight, and his gaze was determined as he stared at what was left of the building.

Lowering his head to mine, he pressed a soft kiss to my lips, and when he drew back, there was a smile on his face, so small but so sincere. I returned it, my heart full of love for this man.

"Come and look at this." He led me along the line that marked the front wall of the house. When he came to a stop, he curled one arm around my waist, and the other pointed down at the cracked, blackened ground, ashes still remaining.

In the midst of the devastation, sheltered by a small, crumbling wall, tall spikes of flowers bloomed, a pinkish-purple shock of colour against the grey. The sun was just starting to set, the rays touching them with burnished gold, making it look as if they were alight.

"They're wildflowers. Fireweed. It's not the right time of year to see them properly, but when we come back next summer, this whole place will be covered."

Next summer. He was already planning ahead. Something inside me warmed at the thought.

I sank to my knees, my fingers stretching out to touch the delicate petals. There was life here in this barren landscape. Beauty from ashes.

"They grow where nothing else can." Zayde crouched down next to me, his hand covering mine. "After the war, they started appearing in London at sites that had been bombed. After the fires had gone."

He never usually volunteered information like this, and it was clear to me that he'd spent a lot of time researching. A lump came into my throat as I imagined him taking the time to do this for me. I twisted my palm, threading my fingers between his. "It's a sign. I...I think I'd like to take some for Tim's grave."

His smile was like the sun coming out. "Yeah. We can do that."

Carefully, he used his knife to slice a few stems. When we had enough, I laid a hand on his arm. "Z. Thank you for this. I really needed this today."

"I know." Tugging me to my feet, he glanced up at the skyline, shading his eyes. "We should go if you want to get there before the sun sets. Are you ready, or do you want to stay longer?"

Shaking my head, I turned towards the place he'd parked his motorbike. "No. I'm ready to go."

Hand in hand, we walked away.

EPILOGUE 1

fallon

ONE MONTH LATER

"Okay. Yellow team. We need to discuss strategy." Lena beckoned us into a huddle. I couldn't help smiling at her enthusiasm. "There's no way I'm letting West beat me."

"We've got this." Jessa glanced over to where the boys were also huddled, down the side of a strategically placed Jeep. "They think they can beat us, but they underestimate how good we are."

Winter grinned at me. "How're you feeling? Ready?"

"I'm ready." Despite having zero experience in aiming and shooting guns, their excitement was contagious, and I was more than ready to get started. We were at the Battle Fields, a new outdoor laser tag section of Skirmish, the place Creed owned, which offered various activities, including knife throwing, archery, and paintball. He'd asked Z if we were interested in testing it before it was made available to the general public, and the Four had jumped at the chance.

"I've been wanting to plan a girls' day with you for a while. As soon as it was clear how important Z was to you, I knew that we needed this." Winter squeezed my arm, glancing over to Lena, who nodded.

"Yep. You're one of us now. There's no escape."

"You're moving into the house with us at Christmas, right?" Jessa gave me a bright smile as she stretched out her hamstrings. Both of us were officially moving in with the Four around the same time, and after a long debate with myself about whether I should continue to pursue independent living, Zayde had pointed out that I could still be as independent as I wanted, but living in his house meant that we got to wake up next to each other every morning. How could I say no to that?

I nodded. "I am. I felt bad about leaving Kinslee, but that worked out well."

Jessa straightened back up, her glossy, straight ponytail flipping over her shoulder. "Yeah, me too. But she said she'd always wanted to live in one of the apartments in my building, so it all worked out."

It felt like fate, in a way. After so many things had gone wrong, everything had fallen into place. Kinslee insisted that she liked her own space, and with Jessa moving in with the Four, her apartment was free, and thanks to her connections, she was able to sign the rental agreement over to Kinslee. It also meant that Kinslee was a little closer to our house, too. I'd enrolled on a business course—not at Alstone College but via distance learning, and together with James, we were learning the ropes of what remained of Hyde Consultings. That was no longer its name, of course. Most of the business was in the process of being absorbed into Alstone Holdings, but a small branch remained, focused only on local property. We had an interim manager while we studied for our qualifications, but eventually, the two of us would run TL Properties, aka Tim Lewis Properties, named after my brother. We'd signed a partnership deal with Alstone Holdings, and the terms had been very generous. There was a no-competition clause, and as long as James and I managed to get our heads around the ins and outs of the business, it would be a success, bringing us both a decent, guaranteed income.

As for Joseph and my mum...Zayde had taken care of everything, just as I'd trusted him to do. He'd arranged for the Hyde mansion to be sold, and as I wanted nothing to do with it, he generously arranged for my mother and my brother to keep the proceeds of the sale, provided they moved away from Alstone and agreed not to speak to me unless I initiated contact. The last I'd heard, Joseph had been looking at properties in Oxfordshire, and there had been rumours swirling around that my mum had latched onto some widowed minor royal in the home counties. She'd shown no interest in changing her habits, but I had to remind myself that it wasn't my place to interfere. It had to be her decision to want to change, if she wanted to change. And as far as I was concerned, she had no interest in my life —in fact, she held me responsible for everything that had happened with my dad, and so, that was the end of our relationship, at least for the foreseeable future. Things didn't always work out perfectly.

But that was life. Messy. Imperfect. Precious.

"Where is Kinslee, anyway? I thought she'd be here." Lena glanced around like she was expecting Kinslee to pop up suddenly.

Winter smirked. "She's inside with Creed and Austin."

"And Mack," Jessa added. "It's all very secretive, but I think Creed might be trying to recruit her."

One of Lena's brows arched. "Recruit her for what?"

"Who knows what goes on at Pope Industries?" Winter shrugged, her eyes sparkling. "But if he does recruit her, maybe we can find out."

A klaxon sounded, making us all jump, and Lena swore under her breath. "We didn't get to discuss strategy."

I hoisted up my laser gun, looking down the scope like I'd seen people do on TV. In the distance, I caught sight of the top of someone's head, the rest of them hidden behind an oil barrel. It looked like Cassius. "Hmmm. Don't get shot?"

Lena laughed. "Yeah, I think that's probably the best strategy. Stay low, stay covered, avoid the boys."

With that, we all dispersed, aiming for separate hiding places where we could hopefully pick off the boys one by one.

I ducked down behind a large crate, one of the many hiding places scattered around the hilly fields, along with dips and rises, tunnels and walls. Steadying my gun on the top of the crate, I carefully lifted my head to peer through the scope. There was no sign of anyone. In fact, it was almost too quiet. I couldn't even hear any birds.

Glancing around me, I decided to make a run for the low wall made of stacked sandbags that lay around twenty metres to my right. There was a tunnel to the left of the wall, burrowed into the side of a small hillock, that I could probably crawl inside and pick someone off.

My heart pounded as I sprinted for cover, adrenaline fuelling me with extra speed. I threw myself down behind the wall, and then all the breath was knocked from my lungs as a hard body pinned me in place.

"Got you."

I twisted, and Zayde let me turn so that my back was against the ground, but he kept me pinned beneath him.

"Did you really think you could escape me?" He raised a brow, amusement dancing in his eyes, and I loved him so much.

"Zayde." Sliding my left hand up the tense muscles of his thigh, I slowly, deliberately licked my lips. As his eyes darkened, I curled my right hand around my gun, my finger slipping into place over the trigger.

Then in a movement that I thought Lena would've been proud of, I swung the gun up, aiming the red dot of the laser and shooting his chest at point-blank range.

His mouth fell open, his eyes wide with shock, and I was helpless to stop the huge grin that was spreading across my face.

"Fallon," he growled.

"Mmm?" I gave him an innocent look.

Shaking his head, he studied me intently, and then he huffed out a small laugh, tugging the gun out of my hands.

"I love you. So. Fucking. Much."

"Wh—"

His mouth came down on mine, cutting off my words. I instantly wrapped my arms around him, kissing him back with everything I had. *He loved me.* I knew that he did, because he'd shown me every day, but to hear those words coming from his mouth, at the most unexpected time, when we were halfway through a battle simulation in a muddy field in the middle of winter...

I wouldn't have changed this moment for anything in the world.

"I love you so much, Zayde." There were tears in my eyes, but I blinked them away, smiling so hard that my cheeks hurt. He returned my smile, dropping kisses across my cheeks, my nose, and then my mouth.

"You're mine, and I'm never letting you go."

We remained that way for a perfect, still moment, breathing each other's air. Happy. Together.

Then my boyfriend swung himself into a seated position and shot me in the chest.

"You were the one that lost us the game." West elbowed Cassius with a smirk. "Can't stop thinking with your dick, can you?"

"Jessa cheated! It wasn't my fault."

Jessa shook her head, the picture of innocence. "All I did was promise you a blowjob if you let me shoot you. I'm no match for your shooting skills, so I had to improvise."

"But your blowjobs are so good, how—"

Caiden clamped his hand over Cassius' mouth, muffling the rest of his words. "Let's call it a draw."

"No," Winter and Lena said at once. Zayde wasn't even paying attention for once, hugging me from behind and pressing kisses into my hair. I melted into him, turning my head so I could meet his gaze.

"While they're distracted, can I show you something?"

He nodded, releasing me to take my hand, and we made our way through Skirmish to the locker area. My package had arrived this morning, and I hadn't had a chance to open it before I came, but I also hadn't wanted to wait to show Zayde.

I unfastened the key from my wrist and unlocked the locker door. Unzipping my bag, I withdrew the small parcel and handed it to him. "Open it."

Taking a seat on one of the benches, he pulled off the tape and brown paper to reveal a small cardboard box. When he opened it, he inhaled sharply, his throat working as he stared down at the contents.

I swallowed hard. "I...um. When I left Switzerland, I left them behind. At the time, my head wasn't in the right place. I hadn't...I wasn't sure if I'd be able to get them back, if they were gone for good. But Selma—she works in the sanctuary—she kept hold of them for me. She had the chain fixed." Gathering my courage, I met his eyes. "I'm so sorry, Z. I'm sorry that I treated them so badly. I know how important they were to you—to *us*. I just—"

Placing the box down, he stood, tugging me into his arms. "I know, baby. It's okay. You don't have to explain. I get it."

When we drew apart, he carefully lifted the chain from the box, directing me to turn around. He gathered up my hair, smoothing it over one shoulder and pressing a soft kiss to the back of my neck before he fastened the chain. My hand came up, my fingers stroking across the angel wings. They'd been a gift from him when I turned sixteen, designed by him to show how much I meant to him, but only when I'd come back to Alstone had I realised just how deep those feelings went. He had the tattoo inked into his skin, and the same symbol hung over our bed.

"My angel," he murmured, his hand covering mine, his thumb stroking across the platinum feathers.

"Always," I whispered. "I love you."

Reaching back into the box, I drew out his copy of *To Kill a Mockingbird*, forever grateful to Selma for having the insight to put it aside instead of throwing it away. I turned around, holding it out to him.

He smiled as his fingers curved around the spine of the

book, his thumb stroking across the corner of the battered front cover.

My heart skipped a beat.

I'd righted a wrong, and he was happy.

EPILOGUE 2

zayde

TWO MONTHS LATER

Another party. But this time, it wasn't Cassius' idea. This was all the idea of the Alstone Holdings board. A double celebration for the newly reopened AH offices, rebuilt in record time—the benefits of owning our own construction businesses—and for Alstone Holdings' partnership with TL Properties. Arlo Cavendish had appointed Grant Wilson, one of his most trusted colleagues, as the interim manager, and I was so fucking happy for Fallon that she had this company to run when she was finished with her business qualifications. She deserved the world.

When I pulled up outside the large Georgian manor house where Arlo lived, gravel spraying under my bike's wheels, I whistled under my breath. Caiden's dad had spared no expense. Fairy lights were fucking everywhere, making the house stand out like a beacon on the headland. The sounds of a string quartet or some orchestral shit drifted out from the open door, and there was even a red carpet running down the stone steps, with a uniformed butler at the top, greeting people as they entered.

Welcome to the Alstone elite.

I patted my pocket, feeling the reassuring combined weight of my knife and the small tin that held an emergency blunt. I might be wrapped in a tailored designer suit, but underneath, I was still me.

From behind me, car doors slammed, and then there was the crunch of shoes on gravel. Caiden, Cassius, and Weston came to stand beside me. Caiden glanced between us all and then faced the house. "Ready?"

As one, we moved towards the door, and when we were inside, we headed for the staircase to wait for our girls, who were getting ready upstairs.

"We look hot as fuck. C'mon, selfie for my social media. Let's make everyone jealous." Cassius held out his phone, slinging his arm around West's shoulders. Cade yanked me in closer, and Cass snapped a photo of the four of us.

He was right. We did look hot as fuck—freshly shaved, hair styled, all of us in black-on-black suits.

"This is gonna get me so many likes." Grinning down at his phone, Cassius tapped quickly at the screen. "I've tagged you all in—"

West's elbow to his side cut him off, and his gaze flew up, his sharp intake of breath echoed by the rest of us.

Our four girls stood poised at the top of the stairs. Each of them had on a variation of a short black dress and towering heels, but I'd have been hard-pressed to give any details of what Winter, Lena, or Jessa were wearing if anyone had asked me. I only had eyes for Fallon, who looked so. Fucking. Sexy.

Her body was clad in a tight black dress that was so short it made her legs look a million miles long. It was strapless, the neckline dipping down to give a mouthwatering view of the swell of her tits, and on her feet were spiked black heels. Her hair hung down her back in soft platinum waves, and her eyes were huge, ringed in smudged black that gave her a heavy-lidded, sultry look. In short, her entire look was a giant fuck-you to her parents, who would have never let her get away with wearing anything that came above the knee or even showed a hint of cleavage. When she saw the way I was openly eye-fucking her, a flush stole over her high cheekbones, and her soft lips curved into a pleased smile.

The girls descended the stairs, arm in arm, splitting off when they reached the bottom. I tugged Fallon into me, lowering my head to her ear with a groan as I pressed my erection into her thigh.

"You look so good, baby. Feel that? You made me so fucking hard."

A breathy laugh fell from her throat. "Have you seen yourself? All I can think about is stripping you out of this sexy suit and riding you until you come inside me."

Fuuuuck.

"Yeah. We're doing that. Now."

Without waiting for a reply, I dragged her away from the others, down the corridor, past the roped-off section that marked the following area as out of bounds. Throwing open the door of the small bathroom to our right, I tugged her inside, slamming the door behind us.

"*Zayde*. I need you now." Her body pressed into mine, her lips kissing across my jaw as her hand went down to palm my erection. "I'm so ready. The second I saw you in this suit, knowing what's underneath—"

I cut her off by slanting my mouth over hers, scooping her up and lifting her onto the counter.

"Fuck, look at you," I groaned, tearing my mouth away and shoving up her dress to expose the tiny triangle of silk beneath. Slipping my fingers beneath the band, I tugged lightly. "How attached to these are you?"

Her pupils were blown, her fists clutching my suit jacket as she panted against me. "Not...very. Why?"

In answer, I tugged my knife from my pocket, flicked open the blade, and sliced her underwear right off her.

She moaned so fucking loudly, her head falling back against the mirror. "Please, Z. I need you. Now. *Please.*"

Who was I to argue with my girl when she was begging for me so sweetly?

It took me seconds to open my trousers, freeing my hard dick. Dragging her to the edge of the counter, I lined myself up and then thrust inside her.

Fucking. Heaven.

Our fucking was hard and fast and frantic, my hands and mouth all over her, marking her throat with my lips and teeth, palming her gorgeous tits while she wrapped her legs around me, her heels digging into my ass, her fingers gripping my hair, then scraping down my back until she was shaking against me, falling apart on my cock.

"Zayde, Zayde, Zayde," she panted. "So...good." I thrust up, hard, and then I was coming, my dick pulsing inside her and filling her with my cum.

"Sorry," she whispered when I pulled out, the sight of my cum dripping out of her making my dick twitch, despite the fact that I'd just emptied my balls.

My gaze shot to hers. "For what?"

"Um. I messed up your hair a bit. And there's some lipstick..." Trailing off, she waved a hand in the general direction of my face. I glanced in the mirror and shook my head, seeing the amusement in her eyes reflected in mine.

"I hope Arlo still keeps this bathroom well stocked," I muttered with a grin.

Twisting around, Fallon peered in the mirror, laughing when she caught sight of herself. "Oh, bloody hell. Everyone will be able to tell what we've been doing."

"I think they already guessed from the way I dragged my girlfriend away from them the second I had you in my arms."

"True." We smiled at each other, and was it my imagination, or were smiles coming much easier to me lately? They seemed to be happening all the time. If I wasn't careful, I'd lose my reputation as the brooding one of the Four. I made a mental note to throw out a few of my so-called "serial killer" stares when we got back to the party, just to even things up.

When we were cleaned up and all evidence was cleared away from the bathroom, I wrapped my arm around Fallon's waist, and we joined the party.

"Arlo's invited everyone, hasn't he? This doesn't feel like the kind of parties I used to have to go to."

She was right. Scanning the room, I saw Creed deep in conversation with Jessa's brother, Austin, and Paul Drummond. Over by the window, Obie and Mack were standing with West and Lena, studying something on West's phone. In the centre of the huge room, in the space reserved for dancing, West's friend Rumi and two of his other mates were doing a loose interpretation of dancing with Kinslee and a group of girls from uni. And Caiden, Winter, Cassius, and Jessa were over by the bar. Caiden was talking to James Granville, and was that a smile on his face? My eyes had to be deceiving me.

With a smirk directed at my best mate, I pulled Fallon closer.

"Yeah, and look at how well they're all getting on." Alstone Holdings staff members, from the managers to the maintenance staff, mingled with our friends from various different backgrounds, our families, and the rest of the elite, and somehow, it worked. Maybe because Arlo had cultivated the guest list to exclude the snobby asshole types that I had no time for. Whatever it was, this should be the standard for elite parties from now on.

James Granville caught Fallon's eye from his position next to the bar, and she lifted her hand in a wave. Instead of returning it, he said something to Cade and then began to weave his way through the crowd towards us.

"Zayde," he greeted me with a nod.

"James."

After giving me a hesitant smile, he turned his attention to my girlfriend. "Hey, Fal, can I talk to you for a minute?"

"Yeah, of course." She reached up to press a kiss to the side of my face. "I'll be back in a minute?"

"Take as long as you need, baby. I'll get us some drinks."

When I reached the bar, Winter threw her arms around my neck, pressing a kiss to my cheek. I hugged her back, my brows raised at her enthusiastic display of affection—and I realised that hugs were another thing that seemed to be happening more frequently. Fucking hell. I wasn't going to turn into another Cassius, was I? All fucking ultrabright Cheshire cat grins and hugging everyone all the time.

No. Never gonna happen.

"Alright, Winter?" I caught Caiden's eye over her shoulder, and he shrugged, smirking at me.

"I just wanted to say that I'm so happy for you. I love you, and I love Fallon, and I'm just so glad that you found your way back to each other." Her voice lowered. "I used to worry about you. But you...you're different now, aren't you? Lighter."

Oh. Fuck. I swallowed hard. "Uh, yeah. There's ups and downs. But yeah, I'm happier."

"Good. You deserve it." She gave me another bright smile, and then I surprised her and Cade by first brushing a kiss across her cheek and then pulling my best mate into a hug.

"Happy for you, mate," he said quietly.

"Yeah. You too."

We glanced at each other and then both started laughing.

"Fucking hell. Our reputations as the aloof, unapproachable bad boys are completely fucked." Caiden mock groaned as we stepped apart. "No one will fear us now."

"Did anyone ever fear you?" Winter wondered aloud, her eyes dancing with amusement. Caiden shot her a warning look, which was ruined by the fact that he couldn't stop fucking grinning.

"Snowflake. We're the future of Alstone Holdings. One day, we'll be the ones running this town. We have to cultivate our reputation as badass, cut-throat businessmen."

Winter snorted with laughter, and Caiden shook his head.

"Back me up here, Z."

"I'm not getting in the middle of this." Lifting my hands in the air, I started backing away, but Cade stopped me with a look.

"Wait. Can you meet us on the terrace in an hour? Bring Fallon."

I gave him a nod. Oh, yeah. Tonight was the night. "We'll be there."

"Dinner next Thursday?" My dad looked between Fallon and me with a small smile.

I gave him a nod. "We'll be there."

"Good. Good." He held out his hand and then ended up awkwardly patting me on the arm before giving Fallon another smile. We were still a work in progress, probably would be for a long time, but everyone was trying. I now had Nina therapizing me through a series of excruciating Zoom calls—okay, they were a little less excruciating now than they had been in the beginning when I found it too fucking hard to even say anything—and every time I interacted with my dad, I had her voice in my head, forcing me to make more of an effort than I normally would. It was slowly but surely improving our relationship, though. I could admit that, however grudgingly.

"See you Thursday, Dad." I threaded my fingers through Fallon's, leading her through the crowd and outside onto the terrace. It was almost time to meet Cade.

Leaning back against the stone wall next to the doors, I wrapped my arms around Fallon from behind, tugging her into me. "What did James want earlier?"

"Oh! He had a gift for me." She paused. "From Joseph, actually."

I kept my voice neutral. Despite the fact that I hated the guy, he was still her brother, and it was up to her to choose whether she wanted to reconnect with him or not. If she asked for my advice, yeah, I'd give it to her, but I wouldn't try to influence her decisions. "What was it?"

"It was a photo album. Our mother...she'd sold most of the stuff in the house before Joe could go through it, but he found the album when he was clearing out the attic. He printed out other photos and added them to it, too. It's...there are so many photos, Z. Pictures of Tim, of the three of us as kids, selfies from our social media accounts."

Nothing could ever make up for what he'd done to Fallon, but I knew just how much something like that would mean to her. "I'm glad that he sent it to you," I said honestly.

"He...he included a note, too. Apologising for everything. I don't think we'll ever be able to get past what he did, but..." She sighed. "You know."

"One day at a time, baby."

"You're right." Her fingers curled around my wrists, pulling my arms more tightly around her.

"I love you," I murmured with a kiss to the soft skin just below her ear. The words came more easily now, and I meant them with everything I had.

"I love you, too, Zayde." Turning her head so that our lips could meet, she smiled. "Always have, always will."

"Me too." Just as I was losing myself in the hot slide of her mouth against mine, we were interrupted by a throat clearing loudly. I raised my head to find my best mate staring at us with a raised brow.

"Finished?"

I lifted one hand from Fallon's waist to give him the finger, and he gave me one of his shark-like grins. "I'll take that as a no, but come over here for a minute." We followed him to the centre of the stone terrace, where Cassius, Weston, Winter, Lena, and Jessa were all gathered. Cassius handed us each a champagne flute, filled to the brim. When everyone had a glass, Cade clambered up onto the low stone wall in front of us.

"We—me, Cass, West, and Z—wanted to make this official. I'm no good at speeches, so I'll keep it simple. The Four—that's no longer just a number. Our family now includes four more people. Jessa, Lena, Fallon, and my girl, Winter. We're the future of the elite, the future leaders of this town, and we're gonna be fucking amazing at it."

"Yeah!" Cassius fist-pumped the air, sloshing some of the champagne out of his glass.

"Our bond goes deeper than blood. We have each other's backs, and if any one of us has a problem, that means we all have a problem. I said it already, but I'll say it again. We're. A fucking. Family."

As if it had been choreographed—which it probably had, West moved, hitting a small control pad in his hands, and suddenly, the darkness was lit up. Drones spelling out IV in red, the colour vivid against the inky blackness of the night sky. He pressed something else on the control pad, and the drones changed direction to sweep across the sky, coming together again to spell out the number 4, and then EVA.

"That forever bit was my idea," Cassius said loudly. "We didn't have enough drones to spell out the word properly, so we had to go retro."

"I love you all," Winter said finally, her voice cracking. "We've been through so much, and here we are now."

Caiden jumped down from the wall, pulling her into his arms. "Everything we've been through has made us stronger. We've had some dark fucking times, but we made it through."

Fallon cleared her throat, and everyone fell silent. "You all—*we've* all faced things that no one should ever have to face, but do you know what? Even after the darkest of nights, the sun will always rise. And it's beautiful."

"Yes. *This.*" Stepping forwards, Winter lifted her glass. One by one, the rest of us moved, forming a circle, our glasses meeting in the centre.

"To the Four," Caiden said.

THE END

THANK YOU AND A NOTE

Thank you so much for reading Zayde and Fallon's story, and the conclusion to The Four series. Want a bonus epilogue where you can see their university graduation? Download it now: https://bit.ly/zaydefallon

Feel free to send me your thoughts, and reviews are always very appreciated ♥ You can find me in my Facebook group Becca's Book Bar if you want to connect, or sign up to my newsletter to stay up to date with all the latest info. Check out all my links, including my Patreon, at https://linktr.ee/authorbeccasteele

I wanted to share a little note before I go. The struggles that Zayde and Fallon faced were very personal to me, and I wanted to say that if you're also struggling with any of those issues, please know that you're not alone. There is help available. Some resources:

USA:

National Alliance on Mental Illness (NAMI)

American Foundation for Suicide Prevention (AFSP)
The Trevor Project - LGBTQ+

UK:

Mind
MindOut - LGBTQ+
Samaritans
Campaign Against Living Miserably (CALM) - men's mental health charity

International:

Checkpoint - global mental health resources
Samaritans - worldwide links

Thank you,
Becca xoxo

ACKNOWLEDGMENTS

First of all, thank you so, so much to everyone that has read The Four series and has stuck with our guys throughout. I can't believe that it's over. It's a bittersweet feeling, knowing that it has come to an end, but I know this isn't the last we've seen of The Four, and I have no doubt they'll be making appearances in future books.

Claudia and Jenny, thank you for believing in our boys from the beginning, and for being their biggest cheerleaders. I love you guys.

Thank you to Megan, and Sue, for your endless support and feedback. And to my U13 sprinters and to Ivy, thank you for writing with me, for cheering me on, and all your support.

A huge thank you to Alexandria for the sunrise analogy, and another huuuuge thank you to Hallie for believing in this series!

Sandra and Rumi—you are my dream team! Thank you for dealing with my last minute everything, and for keeping my em dashes (or most of them, anyway).

Thanks to Jen and all the team at Wordsmith, my awesome blogger team and ARC team, Laura, Stephanie, and to everyone who helped to promote this book.

To the readers, bloggers, bookstagrammers, and everyone who has shared, read, enjoyed the world of The Four, you are amazing!

I also have to thank my husband, who will never read

these words, but read the entire story prior to editing and gave me invaluable (and not so valuable) feedback. You're pretty amazing.

And lastly, thank you so much to everyone who waited patiently for Zayde's story. It was a long time coming, but finally, our boy got his girl.

Becca xoxo

ALSO BY BECCA STEELE

LSU Series

(M/M college romance)

Collided

Blindsided

Sidelined

The Four Series

(M/F college suspense romance)

The Lies We Tell

The Secrets We Hide

The Havoc We Wreak

*A Cavendish Christmas (free short story)**

The Fight In Us

The Bonds We Break

The Darkness In You

Alstone High Standalones

(new adult high school romance)

Trick Me Twice (M/F)

Cross the Line (M/M)

In a Week (free short story) (M/F)*

Savage Rivals (M/M)

London Players Series

(M/F rugby romance)

The Offer

London Suits Series

(M/F office romance)

The Deal

The Truce

*The Wish (a festive short story)**

Other Standalones

Cirque des Masques (M/M dark circus romance)

*Mayhem (M/F Four series spinoff)**

*Heatwave (M/F summer short story)**

Boneyard Kings Series (with C. Lymari)

(RH/why-choose college suspense romance)

Merciless Kings

Vicious Queen

Ruthless Kingdom

Box Sets

Caiden & Winter trilogy (M/F)

(The Four series books 1-3)

**all free short stories and bonus scenes are available from https://authorbeccasteele.com*

***Key - M/F = Male/Female romance*

M/M = Male/Male romance

RH = Reverse Harem/why-choose (one woman & 3+ men) romance

ABOUT THE AUTHOR

Becca Steele is a USA Today and Wall Street Journal bestselling romance author. She currently lives in the south of England with a whole horde of characters that reside inside her head.

When she's not writing, you can find her reading or watching Netflix, usually with a glass of wine in hand. Failing that, she'll be online hunting for memes or making her 500th Spotify playlist.

Join Becca's Facebook reader group Becca's Book Bar, sign up to her mailing list, check out her Patreon, or find her via the following links:

facebook.com/authorbeccasteele
instagram.com/authorbeccasteele
bookbub.com/profile/becca-steele
goodreads.com/authorbeccasteele
patreon.com/authorbeccasteele
amazon.com/stores/Becca-Steele/author/B07WT6GWB2

Made in the USA
Middletown, DE
06 October 2024